'Irresistibly compelling.' *Sydney Morning Herald*

'Nothing short of outstanding. Tony Birch could take home a few prizes, deservedly so. *Blood* is a humanist masterpiece that has been worth the wait.' *Australian Book Review*

'*Blood* keeps us on edge from the outset. Jesse is an endearing mix of love, cynicism, patience and survival instincts.' *Good Reading*

'A novel about what makes and what breaks a family. It is emotional. It is at turns tender and intense. It is a novel worth reading.' *Avid Reader*

'Darkly suffused with the gritty realism of young children doing it tough in a world of dysfunctional adults'.' *Sunday Canberra Times*

'An absorbing and endearing tale of children in adversity. The story is told from Jesse's point of view, and Birch pulls this off beautifully with a compelling combination of flinty Australian vernacular and boyish candour. It's impressive stuff.' *Weekend Australian*

'This is a fractured fairytale, a dark Australian road story, but also an affecting tale about the bond between a brother and sister, and how the most unexpected people can transform lives. Birch delivers edge-of-your-seat suspense and engrossing characterisation in equal measures.' *Readings Monthly*

'The story is gripping, and I am in awe of Birch's ability to paint brilliant scenes and emotions with so few words.' *Manly Daily*

'The book explodes in its last third with equal parts exhilaration and dread, racing to a seemingly inevitable end that is awful, but not without hope, and leaves you bruised. A fantastic book.' *Newcastle Herald*

'Birch develops a gripping tale and readers will be left thinking even after they turn the last page.' *Port Macquarie News*

Tony Birch is the author of *Shadowboxing* (2006) and the short story collection *Father's Day* (2009). He lives in Melbourne, where he teaches in the School of Culture and Communication at the University of Melbourne.

BLOOD

TONY
BIRCH

UQP

First published 2011 by University of Queensland Press
PO Box 6042, St Lucia, Queensland 4067 Australia
www.uqp.com.au

This edition published 2012

Cover design by Design by Committee
Cover photographs © Bigstockphoto
Originally typeset in 12/17 pt Bembo by Post Pre-press Group, Brisbane
Printed in Australia by McPherson's Printing Group

Twenty-seven words from 'The Bitter Boy' © Kate Rusby
reprinted by permission of Pure Records Ltd.

 This project has been assisted by the Commonwealth
Government through the Australia Council,
its arts funding and advisory body

National Library of Australia Cataloguing-in-Publication Data
is available at http://catalogue.nla.gov.au/

Blood / Tony Birch
ISBN: 9780702249549 (pbk)
           9780702247590 (epub)
           9780702247606 (kindle)
           9780702247583 (pdf)

University of Queensland Press uses papers that are natural, renewable
and recyclable products made from wood grown in sustainable
forests. The logging and manufacturing processes conform to
the environmental regulations of the country of origin.

For Brian and Debbie –
with all my love,
for taking my hand.

'Then the boy, me and the boy
we walked for miles through stormy weather
hand in hand, we roamed the land
and held the gleaming heart together.'

KATE RUSBY, 'The Bitter Boy'

A policewoman came into the room carrying a tray of food. Two cheese burgers, some fries and a Coke. She put the tray on the wooden table. The top was scratched with initials and messages – FUK THE COPS. I kept one eye on her and the other on a TV sitting inside a padlocked cage in the corner. She was pretty, the policewoman; blond hair and big brown eyes. She looked like she could be a pop singer, if it wasn't for the uniform.

I was busting for a piss so I asked if it was okay to go. She shrugged. As soon as we walked out the door she grabbed hold of a belt-loop in the back of my jeans and stuck a couple of fingers through it. We walked along a narrow corridor. The offices on each side were crowded with police, some of them in plain-clothes, others in uniform. She followed me into the toilet, stood behind me and held onto me as I unzipped my fly. I could feel her warm breath on my neck and I was so embarrassed I couldn't piss. I asked her if she would let go of me for

1

a bit. She laughed. 'You got stage-fright? I'll help you.' She let go of the belt-loop, reached across to the sink and turned on the tap. 'Try now.'

When I'd finished she told me I couldn't wash my hands. I'd have to wait until after I'd been interviewed. I took a look at my face in the mirror over the sink. It had a crack down the middle, splitting my face in two. My hair was plastered to my face. One eye was swollen shut and scabby. She leaned forward, put a hand on my shoulder and spoke into my ear, real quiet. I could feel her tits pressing against my back. I watched her face in the mirror. 'Jesse, if you help us out here, tell us what went on back there at the house, I'll make sure you get a hot shower, some clean clothes and something decent to eat. No takeaway shit. What about it?' She sounded so friendly I was about to ask her where Rachel was, and if she was okay. But I didn't. If I opened my mouth once, I might keep on talking and get myself in more trouble. Jon Dempsey had taught me that. 'Once you start humming a tune, you can't help but sing the whole song.'

We walked back along the corridor. The policewoman left me in the room with the cold food and TV for company. I tried to remember the last time I'd eaten but I was too tired to think. I had an ache in the guts and a hammer in my head. I grabbed one of the burgers, tore it apart with my teeth and washed it down with the Coke. I'd knocked off both burgers and most of the fries when my guts started aching even more. My head was spinning and I thought I was going to be sick. I looked around the room but couldn't see anything I could spew into. I wondered if I was being watched. I couldn't see any cameras, so I guessed not.

Pretty soon the dizziness went away. I took off my wet smelly runners, lay down on the floor, and stuck the shoes behind my head for a cushion. The TV was turned to the home shopping channel. A woman in a sparkly dress was selling gold and silver jewellery. I tried to guess the price each time she held up a piece. I wasn't even close.

I heard the door open and looked up. It was the skinny detective I'd seen earlier that night. The policewoman was standing behind him. He had a folder under one arm and was carrying a clear plastic bag. He yelled at me to get to my feet and sit back at the table. He pulled a chair over to the table, sat across from me and threw the bag down. I could see the gun inside. I shifted my eyes to some of the names scratched into the tabletop and pretended I could see a J and an R carved in the wood. Jesse and Rachel.

'Jesse and Rachel Were Here.'

ONE

We'd always been on the move, shifting from one place to another, usually because she'd done the dirty on someone, or she was chasing some fella she'd fallen for. And when Gwen fell for a bloke, she had to have him. I didn't mind so much when it was just the two of us. All I had to concentrate on was staying out of her way and the trouble she brought home. But when Rachel came along everything changed. I was only a kid, just five years old. But from the moment I saw her, wrapped in a blanket in the hospital, I knew I'd be the one that would have to take care of her.

We were heading for Melbourne from up north, when Gwen said we'd have to stop because she was going to have the baby soon. 'The place has a set of traffic lights,' she noticed when we stopped outside a pub in the town we were passing through. 'So it has to have some sort of hospital.'

She rented a room upstairs at the pub. It was hot and stuffy and smelled of something terrible that I couldn't make out.

She ordered us toasted cheese sandwiches from the bar, picked up a couple of beers and sat on the bed and waited. The pains went away in the night and she slept in until around lunchtime the next day. We shared a ham sandwich in a shop next to the pub and went for a walk around the town looking for the hospital, but couldn't find it. 'Gwen, maybe we should stop and ask someone for directions?' She ignored me and kept on walking. We followed the sounds of kids yelling and music playing, and turned a corner to see a brightly coloured tent in a paddock, with flashing lights and rides. It was a carnival.

I stood and watched kids crashing into each other in dodgem cars while Gwen counted our money. We had just enough for lunch. We were sitting at a table in the food tent eating hotdogs when I saw that her hands and ankles were swollen. She held up a hand and said the same had happened when I was about to be born and when she went into labour another time, a couple of years back.

'You remember that, don't you, Jesse? The last time I got pregnant?'

She smiled when she said it. Didn't bother her at all.

'No, I don't remember,' I said.

But I did. I remembered lots of stuff I never spoke to Gwen about. She'd lost that baby. I'd watched her belly get fatter and was excited about getting a baby brother or sister because I didn't want it to be just Gwen and me, any more. The day she was supposed to have the baby she left me on my own and went to hospital in a taxi, holding her belly like it was about to collapse on her. When she came back the next afternoon she had a flat tummy and no baby. She wouldn't talk to me and just lay down on the bed and went to sleep. She tossed and turned in the night, moaned in her sleep, and woke us both up. I sat up in bed and asked her where our new baby was. She looked at me as if she didn't understand what I was talking about.

'There's no baby, Jesse.'

'Why not? You said we were going to have one.'

'I've got a shocker of a headache. Leave me be.'

She got out of bed, went through her bag until she found some tablets, threw a couple in her mouth, and stuck her tongue under the tap in the sink across the room. She came back to bed, rolled onto her side and faced the wall. I was upset and pulled the bed sheet off her.

'Where's the baby?'

She pulled the sheet back.

'Jesus Christ, Jesse. You ask too many questions. The baby couldn't breathe when it came out. It was born blue. That's what they call it. It died, Jesse. The baby's gone.'

'Blue? What's that mean?'

'No more, Jesse. Get back to sleep.'

She pressed her body into the wall and left me with no sheet.

I wanted to cry, but knew if I did she'd probably give me a whack, so I squeezed my eyes shut to stop the tears from coming out.

One night, months later, I had a dream about the blue baby. It was night and the sky was full of stars. The baby was a boy and he was floating above my bed. He had a jumpsuit on and looked like an astronaut. When I reached up and tried to touch him he drifted away. I was sure he'd been real, even after I woke up with a fright. I jumped off the couch and ran to the window, hoping to see him. Outside, the sky was dark. There were no stars and no baby.

When Gwen told me she was pregnant again I worried that she would have another blue baby and it would float away too and meet up with the other baby. But when it came it wasn't blue. It was a girl. And it was Rachel.

Gwen felt the pains when we were standing in line at the supermarket after we left the carnival. She was wearing maternity pants with elastic in the front. They made it easier to knock stuff off. She'd just shoved a smoked ham down her front when she buckled over with pain. It went away pretty quick but she got another one a few minutes later. I ran to the lady on the checkout. She told me where the hospital was and we walked there, as fast as we could. On the way Gwen handed me the ham and a packet of cheese and some dry biscuits and told me to hang onto them.

At the hospital she was put in a chair and wheeled away and I was sent to an office to wait for somebody. I'd only just sat down when there was a knock at the door and a woman came in. She had frizzy hair and wore a dress with big flowers all over it. She didn't look like a nurse or doctor. She looked down at what I was holding in my arms.

'Where did you get the food?'

'We paid for it, at the supermarket.'

I don't reckon she believed me but she didn't seem to care. She picked up a jar from the table and unscrewed the lid.

'Would you like a lolly?'

I took one, my favourite, a sherbet bomb. She read from a blue slip of paper in her hand.

'Gwen Flynn. She's your mother?'

I bit into the sherbet bomb. It exploded in my mouth.

'Yep. My mum.'

'And you are?'

'Jesse.'

'Tell me, Jesse, how did you end up here, in our town?'

I took a deep breath and then told her the story Gwen had been drilling into me since I could talk. She called it the 'Nosy Parker' story. I told the woman we'd left our hometown across the river and were on our way to Melbourne to stay with our relations because my grandmother was sick and 'probably about to die'.

'Gwen . . . my mum started to get pains in her guts so we had to stop here.'

She looked a bit sad and offered me another lolly. She even took one herself. The truth was we had no place to live, on this side of the river or the other. And my nan had died years before I was born. I only knew her from a couple of photographs.

The woman stood up, came around my side of the table and put an arm on my shoulder. She told me she was sorry that my grandmother was 'gravely ill'. Then she went back to her side of the desk and signed the bottom of a ticket. I had to hang it round my neck in a plastic wallet. It let me eat anything I wanted.

I caught a lift upstairs and followed the smell of hot food, to a cafeteria where a lady behind the counter helped me pick out a meal, finished off with a bowl of chocolate ice cream. She piled the ice cream so high it spilt over the side of the bowl. After I'd eaten I sat and watched TV until a nurse came for me. She had good news. I had a baby sister.

The baby was wrapped up tight in a pink blanket with just her face poking out. She had bumps and bruises over her eyes and looked like she'd been belted or dropped on her head. I touched the side of her face with a fingertip. Her skin was softer than anything I'd felt.

'Gwen, what's wrong with her face? Did somebody hurt her?'

'Nothing's wrong, Jesse. Most babies look like that when they come out. Don't get yourself worked up about it.'

I didn't trust anything Gwen said. Once, when she was having an argument with my pop he'd called her a 'born liar.' It sounded strange because I didn't see how a person could be born a liar. But as I got older I thought that if anyone could have, it would be Gwen.

I walked around the ward and looked at the other babies in their cribs. A couple of them looked perfect, like the babies I'd seen on the covers of magazines, with fat faces, big round eyes and red cheeks. Others though, like Gwen said, had faces more like a beaten-up boxer than a baby. I came back to the bed and touched the baby's cheek again.

'Have you picked a name for her?'

'Yep. I'm calling her Rachel. Do you like it? It's from the Bible.'

I couldn't see how Gwen knew any names from the Bible. I'd seen a few Bibles before, lying around the hotel rooms we'd stayed in, but I'd never seen Gwen reading one.

The day after Rachel was born Gwen got an infection and had to stay in the hospital. There was no one to look after me while she was sick. The social worker tried finding me a foster place but couldn't get one, so, in the end, they let me stay at the hospital. I spent most of my time in the TV room watching the soap operas and quiz shows with some of the new mums breastfeeding their babies and a row of old women who'd fallen over and hurt themselves and had their hips replaced.

The women were friendly and gave me chocolates and lollies. I made them cups of tea in the kitchen next to the TV room because some of them couldn't walk so good. I enjoyed myself so much I'd have been happy to stay there. But after a week, we were on our way again. Gwen picked up a second-hand baby seat at the Salvation Army down the street and we headed straight for Melbourne with baby Rachel in the back. A friend of hers, called Midnight Mary, had a place over the office at a tyre yard. We'd stayed with Mary a few times before, but we never lasted long because she and Gwen would end up fighting over money, or men.

Mary grew marijuana plants for a living, under special lights, in a spare room. She said we could stay with her, rent-free, if Gwen kept an eye on the plants and checked the timers on the lights when Mary was out dealing. There wasn't much for me to do but watch the baby or go downstairs to the workshop and listen in on the tyre fitters talking about drinking and girls. Across the street, there was a block of flats with heaps of kids, so I sometimes wandered over there. A police car would pull into the flats most days. Gwen told me to stay away from the kids, unless I wanted trouble.

She also said I'd be going to school for as long as we were there.

'If the police get a look at you, they'll get suspicious and call the welfare. Or worse. Take you in.'

'School? But I don't want to.'

'You bet, sport. School. I need you off the streets while I'm helping out here.'

So I went to school for the first time. We had our own desks and had to sit in the same seat every day and weren't allowed to move around. After a week I told Gwen I wasn't going back. She snorted and said, 'No fucken way. I can't be taking off with this baby. This is our home now, Jesse. For a while, at least.'

It was hard to believe what she'd said. We'd never had a home and I didn't reckon we'd last with Mary. And we didn't. We took off when Rachel was about four months old. Gwen went to bed swearing and yelling at me for no reason and woke up the next morning and told me we were leaving. She waited until Mary had taken off for the morning, packed up our stuff and we left.

'What about school?' I asked, as we were driving out of the tyre yard.

She wound down the car window and sniffed the air. 'Don't worry about school. You're no Einstein. You won't be missed.'

I skipped a lot of school after my first taste, moving around with Gwen and Rachel. We spent as much time on the road as we did staying put. She was either running away from someone or chasing a crazy idea she'd picked up from the horoscopes she read in old magazines or her tarot cards. She'd always mucked around with the cards. She'd even made a bit of money telling people their future when we were broke. The luck in our life, which was mostly bad, she put down to the fall of the cards. Just about everything that happened to her was the result of being dealt a 'bad hand'.

'I can only work with the cards I got,' she'd say whenever we took a knock.

If we did stop in the one spot long enough for me to go to school, I was always a mile behind the other kids. I got teased a lot and ended up in fights. I didn't read well and couldn't add up much more than what I could count on the fingers on both hands. But I could tell a good story. I'd learned that from watching TV.

Whenever Gwen got a job she did nights. The only baby-sitter I'd ever had while she was out working or partying was the TV. I did the best I could looking after Rachel, but sometimes she'd start bawling and wouldn't stop until I propped her in front of the telly. It did the job, and shut her up straight-away. One time when the power went off for half the day during a heatwave, she sat in a beanbag and stared at the blank screen like the world had come to the end.

Until she was around five Rachel was happy to watch the shows I picked out. But once she'd worked out her own favour-ites we had to take it in turns. I liked cop shows and gangster movies. She went for anything about families, especially if they got through hard times and ended up happy-ever-after. Her stories were all the same and I liked spoiling the ending by giving it away.

We missed out on a lot of stuff that other kids got. Birth-days. Family parties. Food, sometimes. But we never missed out on TV, even when Gwen was flat broke. She once told me that in the old days, when she first started working behind the bar in pubs, you could buy a stolen TV for about a quarter of the real price, and brand new in the box.

These days, you can pick up a TV for nothing, off the side of the road. When someone buys a new model, a flat-screen, they end up putting the old set out with the rubbish. The last telly we had, before the three of us took to the road for the last time, I found sitting at a bus stop. I was walking by, after school, when I spotted it. It looked lonely, like it couldn't wait to be taken home, plugged in and sat in front of.

It was big and heavy and I could hardly get my arms around it. I wrestled it like a bear down the road, back to where we were living, a rundown farmhouse out behind the airport. We were just off the old highway that runs in a straight line all the way from Melbourne to Sydney. A freeway had gone in further up from us and our road took only a few trucks. It would have been a quiet place to live except that the planes from the airport went straight over the house about a hundred times a day and rattled the windows. It was peaceful at night, and quiet, except when a storm rolled in from the west and it sounded like another plane coming over, as the wind tried to tear the tiles off the roof.

Gwen had a job dancing at a beer barn along the highway called 'The Road Train'. It was stuck between a used car yard and takeaway food place. A neon sign out the front advertised 'Topless Asian Hostesses'.

When I got up of a morning and went into the kitchen the smell of cigarettes and booze would be hanging around. It was also in Gwen's hair and her clothes and on her skin. The men at the beer barn left that smell on her. I felt bad that maybe she was dancing topless too. I couldn't stop thinking about it, so in the end I asked if she was taking her clothes off.

'Of course I'm not.'

'I bet you are.'

'I told you, I'm not.'

'I don't believe you. I saw that sign out the front.'

She ended the argument by slamming her fist down on the table and screaming in my face, 'Do I look fucken Asian?'

She never got out of bed before lunchtime and left for work in the afternoon. She'd sold our car for bond and rent and had to walk to the bus stop where I'd found the TV. Her boss, Larry, dropped her back at the front gate early in the morning. Whenever she was away Rachel and me were left at the farmhouse on our own. I didn't mind her being away, except when the storms came, and the old house got thrown around like a boat. If the wind moaning through the house didn't keep us awake, wild dogs howling off in the darkness did.

As soon as she heard the first cry of a dog Rachel would jump down from her bunk and slip under the blankets next to me as quietly as she could. She knew that if she didn't make a nuisance of herself, the better chance she had of staying. I was usually awake anyway. I would never have told her so, but I was just as frightened as Rachel, and felt safer myself with her warm body pressed against mine.

Gwen carried a red plastic wallet everywhere she went, in her handbag, filled with photographs of herself, taken when she was younger, when she first started dancing. She flipped through the wallet every chance she got just to be sure she'd once been beautiful. One time I heard her talking on the phone, telling whoever was on the other end that she was too old and ugly for the game. She'd been knocked around and it showed on her face. She was worn out.

On warm days she would sit out back in her underwear, slap her thighs and tummy and ask us if we thought that she still had a good body.

'I've still got it. What do you reckon?'

Rachel would tell her she looked as beautiful as ever. I didn't think she looked good at all, but I always kept my mouth shut. There must have been something about her that was still attractive. She made as much in tips as she did in wages and men still came around asking after her, even if they were older and looked worn out too.

At first the picture wasn't too good on that old TV I brought home, like watching a giant snow globe. But it beat having no TV at all. The problem with the picture got solved when Gwen brought a fella home from the pub the next week. He stayed the night and made himself useful the next morning by fixing the telly. I stood in the kitchen and watched as he ran a piece of wire from the back of the set, out the window and onto the roof, where he hooked it to the downpipe. The new picture wasn't perfect. But it was a lot better than it had been.

His name was Jon Dempsey and he looked mean. I was getting Rachel's breakfast when he came out of Gwen's bedroom wearing jeans and a singlet and introduced himself. He was covered in tattoos; Gwen's boyfriends always had tattoos. She said it made men look tough and sexy.

He stood in the middle of the kitchen, spread his arms out and turned his hands over to show us he had nothing to hide. He lifted his eyebrows.

'And you two are . . . ?'

Gwen had taught us to keep our mouths shut and not answer questions to strangers. I wasn't going to open mine for someone I'd never met before. When neither of us spoke he shrugged his shoulders like it didn't matter to him, filled a bowl with Weet-Bix and milk, and sat down at the table. We watched him closely as he ate. He chewed the food slowly, like he had all the time in the world. When he'd finished the cereal he lifted the bowl to his mouth and drank the slops. It left a milk moustache across his top lip. He looked silly but I knew better than to tell him so. I reckoned he could chop the table up with his bare hands if he felt the need.

He smiled across at us and tapped the tabletop with his knuckles.

'I'm gonna be straight with you kids. I've only been out of the clink for four months. Your mum says that maybe I can stay here for a bit.'

He rested both hands on the table, flattened his palms and looked me in the eye.

'Is that all right with you? I hear you're the man of the house.'

I looked down at the picture of flowers at the bottom of my empty bowl. Gwen had come home with plenty of dodgy-looking men over the years and Jon was scarier-looking than all of them put together. He had a shaved head and scars criss-crossed it like a railway map. He also had a piece missing from one ear and rock-hard muscles under his tattoos.

He told me some time later, when I got to know him better, that most of the tattoos had been done in gaol. I thought that maybe they'd been done in the dark as well, but kept the idea to myself. His shoulders and what I could see of his chest were a mess of initials, names, dots and numbers, and drawings of animals I couldn't recognise.

Rachel was so frightened of him, that first morning, she ran out of the kitchen into our room, slammed the door behind her and hid under the bed. When she wouldn't come out Jon got down on his hands and knees next to the bed and flicked his cigarette lighter on and off. He waved a ten-dollar note in front of her eyes but she still wouldn't budge.

Gwen had a habit of latching onto men who were good with their fists, and Jon didn't look too different. I didn't exactly hide from him, like Rachel, but I made sure to stay out of his way when he moved into the farmhouse later that day. He took off after breakfast and came back a few hours later carrying everything he owned in an old bag. That night after tea he stood up from the table and announced he was going to get a job and pay his own way. I soon learned he was like that; always saying whatever was on his mind, and loud enough that we all heard it.

He walked the half-hour to the shops the next morning, bought a newspaper and went through it looking for work. He rang some places and cleaned himself as best he could for a couple job interviews. No one would hire him.

'I got no fucken hope,' he screamed one afternoon after he'd got back to the farmhouse with dust on his boots and the clean shirt he'd put on that morning soaked with sweat. I was sitting on the front step watching Rachel ride around in circles on a rusty two-wheeler we'd found in the yard when we moved in. Jon sat down next to me, pulled the polka-dot tie from his neck, ripped it in half and threw it on the ground.

'They say I'm "legally bound" to tell them I've been inside. Parole officer has some fucken idea I'll be rewarded for my honesty. Well, fuck that. It's got me nowhere. It's the same shit every place I go. I tell em I've done years, they take a couple of steps back and look at me like I'm Charlie Manson.'

'Who's Charlie Manson?'

He kicked the ground.

'A hippy serial killer.'

'He kills hippies?'

'No. He was a hippy. Sort of.'

Gwen stayed on at The Road Train and Jon settled into the farmhouse. He did the cleaning and cooking, some fixing up, and kept an eye on Rachel and me. I was at a school twenty minutes away by bus and made my own way to and from the house. Rachel's school was a ten-minute walk if you jumped the creek behind the house, walked across a paddock and cut through a new housing estate and a big sign that read: 'And only twenty minutes from the CBD – door to door'. When Jon first saw the sign he laughed. 'Twenty minutes? You'd need a rocket up your arse.'

He wouldn't let Rachel walk to and from school alone. Once she got over her fear of him Rachel was happy that Jon was waiting for her by the gate when the bell went at the end of the day. She told me she could tell by the way they looked at him that some teachers and parents didn't like Jon.

'They stare at him. But only when they don't think he's looking back. When he does they go all red and turn the other way.'

Before Jon came to stay with us Rachel had been a quiet kid, afraid even. It didn't help that Gwen was forever telling her how bad the world was, and how something terrible could turn up out of nowhere and bite you on the arse just when you were thinking how good things were going. She said people were not to be trusted, even your friends, because they'd likely be the ones doing the biting.

Rachel had believed every word Gwen said and kept to herself. After Jon came along kids in her grade wanted to know all about him. She told me Jon reminded one boy of the road warrior in his Nintendo game. Rachel nodded her head and said, 'Yeah, he is, a warrior. And a killer. He's been in gaol for killing people. Lots of people.'

I reckon that Rachel's classmates believed every word she said about Jon. She told me they would stand back and watch as he picked her up with one arm and slung her on his shoulder to piggyback her home.

We did lots of exploring through the paddocks with Jon on weekends. He would tell us stories as we walked. He told us that before he went to gaol for the first time, he'd been in and out of boys' homes for most of his life.

'There were not many foster places back in them days. No pretend mums and dads for me,' he told us when we were walking back to the farmhouse one afternoon after yabbying down at the creek. Rachel was riding on his shoulders and I was lopping the fat purple heads of Scotch thistles with a piece of rusted wire.

'I was locked up by the time I was twelve. They might have called it a home but it was run by screws with batons and steel-capped boots. They belted the shit out of you the same as they would a grown man.'

He stopped and looked across the paddock and thought about another time.

'I know kids that went off their heads in there. More than one of them knocked themselves off.'

He said he wasn't ashamed of having been in the homes, or prison, and would never hide it from anyone who asked him.

'Even if it cost me. Like not getting any of them jobs. I done my time and I owe nobody nothing.'

He never once spoke about the reason he'd gone to gaol, so I guessed he must have been ashamed about something he'd done.

We were sitting on the bank of the creek another afternoon, keeping one eye on our yabby nets and the other on the sunshine, when he spotted the three round scars on my left shoulder.

'Seen scars like these before. How'd you get them?'

I'd been in foster care myself, just once, when Gwen was off the plate on speed. We hadn't eaten for a couple of days and to stop me nagging her about it she'd given me money to take myself to the movies. When I got back I found Rachel in the bathroom, asleep on some dirty towels. Gwen was sprawled out on the couch. She had no clothes on and her skin had turned grey. I tried waking her up but she didn't budge. I thought she might be dead, until I heard her moan a couple of times.

I should have called an ambulance but I was hungry and there was no food in the cupboards. I changed Rachel's dirty nappy, put some clean clothes on her, sat her in the pusher and wheeled her down the street to the milk bar. The shop owner was an old man who could only talk by putting a microphone up to a dark round hole in his throat. He caught me stealing a loaf of bread and some sausages from the freezer. But not before I'd grabbed two chocolate bars and shoved one into Rachel's mouth and eaten the other one myself.

He locked us in the shop and called the police. They could have charged me but didn't. The way we looked, dirty and hungry, maybe they felt sorry for us. We were handed to the welfare at the police station and Rachel and me were separated for the first time in our lives. She was the only person I knew in the world other than Gwen, and I felt sick being away from her. I didn't know where they'd taken her and felt bad because it was my fault in the first place for getting caught.

I was sent to a foster home run by a woman named Claire. She took care of three other kids and had looked after dozens of others. There were photos of them stuck up around the house. And nice letters from the ones who'd moved on and wanted to let her know how grateful they were and how they were getting on in life.

On my first night in the house I was sure I'd be jumped by one of the other kids. Even though it was a hot night I slept with my clothes on and my jacket zipped all the way up to my neck. Nothing bad happened to me that night, or the night after, so on the third night I took my clothes off and slept in my underwear.

'What's this got to do with the scars on your shoulder?' Jon asked.

'He's getting there, Jon,' Rachel said.

'You heard this story before?'

'Yep. Heaps of times.'

Jon listened as I told him how I'd been at the house for a week when Claire sent the other kids off to the local pool and called me into the kitchen. She sat me down and told me I had some 'trouble to answer for'.

'You'd done the wrong thing?' Jon asked.

'Nup, I hadn't. She said I'd been stealing food from the fridge in the night. I hadn't stolen anything, and said so, but she didn't believe me. She screamed at me and said I was a liar and a little thief.'

I put my hand over the scars and rubbed them like they still hurt.

'When she couldn't get me to own up to stealing, she told me I'd be punished double because I'd lied too. She got angry, held me down and burned me with a cigarette. Three times.'

'She was a bad lady,' Rachel piped up, while Jon nodded quietly, as if he understood what I'd gone through.

'Doesn't surprise me, what happened. The bitch. Did you lag on her?'

'Yep. I didn't want to. I'd never told on anyone before. I waited for my next meeting with the social worker and told her. Do you think I shouldn't have told on her?'

'Well, lagging's wrong. No one wants to be called dog for the rest of their life. But you were just a kid and she'd tortured you. You done the right thing, Jesse.'

Jon believed every word of the story. Just like the social worker had when I'd told her. Gwen had believed it. And Rachel. Even though the story frightened her, she liked hearing it again because it was the cigarette burns that got us back together.

But not a word of the story was true.

Claire, the foster mother, was a nice woman. Her house was clean, the food was good, and the other kids were mostly okay. The only thing she kept on at me about was getting me to eat with my elbows off the table when I was using a knife and fork. I could never get the hang of it.

I missed Rachel and never stopped feeling bad about what had happened to her. My plan was to get back to her by running away, until one of the other kids at the home, Noah, told me it was a shit idea.

'If you split from here and get caught they'll only drag you back. Even worse, they could put you in the lockup. You'll never see your sister then. By the time you're out she could be anywhere. You want her back, you got to make yourself the victim, not the crim.'

Noah lifted his shirt and showed me a jagged scar in his side, just under his ribs.

'Did this with a piece of glass at the last place I was at. Blamed it on the manager. I rang the cops myself when he had some of the boys out on a hike. They let me go home to my mum in a couple of days. It was easier than them finding another place for me, even though she was using heaps.'

The next night Noah and another boy at the house, Tran, who always smelled of piss because he wet the bed, held me down and burned me three times with a cigarette. It hurt like hell, but was worth it. I was out of there and back with Gwen before the scabs had come off. And a few weeks later, Rachel came back too.

Jon did the cooking at the farmhouse. He could fry up a breakfast, do a roast of a Sunday, and sometimes made what he called the 'B division version of the dagwood sandwich' for lunch. The ingredients were layers of cheese, tomato and onion and lots of salt and pepper, stuck between two pieces of white bread.

Jon could even bake a cake. One Saturday afternoon he walked all the way to the shops and came back with a brown paper bag carrying his 'secret ingredients'. He ordered us to stay out of the kitchen while he cooked. I could hear him banging away with pots and pans.

'What do you reckon he's making?' I asked Rachel.

She shrugged her shoulders. 'Dunno. It's not near teatime yet.'

A little later he called out to us, beating a drum roll on the edge of the kitchen sink with a couple of forks.

'Take a look kids. This is what you come up with after two years in the prison kitchen. Couldn't find a baking tin, so I greased an old biscuit tin I found in one of the cupboards. Thought I might have stuffed it up. But she's a beauty. Wish I had a fucken camera.'

A chocolate cake, topped with whipped cream, sat on a chipped plate in the middle of the kitchen table. We sat at the table while Jon cut a piece for each of us. Rachel stuck her hands under her chin, rested it on the table and stared at her slice of cake. Jon pointed the knife at it.

'You gonna eat it or what?'

Rachel wiped her hand across her mouth, catching some dribble. 'I don't wanna spoil it.'

'Spoil it all you like, sweetheart. There's plenty more to come.'

Before he'd gone to gaol, Jon told us he could cook only two meals other than toast and a boiled egg: the 'Ned Kelly', which was a main course, and a dessert he'd invented and christened the 'Can-Tam'.

'With the Ned Kelly you take a tin of crushed tomatoes, a tin of tomato soup and a tin of baked beans. Then you add a tin of water. Two if you want the feed to last a couple of meals. And it doesn't hurt to add some salt and pepper. Same rule as the dagwood. Plenty of salt and pepper.'

'Why's it called the Ned Kelly?' I asked. 'Because murderers eat it?'

'You're not saying I'm a murderer are you, Jesse?'

He smiled when he said it, so I guessed he wasn't angry with me.

'It's got nothing to do with being a murderer. It's all the tin cans in the recipe. You know, like the Kelly Gang and their tin hats.'

He shook his head and laughed.

'Jesus, he might have been brave. But what a fucken dumb idea.'

We never got to try the Ned Kelly, but we had the Can-Tam, lots of times. It had only two ingredients, sliced cantaloupe and chocolate Tim Tam biscuits, broken into pieces. Jon would put the biscuits into a tea towel and beat them with the heel of his shoe and sprinkle the mix over the top of the sliced cantaloupe.

The colours, brown and orange-yellow, didn't look all that good on the plate, but when you bit into it, the Can-Tam tasted sweet and juicy and crunchy all at the same time.

We usually ate it in front of the telly after we'd finished tea and cleaned up. Jon loved his dose of TV as much as Rachel and me. He said it was 'sacrilegious' to switch it off.

'Once you've got a hold of freedom, a taste of the good life, never let go of it,' he called out from the kitchen bench one night, where he was peeling potatoes, while Rachel and me were at the table trying to answer the questions on a quiz show.

'When I first went inside they doled out TV time along with cigarettes and chocolate milk. The set was bolted to the ceiling in the day room, where we all sat of a night.'

Rachel put her hand up to ask a question, like she was in class at school.

'You said it was the day room, Jon. How come you went in there at night-time?'

I thought it was a dumb question. I rolled my eyes and told her to stop interrupting. Jon was more patient with her. He leaned across the bench and patted her on the head.

'See, Jesse. She's sharp. She understands they were trying to fuck with us. They put us in the day room of a *night*. Good one, girl. Treated us like kids. One word out of line, one misdemeanour, and you could miss *The Bill* for a month. By the time you'd begged your privileges back you'd lost track of what was going on. Since I've been out, I've watched all the TV I can get. Flatline on it.'

He loved cop shows. I was surprised that he didn't seem to mind the police. He even barracked for them to catch the crooks. It was the lawyers in their suits and ties that got to him.

'A lawyer's like a sly old fox crossed with a snake,' he said from the couch one night.

He was smoking the fattest joint I'd ever seen and watching a repeat of *Law & Order*.

'I come across lots of fellas in the can who were done over worse by their lawyer than the Jacks.'

All Jon missed about prison, he said, was cable television. I thought he was making it up.

'You had cable TV in gaol? For free?'

'Yep. And computers.'

'Did they ration it? Like you said before, with the telly in the day room, if someone played up?'

'Yep. But when cable came in, they could shut them down, cell by cell. So, if the bloke in the next cell did the wrong thing, he paid the price, not the whole division. A fairer system, the old cable.'

'What did you like best on the telly?' Rachel asked.

'Well, I loved my sport. Specially the wrestling. All the boys went for the wrestling. Cooking shows were popular, of course. Although it could be torture, looking at all that top-shelf grub and not being able to get a mouthful.'

'Did you watch cartoons?'

'Too right. Watched a lot of cartoons, mostly old-school stuff, like *Top Cat*, *The Flintstones* and *The Rocky and Bullwinkle Show*. We all love cartoons, don't we?'

'Not Jesse,' Rachel said, laughing. 'Not when he was littler than me.' She held her hand over her mouth. 'Tell him that story, Jess.'

The story was embarrassing and I wouldn't have repeated it except that Jon wouldn't stop at me.

'Come on, Jesse. I really want to hear it. Give us the story.'

I don't know why but I stood up to tell it.

'Well, before Rachel was born Gwen and me were living in a bungalow in the backyard of this Greek fella, where we had this little TV, a portable one. It was mostly made of plastic. Orange plastic. After I turned it on I complained that we had a cheap telly. Well, Gwen said, "What do you mean a cheap TV? The picture looks okay to me." I told her the picture was fine but I couldn't understand why the people inside our TV were drawn with pencils and crayons. I wanted real people instead of drawn ones, I told her.'

Jon liked the story and couldn't stop laughing. Rachel laughed too, even though she'd heard it before.

'And what'd Gwen say?'

'She said if I didn't want to watch it she'd be more than happy to chuck it out the window for me.'

Rachel and me usually watched our favourite cartoon, *The Simpsons*, while we were having tea. Jon tried to get into it but didn't like it.

'This is a sitcom pretending to be a cartoon,' he complained. 'If that's what they're trying to do, then they should use actors in the first place. It's sort of like your portable telly story, Jesse. They should use real actors for this stuff.'

If we helped him with the dishes and cleaning up of a night, he'd tell us a prison story. They were crazy, wild stories. Some were so scary I hoped they weren't real. If I thought about them after I'd got into bed I couldn't get to sleep.

Jon said prison was a place of rules, and new inmates had to learn real quick that while some rules were written down, most of them you had to work out for yourself as you went along. If you didn't learn fast, he said, you could get hurt, even killed.

Rachel was fascinated by what he'd said. 'How would they kill you?'

'Don't you worry yourself about that, sweetheart,' he winked. 'There's some things you don't need to know.'

The first unwritten rule of prison was that you never asked another inmate what he'd done to end up in the lockup.

'That's your basic starting point, which every new boy should know. If a cellmate gives up his story, that's fair enough. Otherwise, you don't mention it.'

He said if you had 'half a brain' you tried your best to stay out of trouble.

'You look the other way. Say nothing. But once another inmate had made his mind up to get you, you can't take a backward step. Don't matter how frightened you are inside, you have to step up.'

Jon looked at me and repeated what he'd said, nodding his head up and down as he spoke, like it was important that I understood.

When he wasn't cooking or telling us stories he did jobs around the house. The roof was full of leaks and the floorboards were rotten. He'd fixed most of those within a couple of weeks. He built a set of shelves from planks of wood he'd dragged home from the highway. They'd fallen from passing trucks. When he'd finished the shelves he looked around the house to see what he could put in them. All he could find were a few cups, some old magazines and a book or two.

He also built a funny-looking toy for us to play with. It was a cross between a skateboard and a billy-cart and was made from more scrap timber and the wheels off an old pram he found in the shed out back. On warm nights he'd sit on the veranda steps, smoking a joint and listening to the radio, while I pushed Rachel up and down the road in the cart.

Jon started to worry that he'd 'gone to blubber' since getting out of prison so he also made himself a set of barbells from a metal star picket and two empty paint tins that he filled with cement. He poured cement into one of the tins and stuck the end of the picket in the tin. When it was hard, he filled the second tin with muddy cement and stuck it in the other end of the picket.

After breakfast he'd go out to the yard, wearing just a pair of jeans, and throw the barbell round like it weighed nothing. The muscles in his arms turned to knots of rope each time he lifted the bar, and I could see the blood pumping through his veins.

As he exercised I read the tattoos on his arms and on his back and chest. They were mostly the one colour, dark blue, and looked nothing like tattoos I'd seen before. Names ran up and down both arms. Some had dates with R.I.P. written under them. He had a pair of hands gripping a set of prison bars on his stomach and a large picture of a winged demon on his back.

It was a bit like the demon in Gwen's deck of tarot. It was a card she never liked dealing herself. Whenever I looked at his bare back I got a little scared that maybe I'd been wrong about Jon and he'd turn out to be no good and bring us more bad luck. We were watching him exercise one morning when Rachel pointed to one of the tattoos.

'What does R.I.P. mean, Jon?'

He lifted the barbell a few more times and put it on the ground before answering.

'R.I.P., Rest In Peace, love. They're dead. All these people listed here.'

Rachel ran her eyes up and down one arm. 'There sure is a lot of them.'

'Yep. There is. Two of them died inside but the others were citizens when they passed.'

He laid a hand on a name on his shoulder – Rodney.

'This bloke I'd known all the way back from the homes. Little kid, he was, when I met him. In for stealing cars. When the cops pulled him over, the night he was caught, he was sitting on the spare wheel from the boot so he could see over the steering wheel. Died a few years back, in a fight out the back of a country pub. A blue over a five-dollar bet on a game of pool.'

He pointed to the name below it – Shannyn Lee.

'She was a beautiful girl, Shannyn. Knew her before I went in last up. You know, some of your so-called friends drop off soon as you're away. You're as good as dead to most of them. Not Shannyn. Visited me whenever she could. Her old man wasn't happy about it, so she'd come out on the train when she could sneak away. We was never together or nothing. She was someone who cared about you. No matter what you'd done.'

'How'd she die?'

He looked across at Rachel. 'Just lost her way, mate. Lost her way.'

He picked up the barbell, looked at it like he wasn't sure what he had in his hands and dropped it back in the dirt.

'Any fella inside for the time I did, they carry their history with them. Your body is a map. Or a book.'

He stuck his fists under his chin, pushed his elbows forward and showed us the cobweb tattoos wrapped around both elbows.

'In the old days you'd count the number of rows in the web. That's how you worked out the years a man had done. A row for each year.'

I counted the rows on Jon's left elbow under my breath, five – six – seven.

'These days every man and his dog has ink. Have you see the old girl who works behind the jump at the post office down the road? She has a tatt. Got it for her sixtieth birthday, I heard her telling one of the customers. Ink means nothing these days. Movie stars have got it. Teachers. Even coppers. A mate of mine told me that when Princess Diana got killed in that car crash with the Arab bloke, they stripped her down on the slab at the morgue and saw that she had a pussy cat tattooed on one cheek of her arse, and a big dog on the other, with his tongue hanging out.'

He chuckled to himself. 'Jesus, wonder what the prince would have thought of that when he found out?'

The only tattoo he had with colour in it was a red heart and a scroll across his chest. The scroll, with R.I.P. under it, was blank.

'Who's that one for?' I asked.

'Me.'

'For you? But you're not dead.'

'Not yet. But one day, when I am, and they find me, people will see this. Then I'll be remembered.'

He covered the heart and scroll with his hand. 'I haven't seen any family for years now. And don't expect to. No one's gonna say any words for me when I'm gone. Except what I put here.'

He slapped his breast. 'Jon Daniel Dempsey – Rest In Peace. That's what I'm gonna have put there. I'm a little too superstitious to have it filled out yet. I've still got a bit of life in me. I don't want to be stirring the demons just yet by telegraphing my end. Tatts can do that. Fuck you up if you're not careful. Knew a bloke in gaol, went by the name of Pistol. Had a smoking snub-nose inked into one of his thighs. Surprised no one when he took a bullet in the back of the head.'

He pointed at his cheek, just below his eye. 'You come across a fella with a teardrop here, you give him a wide berth. Can only be bad news. He's probably killed. Most likely in gaol. Another inmate. A screw, maybe.'

He tapped his cheek a couple of times more to be sure we were paying attention. 'You two with me?'

'Yeah, we're with you,' I said, although I didn't reckon Rachel got much of it. She was looking bored and wandered off and picked up her bike. I thought that maybe I understood what Jon was getting at.

'It's like Gwen with the tarot cards,' I said. 'You look at some of them pictures and you know they mean trouble. There's one card with a dead body lying on the ground. A soldier, face down in the dirt, and he's got ten swords in his back. Been stabbed ten times. That has to be a bad sign, doesn't it, Jon?'

He raised his eyebrows and whistled. 'Stabbed in the back ten times? Yeah, I'd reckon that'd be about as bad a sign as a man could get. If I drew that card I'd be laying low for a while.'

Things were going along real well at the farmhouse until it went sour between Jon and Gwen. She turned on him, just like she had on other boyfriends. Trouble came out of the blue, on her night off from the pub. They usually sat on the couch, her with a drink, and him with a smoke, watching a DVD.

After we'd finished tea, she went into the bedroom and slammed the door.

'What's up her arse?' Jon asked, as I handed him the plates from the table.

'Dunno.'

When we'd finished cleaning the kitchen Jon asked Rachel to go tell Gwen he was about to start the movie. He picked up the remote and fired it at the telly. We could hear Gwen yelling at her over the volume.

'She says she won't be watching,' Rachel said, standing in the doorway.

'Suit herself then. Come on. Sit down with us.' Jon smiled and made some room for Rachel on the couch.

Gwen came out of her room a while later wearing a skin-tight black dress and lots of make-up. She stood in front of the telly and told Jon she wanted them to go out for the night.

'Sorry, babe. You know how it is. I'm on the wagon. Too much temptation down the road for me.'

'On the wagon? Bullshit. You're not on the wagon from the choof. You're never off it. You smoke more dope than fucken Bob Marley. Seeing as you don't mind taking money off me for your smoke, you can take me out for a drink.'

'Can't, love. It's not the same. It keeps me calm and off the grog. And the other stuff.'

She walked into the kitchen and sat at the table with a bottle of vodka for company. She poured herself a drink, then a second, and a third. She stood up, choked the neck of the bottle, walked back into the lounge and sat on the arm of the couch. Jon didn't take his eyes off the telly and wouldn't look at her when she called his name. She started poking fun of him, saying he was a 'fucken old bore', who never left the house.

'I dunno if you're just a big kid, the way you hang around with these two all day, or if you're turning into an old woman, with all your mopping and dusting. Dusting? For fuck's sake. Jesus, they sure fucked you up in gaol. Turned you into a robot.'

She teased him over his cooking, which wasn't fair, seeing as she always finished off the food he left out for her when she got home from work.

'And all those cakes and biscuits? What's that about? You've gone from being a gunnie to Jamie Oliver.'

Rachel was now on the floor with her colouring pencils. She loved the Jamie Oliver cooking show and started laughing.

When the bottle was empty Gwen went back to the kitchen. She banged around in the cupboards and the fridge, hunting for another drink. All she could find was a stubby of beer. She stood in the doorway between the kitchen and the lounge.

'You start showing me some attention or you can pack your bags. I want a night out. Tonight. You pick up your game, or you can fuck off now,' she screamed.

Rachel scooped up her pencils and ran out of the room. Jon didn't say a word. He looked from the telly to Gwen and back again, like she wasn't there. When she couldn't get his attention she stormed out of the lounge, slammed the front door and marched up and down the veranda.

When the movie was over Jon asked me to help him in the backyard, moving some scrap timber into the shed.

'There's something in the air. I don't want the wood getting wet if it rains. It'll go all out of shape and bend like fuck when it dries out. Won't be able to make a thing from it and we'll have to burn the lot.'

He was as calm as ever. Nothing Gwen had said seemed to have upset him. When we'd finished with the wood he made us a cup of tea and we sat on the back step. I heard a rumble of thunder and looked up. There wasn't a cloud in the sky.

'Where do you reckon it's coming from?' I asked.

'Could be hundreds of miles away. Sound travels a long way at night. When I was a kid I stayed with one of my aunties one time, in the country. She had a farmhouse, a bit like this place, but in better nick. They had chooks, and goats, a couple of cows. Late at night you could hear the train off in the distance, thump-thumping along, even though it was miles off. Miles and miles.'

A flash of lightning cut across the sky, with more thunder before it went quiet again. Too quiet.

'Jon, do you reckon it's gonna rain?'

'There's a storm coming, but not yet. This one might pass us by. It's hard to tell.'

He surprised me by grabbing hold of my arm and tugging at it until I looked him in the face.

'Will you be ready for it, Jesse? When the storm comes? You remember what I've told you. Sometimes you can stay out of trouble and other times you have to step up.'

He stood up without saying another word and walked back into the house.

Later on I lay in bed and thought about what he'd said as I listened to the thunder. When I got up in the night to pee, I saw he was asleep on the couch. The next morning he was nowhere to be found. His denim jacket, which always hung on a nail inside the back door, was gone. I walked out the front, down to the gate and searched for him. I saw nothing but empty road. When I walked back onto the veranda I spotted a piece of paper rolled around the handlebar of our homemade cart.

It was a note from him.

He wrote that he was was sorry he had to leave in a hurry, but he had to go to the city for some work, 'or my parole office will fuck me up.' The note ended on a p.s. – 'Don't forget to get stuck into a Can-Tam now and then, if you can remember the recipe!'

I tore the note into pieces, went into the backyard and locked myself in the shed and cried. I stayed in there a long time, until I heard Rachel calling my name. I didn't answer but I heard her footsteps at the shed door and then saw her eye blocking the light in the keyhole.

'I knew you'd be in there,' she whispered through the door. 'Please come out, Jesse. Or let me in. I want to be with you. She's going to be crazy at you. And then she'll be crazy at me too.'

When I went back into the house Gwen was at the table with a glass of water in one hand and some tablets in the other. She smiled at me like everything was fine.

'Why'd you let him go?' I yelled, my fists clenched by my side.

She swallowed the tablets, took a drink from the glass and put a hand to her head. 'Give me a break, Jesse. Can't you see I've got a hangover? Jesus Christ. He's just a fella. One fucken fella. Plenty more than him. And better. Stop sooking and get over it. If it'd been up to him we'd be sitting around like a pair of old-age pensioners waiting to cark it. I'm not ready for that. I've got life in me. Life.'

I'd never had a dad and couldn't have cared less about one until Jon came along. I wasn't sure if he was what dads were supposed to be like, and maybe I was wrong, because I'd met some pretty mean ones who'd spent the night with Gwen rather than be home looking after their own kids. But I did know I'd been happy when Jon was around. And I didn't want him to leave Rachel and me.

She was just as upset as I was. I found out how much she missed him when we were at the table the night after he left. Gwen was smoking a cigarette and doing her nails. Rachel got up, scouted the house a couple of times and came back into the room. She put her hand on Gwen's arm. 'Where's Jon gone to? When will he be back?'

'Won't be,' Gwen mumbled, and she took a long drag on her cigarette.

'Why not?'

When Gwen didn't answer, Rachel pulled at her dressing gown and asked again where he'd gone. Gwen was getting angry. I tried signalling to Rachel to stop with her questions, but she kept on going and grabbed at the dressing gown one time too many.

Gwen jumped up from the table and pushed her in the chest, sending her flying across the room. Rachel slammed into the cabinet against the wall and fell. Cups and plates crashed around her and a dirty plate of leftover casserole, the last meal Jon had made for us, landed in her lap.

'I said he's gone,' Gwen yelled. 'He got sick of you two nagging bastards and fucked off out of here.'

'That's not true,' Rachel screamed right back at her. 'You were fighting with him. I heard you. He's gone from you. Not us. And I'm going to go from you. With Jesse. My brother. He will take care of me.'

Gwen bent down and stuck a fist under Rachel's chin. 'Your brother? Take a good look at him.'

She pointed a finger at me.

'He's only your half-brother. Get it? Half. And his old man was a boong. You get that too, little sister? A drunken no-hoper who left me for dead with a new baby to look after. And your hero brother here, he'll grow up just like him. So don't be thinking he'll look after you when the shit hits the fan. He can't even look after himself, so don't get your hopes up.'

Gwen slammed the fist into her own chest and started crying. 'I'm your mother. Don't you ever forget it. *I* take care of you. No one else. And if you play up I can get rid of you any-time. One call to welfare and you're off. Both of you. Don't fucken push it.'

41

She staggered out of the kitchen and slammed the bedroom door behind her.

That night was the first time I'd thought about running away and knew I could really do it. I could easily go and never see Gwen again. But it would mean leaving Rachel behind.

I left her on the floor with the mess, crying to herself, and went out to the yard. I heard the shower turn on in the bathroom and then more door slamming, and a few minutes later, the whine of the rusting front gate. I walked around the side of the house to the front yard. I could smell perfume. I looked around for Gwen but couldn't see her anywhere.

I sat on the veranda step trying to work out how I might escape for good. Rachel came to the door and looked at me through the flywire.

'Is it true, Jesse?' she cried. 'That we're only half brother and sister?'

I'd always been good at making up a story, on the spot, to get me out of trouble. But I couldn't think of one right then, a lie for Rachel when she needed it most.

'Yeah, it's true. We're half brother and sister. So what? I thought you knew anyway. It's no big deal. We've got the good half,' I laughed.

She opened the door and came out. Her eyes were red where she'd been rubbing the tears away. She stared at me as hard as she could and stuck her hands under her armpits. I noticed she'd put on a clean dress. It was on back-to-front and inside-out.

'It's not funny, Jesse,' she screamed, stamping her foot on the wooden boards. 'I don't want us to be half. We have to be whole. Jenny Lee, the girl with the red hair and the freckles and the plaits from school, she told me that if you have half brothers or sisters and your mum and dad split up, you get separated. Forever. She has a little sister she hasn't seen for ages because her mum and dad had a divorce. It's because they're half, she says.'

'That's not true. Kids always go with their mum when there's a split. Anyway, we haven't got a dad between us, so there's no divorce to get. I don't know Jenny Lee, but I'd bet she's bullshitting, teasing you like that.'

'Don't you swear, Jesse. I don't want you to.'

'Okay. I won't. But only if you stop stamping your feet and screaming your head off. You're worse than Gwen sometimes.'

She stamped her foot again. 'No, I'm not.'

'Then don't act like her.'

She sat next to me. 'What's a boong?'

'A boong?'

'Yeah. Gwen said your dad was a dirty boong.'

'It's an Abo. An Aborigine.'

'Your dad was an Aborigine? Like out in the bush?'

'Don't really know. When I was little, smaller than you, I was always asking Gwen who my dad was, all the time. If she was in a shit mood she'd tell me he was a 'no-good Abo'. Or sometimes, a Wog. Or a Gypo. All sorts of things. And when she was in a good mood she'd tell me he was a musician, a guitar player, someone famous from a rock band she'd met at a pub she was working at. She couldn't name him, she said, because of the scandal it would make. I dunno which story was true. Maybe none of them.'

She frowned. 'What's a Gypo?'

'Maybe like a gypsy. Or an Egyptian. Not sure.'

'Is that why your skin is browner than mine is? And your hair is curly and mine is straight? Cause of what your dad is?'

'I suppose so. But I don't care. You're my sister. All I got.'

'I want to know who my daddy is.'

'Well, you'll have to ask her. I dunno. I swear.'

'I did ask her, one time, but she got angry with me too. Tell me, Jesse.'

'I really don't know, I can't tell you anything. That's the truth, I swear.'

She made fists and banged them against the top of her legs until they turned as red as her face. I grabbed hold of her again and tried to stop her.

'Don't do that. You'll hurt yourself.'

'I want to. I hate Gwen. I hate her.'

'I hate her too. But you don't see me belting myself up. Stop it.'

She might have hated Gwen, sometimes, but it didn't stop Rachel fretting for her whenever she left us alone for too long. No matter how bad she treated Rachel, all Gwen had to do was put out her arms, pout her lips and ask for a hug. Rachel would run to her without thinking twice.

She wouldn't stop her screaming. I had to do something to shut her up. When I tried dragging her into the house she pulled against me.

'Do you want us to be whole or not?' I asked.

'Whole?'

'Do you want to be my full sister? Me your full brother?'

She dropped her head. 'Course.'

'Good. Shut up then and come with me.'

I marched her into the house and told her to sit at the table while I went through the cupboard drawers, looking for a knife. Because we moved around so much we didn't keep stuff of our own. Just a few cups and plates, a couple of pots and knives and forks. Jon had said it was a miracle he could cook at all with the stuff we had.

I couldn't find a sharp knife in the kitchen, so I took Gwen's razor from the bathroom and smashed it under a leg of a chair by jumping on the seat. Bits of plastic flew across the kitchen floor and the blade came away in one piece.

With the razor in one hand I held my thumb over the sink and sliced across the top of it. I cut myself deeper than I should have and it hurt like hell. I watched the blood as it ran down the inside of my thumb, across my palm and down my arm. Spots of blood, big as raindrops, splashed onto the lino floor. Rachel was holding onto her chair as tight as she could.

'Come on. Now it's your turn.'

She looked down at the spots of blood. 'Nope. It's not my turn, cause I'm not doing it. You're like Gwen. You're being crazy, Jesse.'

'No I'm not. We're gonna be whole. You said that's what you wanted.'

She shook her head and wouldn't move. I showed her the bloodied blade, which was maybe a bad idea.

'Come on, I said. I'm losing all my own blood here while I'm waiting. Do you want to be whole or not? You're the one who was crying over what Gwen said, not me. I don't even care. Now, come on,' I said, a little more quietly.

She got slowly to her feet, but refused to come closer to the sink. She couldn't take her eyes off my bloodied thumb.

'I don't want to.'

'Rachel. I promise, if we do this we can never be separated, by anyone.'

'But Gwen said she can tell the welfare people.'

'Don't listen to her. If she called welfare she'd be the one in big trouble. They'd probably lock her up. And she knows it. She won't be calling anyone. Now, give me your thumb.'

'I have to go to the toilet first.'

'No. The toilet can wait until we've done this.'

'Will it hurt?' She pointed at my thumb. 'I bet it hurt you?'

My thumb was throbbing with pain.

'No, it doesn't hurt if you do it quick. I can't feel anything. Now come here.'

She took a step towards me and held out her hand. She squeezed her eyes closed, opened them again and looked at the blade. Her hand was shaking as I took it in mine.

'Look away, Rachel. Over at the TV.'

She looked at the telly, through the kitchen door and on the other side of the lounge.

'It's off.'

'Well, pretend it's on. Or look out the window. Now.'

I wrapped my hand around her wrist, held on as tight as I could and nicked the tip of her thumb with the blade. She didn't cry at all. She let out a yelp like a puppy that had had its tail trod on. I pressed my thumb to hers and we watched as our blood ran together.

'How does it work?' she asked. 'If only half our blood is the same how does this make us whole?'

'It works like a ritual. An American Indian ritual. I saw it on TV.'

'What does that mean?'

'It's a powerful spell and it can't be broken. Not by anyone.'

'A spell,' she repeated a couple of times.

'Yep. And we have the same blood in our bodies now.'

'Didn't we always have our blood together? Some of it?'

'Yeah. But not like this. Not in the ritual. That's where the magic comes from.'

She drew her thumb away, looked at her cut and then at mine.

'Your cut is bigger,' she said, as she turned her thumb to mine. A lid of skin moved up and down on the top of my thumb as she pressed against it.

'Your blood colour is darker too. What's that mean?'

'Nothing. When you mix them together they're the same. Half and half make one. That's all that matters.'

'It's sticky,' she said, laughing. 'Our thumbs are stuck together.'

She jammed her thumb in her mouth and sucked hard. I couldn't make out what she said next.

'Take your thumb out of your gob.'

She had smudges of blood across both cheeks.

'I'm your magic sister,' she said, smiling.

TWO

I really missed Jon. Rachel didn't talk about him much at all, but she was as miserable as I was. She moped around the farmhouse with her head down and didn't know what to do with herself. Getting her to go to school was hard. She lost the friends she'd made on account of Jon, and was off on her own again.

If Gwen was disappointed that Jon had gone, it didn't show. She was drinking more but that was no surprise. She always hit it harder after a break-up. A couple of weeks after he left the police turned up at the gate with a warrant for his arrest. After they'd had a good snoop around to see if he was hiding somewhere in the house, one of the coppers slapped a card down on the kitchen table and told Gwen it would be 'in her best interest' to get in touch with them if Jon showed up.

'We have a series of violent robberies that we need to question him over. Your boyfriend held a weapon to a young lady's throat. These kids are not safe with him around. He's a bad man.'

'You don't have to tell me,' Gwen agreed. 'And he's not my boyfriend. Shouldn't have let him near the kids in the first place. I feel sick just thinking about it.'

Gwen's boss, Larry, started stopping off for a drink when he dropped her home after work. His car would roar off in the middle of the night, sometimes later, when he stayed until the sun was up.

I woke one Sunday morning to the sounds of shouting and swearing outside my window. I got out of bed and lifted the blind. A woman was standing on the gravel pathway wearing skin-tight jeans, white boots and a black top that had sparkles on the front. She was waving her arms around and screaming at Larry. He was barefoot and smoking a cigar, wearing only a shiny pair of black suit pants with the fly undone. He had a gut like a pregnant lady.

Larry's car, a hotted up red ute with chromed wheels, was parked in the driveway. I picked up the words 'Gwen' and 'slut' in the one sentence before the woman picked up a handful of gravel and threw it against the side of the house. She kicked some more gravel at Larry, rushed at him and thumped him so hard in the chest he fell backwards, onto his arse. She stood over him, spat in his face then marched off to a small yellow car parked out the front. She screeched off down the road, one arm out of the window, giving him the rude finger.

For a moment Larry lay on his back looking up at the morning sky, scratched his belly and took a puff of his cigar. He stood up, dusted himself down and walked back to the house. I closed the blind and listened to the muffled talk between him and Gwen, and then a few minutes later I heard him drive off too.

Gwen lay low in her room all that morning and left for work at the usual time in the afternoon, without a word to Rachel or me. We were surprised to see her back within a couple of hours, fuming. She said as soon as she walked into The Road Train, Larry sacked her 'on-the-fucken-spot, with no pay'.

She took a bowl of noodles into her room and slammed the door behind her. I made some toast and vegemite for us then put Rachel to bed and told her stories until she fell asleep. I was asleep myself later that night when our door crashed open and Gwen came into the room and shook me awake.

'Jesse, in the morning you pack that case under the bunk with as much of Rache's and your stuff that you can fit into it. We're leaving.'

'Leaving? Where we going?'

'Do what I say and just be ready.'

My stomach starting churning up and it took me ages to get back to sleep, worrying over what would happen to us. I didn't want Gwen moving us on again. But I knew we were flat broke and if we stayed at the farmhouse we'd starve.

I was so tired the next morning that I slept in and Gwen had to drag me out of bed. Rachel pretended she was asleep until Gwen left the room, then poked her head over the side of the top bunk and watched as I stuffed the suitcase with clothes. A couple of times I yelled at her to get dressed but she wouldn't move.

'If you don't get some clothes on soon, Gwen'll whack you, so get moving. She told me to do this job and get you ready. If she starts on me, I'll start on you because it'll be your fault.'

She shook her head from side to side. 'I want to stay here. What about if Jon comes back? He won't be able to find us if we go away.'

'Don't be stupid, Rachel. Jon's not coming back. The cops were after him.'

'If I'm the one who's stupid, why do you pray for him to come back? I heard you.'

'That's not praying. I was making a wish. It's not the same thing.'

'You still do it and it's cause you want him back too.'

'Maybe I do. But I know he's not coming.'

She climbed down the side of the bunk and changed out of her pyjamas into a flowery shirt and a denim dress I'd left on the floor for her. She pulled on an old pair of runners and was about to leave the room when I laughed at her and pointed.

'Hey, don't forget your undies.'

She grabbed hold of her skirt and pulled at it. 'Oops.'

We shared a can of peaches and some flat lemonade for breakfast. Even though there didn't seem much point in doing it, I rinsed the dishes under the tap and left them on the sink to dry, like Jon had shown me to. I then stood in the middle of the kitchen and took a last look around. We'd been at the farmhouse less than a year but it was the longest I'd spent in one place and knew I'd miss it.

Gwen came into the room, dragging her suitcase behind her. Rachel grabbed hold of my hand and squeezed tight.

'Come on, you two,' Gwen barked.

When neither of us moved she nodded to the front door. 'Go. Now. Both of you.'

She followed us out of the house and shut the door behind her.

I couldn't look back as I marched down the road carrying one case while Gwen lugged the other. Rachel wouldn't carry anything except for the teddy bear she'd bought for twenty cents in an op shop three birthdays ago. I don't know how she did it but she'd held onto that bear through all the moves we'd made since. When she bought the bear it was all grubby, the lining had split down its side and half the stuffing was missing. Rachel washed it and mended the hole with two safety pins. She named the bear Comfort, in honour of a bear on the TV that advertised clothes softener and, according to her, had to be the twin of the one she'd bought.

With Comfort tucked under her arm she trailed behind me along the road, walking as slow as anyone could without stopping. She was doing it so Gwen would know just how angry she was about having to leave. By the time we reached the bus stop she was way back on the road. Gwen called out to her that if she didn't catch up she'd miss the bus and be left on her own. If Rachel heard it didn't make any difference. If it was possible, she walked even slower.

By the time the bus turned up Rachel was moaning that she was tired and hungry.

'Tired?' Gwen screamed. 'How could you be tired? You just got out of bed. And you had your breakfast. I saw you eating.'

'Peaches,' Rachel fired back at her. 'Peaches aren't breakfast.'

The driver got down from the bus and picked up one of the cases. As Gwen was counting out our bus fare, in small change she'd scrounged from around the house, he couldn't take his eyes off her tits, popping out of a black bra under the dress she was wearing.

When she handed him the coins he jangled them in his hand. 'You're a dollar short, love.'

'You sure? I thought I counted it right.'

He bent forward to get a better look at her tits. The tip of his tongue was sitting on his bottom lip. Gwen followed his eyes and looked down her front. She didn't move or try covering up.

Once he'd had a good perve he smiled at her and winked. 'That's all right, love. Hop on. Take a seat, kids.'

After the bus took off Gwen put a hand under her chin and stared out the window. Rachel leaned against me and held up her thumb, showing me the neat pink cut across the top. It was already scabbing at the edges.

We took the bus to the end of the line and pulled in at a depot with lots of other buses, painted different colours. The drivers were standing in a group at one end, talking and having a smoke before they had to take off again.

Rachel and me sat guarding the cases in front of some shops while Gwen walked to a telephone box on the corner. I watched as she dialled a number. She'd always known how to con the operator with a sob story about losing her money, or some kind of emergency that she was in. She stopped for a bit and then started talking again, to somebody else, I guessed. I watched as she pulled the receiver away from her ear. She stared at it with a weird look on her face, like she didn't know what she was holding in her hand, or maybe who was on the other end of the line.

When she started talking again I could just about hear her from where we were sitting. She was arguing with somebody. She stopped and rested against the side of the telephone box. She held the receiver to her chest, closed her eyes, and slipped down the box until she was just about on her knees.

Rachel had been watching too. She stood up and walked along the footpath to the phone box. Gwen tried shooing her away but Rachel wouldn't move, so Gwen opened the door and yelled, 'Piss off.'

'What's gonna happen to us, Jesse?' Rachel asked, when she came back. She tapped the edge of the footpath with the toe of her shoe. It had a hole in it and her big toe was poking out. 'I bet it will be something bad.'

'No it won't. Gwen'll think of something. She always does. Maybe she's talking to Mary. I think she lives round here somewhere. I remember these shops. When we stayed with her I reckon we came down here for fish and chips.'

'I don't like Mary. She's mean. I'm not going to her house.'

I didn't like Mary either, and hadn't from the first time I'd seen her, but if Gwen decided we were going to stay with her there'd be no arguing over it.

Gwen hung up the phone and I watched as she walked slowly along the footpath in front of the line of buses, reading the names of the places each bus was heading to. When she got to the end of the line she spoke to the drivers. One of them held up his watch, shook his head a couple of times and smiled. Gwen just about ran back to us and snapped her fingers at me.

'Jesse, get your case down to that bus, the blue and white one on the end of the row. Rachel, you too. Go. The driver'll let you know when it's your stop. You're gonna be picked up from there.'

As soon as she said 'picked up' I thought about the welfare. Maybe that's who she'd called on the phone?

'What do you mean? Who's picking us up?'

'Your grandfather. Your pop,' she said, quietly, almost like she was embarrassed. 'He's going to meet you with his car. He'll pay the driver the fare when you get there.'

Rachel was getting worked up. She scratched the side of her face. 'We don't have a pop. Isn't he dead, Jesse?'

Maybe he was. I wasn't sure. The last time we'd seen him had been for only a few minutes. We'd met at a café in the city. Rachel was still in her pusher and Gwen bought me a milkshake and told me to push her up and down out the front while they had a talk. It wasn't long before she came running out and left Pop on his own. They'd had a fight.

Rachel screamed that she didn't want to go to a stranger's house and started to cry. She grabbed hold of Gwen and begged her to come with us.

'I can't.'

'Why not?' I asked.

Gwen's face was pink and sweaty. 'Because . . . because he doesn't want me there. We don't get on.' She pushed away Rachel, who couldn't stop herself from sobbing.

I grabbed the handle of the suitcase with one hand and yanked Rachel's arm with the other. 'Come on. We have to go.'

'No,' Rachel cried.

Other people waiting for their buses started looking at us. Rachel dug her heels into the footpath and wouldn't move.

Gwen pressed her face against Rachel's. 'You're going with your brother. Don't you get it? I've got no money. I can't even feed you.'

'You said he wasn't my brother. Why do you want me to go away with him now?'

I pulled at her shirtsleeve. 'Come on, Rachel, please. You don't want us to miss the bus. We'll have to walk all the way with this case. When we get to the other end I'll ask Pop to buy us a Coke or something.'

'I don't want a Coke.'

She tried grabbing hold of Gwen again. She pushed Rachel away, picked up her own case and walked off. Rachel threw herself on the ground. I left her where she was and started walking the other way. When she'd worked out that Gwen wasn't coming back for her she jumped up and ran after me.

The driver was sitting on the bus, waiting for us with the engine running. 'I'll give you a yell when we get to your stop.'

'Where's that?' I asked.

'You don't know where you're going?'

'No.' He shook his head and groaned.

'Don't worry. I'll let you know.'

As the bus took off I looked out the window, along the shopping strip. Gwen had already disappeared.

The bus headed along a busy road, past some car yards, a soccer ground and a cemetery that went on forever. I started counting the headstones but there were too many and I gave up. The bus stopped and collected more passengers at the next stop.

An old woman staggered on, carrying shopping bags in both arms.

'How much further is it, Jesse?' Rachel asked.

'Can't say. I don't know where we're going.'

'You don't know?'

'Nup. Haven't got a clue.'

After two more stops the driver called out to us.

'Hey, you kids. Here's your stop.'

We pulled into a car park. A couple of old men were sitting on a bench talking to each other.

'Some old bloke's supposed to meet us here and pay your fare. You see him?' the driver asked.

I couldn't remember my grandfather's face, so, of course I couldn't see him.

The driver looked at his watch and shrugged his shoulders. 'Oh well. It's only a couple of bucks. I've got a timetable to meet.'

I reckoned he could see I was looking worried.

'I'll tell you what. When I'm on my way back I'll look out for you. I'll pick you up if you're still here.'

'And what'll we do then?' Rachel asked.

He shrugged his shoulders again. 'Don't know, love. But don't you worry. I'm sure someone'll turn up for you.'

He got back on the bus, waved goodbye, closed the door with a whoosh of air and took off. Rachel tugged at my arm.

'What do you think, Jesse? Will we wait for him to come back?'

'We have to. We've got no place to go.'

She sat down on the case, and I stuck my hands in my pockets and walked along the edge of the kerb, trying to keep my balance. I spotted a man walking towards me. He had on a clean white shirt and grey pants with sharp creases down the front, and black leather shoes. They were shiny as new. His silver hair was parted in the middle and brushed back like an old-time movie star. I was surprised I recognised him straightaway. Rachel stood up, backed away from the case and stood behind me. He looked us up and down like he wasn't pleased to see us, nodded his head and picked up the case.

'Is this all you've got?'

'Yep,' I whispered, a little ashamed. 'I can carry it myself, the case, if you want me to.'

'I've got it.'

We followed him between the rows of cars. Rachel grabbed hold of the back of my shirt and wouldn't let go. He stopped at a battered station wagon with a sticker on the bumper bar – 'Free Yourself With God'. He opened the back door and carefully laid the case down. He got into the driver's seat and lifted the button on both the passenger doors.

When neither of us moved he leaned across and unwound the front passenger window. 'Are you coming or not? I don't see much point staying here.'

Rachel got into the back seat. Before she could close the door I jumped in and shoved her across the other side of the car. He looked across at the empty front passenger seat, then at me, in the rear-view mirror.

'Are you hungry?'

I was starving but I kept my mouth shut. I was still trying to work out what was happening to us. He just about smiled at Rachel.

'What about you? You want something to eat on the way, or can you wait?'

Rachel dropped her head and stuck her chin in her chest. She wasn't about to open her mouth either. He looked at me again and raised his eyebrows.

'Okay. We'll wait.'

As soon as he'd driven off Rachel tapped me on the knee and whispered down to the floor, 'I'm real hungry, Jesse.'

I pushed her hand away and tried ignoring her by looking out the window. She said it again, a little louder. He looked at me again through the mirror.

'We'll stop here.'

He pulled into a spot at a 7-Eleven, and handed me a twenty-dollar note.

'Take your sister inside and get yourselves something to eat.'

I looked down at the money and back at him. I noticed that he was clean-shaven and had a nick of blood on the tip of his chin. His bushy eyebrows were half black and half grey and his eyes were a pale blue, almost grey, just like Gwen's. I took the money.

'What should we buy?'

'Get what you need to.'

I soon learned that our pop used as few words as he needed to say anything. At first I thought he did it because he was unfriendly and didn't want us around. He and Gwen looked a bit the same but they were mostly different. While she was loud and angry most of the time, he was quiet. I reckoned he did a lot more thinking than talking, which was fine by me because I did that too.

His house was tidy and as quiet as he was. It was made of concrete and in a street full of other concrete houses that all looked the same. That first time we drove into the street,

Rachel wound down her window and stuck her head out to get a better look. Some of the houses had car wrecks in the front yards. One had been boarded up with sheets of corrugated iron and had black marks around the windows where there'd been a fire.

We pulled into his driveway. His garden had a scraggy tree in the middle of a dry lawn. As soon as he opened the front door of the house I could smell something like disinfectant. Inside everything was spotless. He dropped our suitcase on the floor in the hallway, and we walked quietly behind him, from room to room, as he showed us around. He opened a door off the lounge room. It was a small bedroom.

'You'll both have to sleep here. I'll get some sheets and blankets for the bed and there's a spare mattress out the back. I'll fix that up for you, Jesse. You'll have to sleep on the floor,' he sort of apologised, and clapped his hands together. 'I'll put the kettle on.'

Rachel was just about strangling Comfort and wouldn't take a step into the bedroom. I walked in, sat on the bed and took a good look around. There were faded pictures stuck on the walls, of movie stars and rock singers with funny haircuts. Bags of stuff were piled on top of a wardrobe. I could see toys and Barbie dolls through the clear plastic.

A photo in a frame hung on the wall above the bed, of a woman and a teenage girl. I could see that the girl was Gwen and guessed the woman was her mum, our grandma. In the photo she was wearing a buttoned-up jacket and a hat and carrying a leather bag. Gwen was wearing a frilly white dress and a veil and some sort of tiara. She had one hand resting on her stomach and was bent forward like she was about to throw up.

I'd never thought about Gwen as a kid before, younger than me, but a bit bigger than Rachel.

I pointed to the picture as a way of getting her to come into the room.

'Look, Rache. It's Gwen.'

Although she was curious enough to take a look, she didn't move an inch.

'How do you know it is? Maybe it's a different girl.'

'It's her, for sure.'

She slowly crept into the room, climbed onto the bed and pressed her face against the photo, close enough that her breath misted the glass.

'You're right. It's her. She looks pretty. What do you think she's doing in that beautiful dress?'

'Going to church, I'd reckon.'

She didn't take her eyes off the picture until Pop came back and told us to come for a cup of tea. The table was set with three cups and saucers and a plate of biscuits, all plain, no chocolate or cream. He went to the back door, whistled a couple of times, then turned around and said, 'He will have crawled under the back fence and gone for a wander,' like we knew what he was talking about.

A minute later a small dog came running into the kitchen. It was white with brown patches over its body and a black tail. It was moving so fast it slipped on the lino floor, skidded across the room and slammed into the fridge. It got straight up and started running again and barking. It skated around and around the table and stopped to sniff Rachel's leg. She jumped down from her chair and started patting the dog. Rachel loved dogs.

'A puppy. What's its name?' she asked.

'Maxie, but he's no pup. He's going on ten years old. He should have slowed by now but hasn't.'

The dog jumped up and butted Rachel on the chin with the end of his nose and licked her all over the face.

'Can we walk him?'

'You can. Be sure, though, to keep him on a lead. He's a bolter. And the side gate, out in the yard, always remember to keep it shut. I don't want him running off and getting himself bowled over.'

When Gwen left us at the bus terminal she told me she'd pick us up in a day or two. I was glad when she didn't turn up the next day. She called the house about a week later. I knew she was on the other end of the line when I heard Pop ask if she wanted to talk to us. She didn't. He got off the phone and said she'd told him she was sick and we'd have to stay with him for another week or more.

While he was cooking the tea, we took Maxie down to the football ground at the end of the street, on his lead. Two kids from one of the houses along the street were hanging over their front fence, giving us the eye.

'Fuck off!' the taller boy yelled out and stuck a finger up.

I looked back at them a couple of times as we walked on, to be sure they weren't following us.

When we got to the oval I let the dog off the lead, even though Rachel said we shouldn't. Maxie ran around in circles, lifted his head in the air and barked and growled like he was crazy or something. He upset a magpie that had been pecking

64

at a brown paper bag with a half-eaten sandwich inside. The bird flew into the air then swooped down on Maxie and tried to take his eye out. Maxie took off across the grass with Rachel and me chasing him and calling out to come back. He ducked under the fence and stopped and waited for us under a tree. He was so puffed out he lay down in the grass and rolled on his side. Rachel put his lead back on and told him how naughty he'd been.

On the way back to Pop's I could see the two boys were standing out the front of their place, waiting for us. I grabbed Rachel by the arm.

'Come on. Cross the street.'

When we crossed, they did too and stopped on the footpath ahead of us, blocking our way. If one of them hadn't been half a foot taller than the other, I'd have reckoned they were twins. They had buzz-cut hairdos, like kids who'd been caught with the nits, and skinny arms and legs with sores all over them. The tall boy was carrying a long stick and I could see that the short one had a rock hidden in his hand. The boy with the stick also had a cockeye.

Gwen had always warned me that it was bad luck to look a cockeyed person in their bung eye, so I looked down at the ground.

'Where ya from?' Cockeye asked, aiming his stick at me. He looked like he was going to spear me, any minute.

'We're from nowhere.'

'Get fucked. Must be from somewhere. Everyone's from somewhere.'

Maxie stepped forward and growled at them. The smaller boy pointed at him.

'Dog belongs to The Preacher. Seen him walk this fucken dog all the time. You seen him, Donny.'

Cockeye Donny spat on the ground, just missing Maxie, who barked and pulled on the lead.

'Yeah, I seen him. You staying with The Preacher then?'

'Come on, Rache. We have to get back.'

They wouldn't move from the footpath to let us pass. I walked onto the road, holding Maxie's lead in one hand and Rachel's hand in the other. Cockeye Donny ran onto the road and blocked our path again. His brother was giggling like a lunatic. Cockeye Donny lifted the stick so we couldn't get around him.

'Where you think you going? You want to pass, you got to pay us. We've been here all our life and this is our place, not yours. So fucken pay up. A toll is what it's called.'

I had no money to pay with and nothing I could give them to pass by. I took a step forward. I was frightened but I remembered Jon telling me there were times when I would have no choice but to step up. I concentrated on Cockeye Donny's good eye and hoped he couldn't see my legs shaking.

'I'm going home, to my grandfather's place. I have to get my sister in for tea.'

I moved in closer to him. As my chest touched his he took a step back. He tried staring me down. I had no choice but to look him in both eyes and accept that it might bring me bad luck later on. He looked at his little brother a couple of times, dropped the stick to the ground and let us pass. I gripped Rachel's hand as tightly as I could and didn't look back as we walked away. I could hear them following us.

'Youse know?' Cockeye Donny yelled out when I reached our front gate. 'Before he was The Preacher, your grandfather, they called him Shit Legs, cause that's what he did, shit his pants all the time when he was pissed.'

He yelled, 'Shit Legs, Shit Legs . . .' until I closed the door behind us.

I couldn't believe that Pop had ever been a drunk, or had done the things that Cockeye Donny said he had. He ran his house and his life like clockwork, and had a set routine for everything. After Gwen's phone call, when he knew we wouldn't be leaving too soon, he gave us jobs to do each day. We had to organise breakfast at seven o'clock 'on the dot', both on weekdays and weekends. Rachel had always found it hard getting out of bed, and I was sure she'd complain about having to get up early, but she didn't. She got straight out of bed when the alarm went off and loved her job, arranging the bowls and spoons and cups on the table. I looked after the toast, the butter and jam, and the cereal and milk. Pop said making a good cup of tea was an 'art form', so we left that to him.

He cleaned the house from top to bottom after breakfast, sweeping and mopping the same floors he'd done the day before, even when they weren't dirty. After lunch he went to his room and read for a while then went off on his own for a couple of hours in the afternoon. Before he left the house he would tell us he had 'a meeting to be at', but said nothing more.

We fell into his routine and did the same things at the same time every day. It could be boring sometimes, but for the first time in my life I knew, pretty much, what was coming next and really liked it. He also had rules and regulations but was fair with them and followed them as much as he expected us to. One rule was that the TV did not go on until after we'd finished our tea and cleaned up. I was used to putting the telly on as soon as I got out of bed in the morning and was a bit lost and lonely without it.

It was the only rule I decided to break.

Once he'd leave the house for his meeting of an afternoon I'd turn on the TV. We loaded up on cartoons, old episodes of *I Dream of Genie*, and half a game show before he got back. I sat in his armchair near the window, where I had a view of the street. As soon as I saw him walk around the corner at the top of the street I'd jump down and turn the set off. Rachel would run into the bedroom and lie on the floor with a book like she'd been there all afternoon.

It was a good plan. And it worked – for about a week. One afternoon, when I spotted him coming home, I turned off the TV and opened up the old atlas he kept on the coffee table and pretended I was studying a map. He came into the lounge, stopped in the middle of the room, sniffed the air and screwed his face up like someone had farted. He walked over to the TV and laid his palm on the screen. We both heard the crackle. As he walked past me and out of the room he said, 'No telly, for a week. And by the way, you've got the atlas upside down.'

That night, after tea, he asked us questions about school, where we'd gone and what grade we were up to.

'Are we going to go to school here?' Rachel asked. 'I don't want to. Those mean boys from the street will be there.'

'We'll see. It depends how long you're here. We'll see what happens after Christmas. And don't worry about any boys. They're not so mean.'

I'd never liked Christmas with Gwen. Whether we were on our own, sharing with one of her girlfriends, or if she was living with a fella, she'd end up drunk or high and get in a fight with someone. Sometimes we got presents, sometimes not. We also got the same story from her, every year, that one Christmas, when she got on her feet, she'd take us to Disneyland. And every year Rachel's eyes would light up like the Christmas tree we didn't have.

On Christmas morning at Pop's house, I woke to the sounds of kids laughing and playing in the street. I lay on the mattress and listened. They were happy and I was jealous. I tapped at the frame of Rachel's bed with my foot.

'You awake?'

'Yep.'

She'd been listening to the kids too. She rustled around under her blanket and poked her head over the top.

'Shouldn't we be up? It's time to set the table.'

I hadn't heard the alarm or Pop moving about doing his jobs. I didn't feel like getting up, but thought it best to not be late.

The kitchen was empty. Pop usually had the radio on and listened to the news. It was turned off and he was nowhere to be seen. Walking to the toilet, I could see across the hallway into his bedroom. The bed was made and he was gone.

As I washed my hands I heard Rachel call out from the lounge room. It sounded like she was in pain. When I ran to the room, she was standing in the middle holding a parcel in her arms, wrapped in Christmas paper. A small tree stood in front of the fireplace, decorated with shining red balls.

'There's one for you too, Jesse. It has your name on it. And look, a real tree, not a fake one. Can you smell it?'

I could and it was a wonderful smell. I was sure I'd smelled it before, a long time ago, maybe even when I was a baby. Another parcel was sitting on the coffee table. I picked it up and noticed straightaway that it was heavy. I didn't want to cry but couldn't stop myself. As soon as I felt the tears in my eyes I turned my back on Rachel, walked over to the window. I could see Cockeye Donny hanging over his fence. He seemed to live in his front yard.

Rachel pushed herself between me and the window. 'Jesse, why are you crying?'

I wiped my eyes. 'I'm not crying. It's sleep in my eyes.'

'It's not. You should be happy. Come on. We can open our presents together.'

'I am happy.' I was about to rip the paper from my present but stopped. 'You go first.'

Rachel sat on the floor with the parcel in her lap. She turned it over and picked carefully at the sticky tape. She was taking too much time.

'Come on, tear it off or we'll be here till next Christmas.'

'I don't want to ruin the paper.'

She slowly removed each piece of tape and opened the parcel. There was a second layer of paper, pink tissue. She gently placed the gift on the floor, still wrapped in the tissue paper and started folding the wrapping paper, over and over, into small squares. Once she'd finished she stuck the gift paper in her pyjama-top pocket and patted it.

'It's for keeps,' she said.

I couldn't wait any longer. I picked up my gift and tore the paper away from the present. It was a pair of binoculars. There were some scratches and marks on them; they weren't new but I didn't care. I looked through the lens at Rachel. She was miles away. I turned them around and looked again and she was all a blur.

She took the tissue paper away from her gift. It was a rag doll in blue checked overalls on a pink blanket of paper. The doll had orange hair tied in pigtails, big eyes and red cheeks. She picked the doll up and hugged it to her chest.

'She's beautiful. I'll have to think up a name for her. Do you think Gwen will like her?'

I didn't want Rachel spoiling everything by mentioning Gwen. 'Who cares?'

'I do.'

I changed the subject. 'I wonder where Pop is?'

'Maybe he's gone to his meeting again. Do you think he'll be angry that we opened the presents without him?'

'I don't reckon he'd have left them out with our names on them if he didn't want us to open them.'

I left her playing with the doll and went into the front yard with the binoculars. I looked through them along the street. I followed a young kid trying to keep a new two-wheeler balanced as a man, probably his dad, ran alongside him, guiding him down the middle of the road with a hand on his shoulder. Cockeye Donny's face bobbed up in the lens all of a sudden, like he was standing right in front of me. I dropped the binoculars. The brothers were walking down the middle of the road, heading straight for me. I could have walked back

71

into the house and closed the door, and maybe I should have. Instead, I rested against the fence and waited for them.

Cockeye Donny stopped outside the gate and pointed at the binoculars. 'Where'd ya get em?'

'Off my pop, for Christmas.'

'How far can ya see through em?'

'Maybe for miles.'

He put a hand out and looked down at the ground as he spoke. 'Can I have a go?'

I looked at his open hand. He had dirt under his fingernails and scratches on the tips of his fingers. I knew if I gave him the binoculars he'd probably run off down the street. His little brother wiped some snot from his nose with the bottom of his t-shirt. I hadn't met too many kids who were poorer than us. I knew they were and felt sorry for them, even though Cockeye Donny could be an arsehole.

'My pop says I'm not supposed to take them out,' I lied, 'until I know how to use them properly. But if you come inside the gate, you can have a look through them.'

I opened the gate and held out the binoculars. 'Come on. You can have a go, then.'

I pointed to the tree right up the other end of the street. I could just make out a bird, high up in the branches. 'Tell me what colour he is.'

Cockeye Donny picked up the binoculars and squinted through the lens.

'Well, what's his colour?'

He handed them back to me. 'I can't see good.' He dropped his head. ''Cause of my bad eye.'

'How'd you get it?'

His brother piped up before Cockeye Donny could answer. 'Our uncle. Our mum's brother. He was looking after us one time and he smashed Donny in the head. His eye was all crooked after that.'

Donny ran at his brother and pushed him onto the dry grass.

'Shut your fat mouth, Kade. That's our business. Not his.'

I offered him the binoculars again. 'I don't care how you got the eye. Like you said, it's not my business. Have another go.'

'Na. I don't want to any more.'

He looked down at his whimpering brother. 'Come on, you fucken girl. I'll get me arse kicked if we're not home. Get up.'

Kade crawled across the yard on his hands and knees and followed his brother out of the gate. I called out to Donny as he walked off.

'Hey. What did youse get for Christmas?'

He stopped, turned around and smiled. He'd never done that. 'I got to have a look through your binoculars and Kade fell on his arse. More than we got last year.'

I lifted the binoculars again just as Pop was turning the corner. He was wearing a suit and tie and carried something in his hand, a book with a gold cross on the front. A Bible. When he got a little closer to the house he slipped the book into his pocket.

He wasn't annoyed that we'd opened our presents.

'I hope you like them.'

I spent the next couple of hours in the backyard looking for birds through the binoculars. I counted three magpies, a black bird with an orange beak that I didn't know the name of, a flock of pigeons, high in the sky, heading towards the football oval, and heaps of sparrows.

We had roast chicken, potatoes and greens for lunch, and afterwards some apple pie. I wanted to thank Pop for the binoculars, but when I tried to say the words they wouldn't come out because I was too nervous. When we sat down to watch TV later that night Rachel tucked her rag doll under one arm and Comfort the bear in the other. I still had the binoculars hanging from my neck. I looked over at Pop a couple of times and practised what I wanted to say to him, under my breath. Finally, after a few tries, I held up the binoculars.

'I really like these. I saw a bird in the yard. It was on the fence, after lunch.'

I looked across at Rachel and rolled my eyes in his direction.

'I like my doll too,' she added.

Pop opened his mouth to say something but the words got stuck. I could see that his eyes were watery. He pointed to the kitchen and marched out of the room. 'I'll put the kettle on for us.'

That night I took the binoculars to bed with me. The excitement of the day had left me restless.

'Rache, are you asleep?'

'Yep. I'm sleeping,' she giggled.

'Did you like today?'

'Yeah. A lot.'

'I wish we had some money. To buy Pop a present.'

'What would we buy him?'

'A book, I suppose. I've seen him reading lots of books.'

'He only reads one book. The one with the cross on it.'

'No he doesn't. I've seen him reading lots of stuff. Have a look at all the books in his room.'

Rachel yawned.

'When do you think Gwen will come for us?'

'You know her. Could be anytime. Tomorrow, maybe. Could be never.'

'Do you want her to come? Or do you want to stay here?'

'Doesn't matter what I want. If Gwen comes for us, we have to go. What about you?'

She didn't answer.

'Are you still awake, Rache?'

If she was, she was playing dead.

Pop had been to church on Christmas morning. He said he went on Sundays as well. It wasn't too hard to work out why kids in the street called him The Preacher. He even knelt at the end of his bed of a night and prayed. I saw him doing it a couple of times when he forgot to close the door. And I'd sometimes hear him mumbling a prayer to himself from my bed.

One afternoon he came back from his meeting with his hair and clothes wet after getting caught in the rain. I was sitting on the bed looking at the frame of Gwen. I had taken the frame down from the wall and didn't hear him come in. He was on his way back from the bathroom with a towel in his hand when he saw me. He stopped in the doorway as he patted his hair.

'She was a lovely girl, your mother. That's the last photograph of them together. Her mum was already sick when it was taken.' He bowed his head. 'We didn't know it then but she had only three months left.'

He hung the towel from the doorknob, took a small plastic comb from his shirt pocket and ran it through his hair. He held the comb up to the light and blew some hairs out of it.

'It was real hard for her, Gwendolyn, after her mother went. It was just the two of us, and I . . . I was a wreck. For years. She more or less fended for herself.'

He put the comb back in his pocket. I jumped off the bed and followed him as he walked back to the bathroom with the towel.

'Where do you go in the afternoon, Pop?'

He placed the towel over the rail, stood back and checked that he'd hung it straight.

'Why do you want to know?'

'Just been wondering. Is it church?'

'Nothing wrong with wondering. It's good for you. But no, I don't go to church, other than Sundays. And Christmas morning, of course. If you want to know where I go, come with me tomorrow.'

The next day, just before three o'clock, we left the house and walked across the football oval where I took Maxie of a night. As we passed the netball courts behind the oval he told me Gwen had played on the local team when she was a girl.

'She was the best player they had. Captained them to a pennant, twice.'

I tried to imagine Gwen playing sport but couldn't.

When we got to her old high school, and he said she'd been 'top of her class, year after year', I was more confused.

'Gwen? Top?'

'You bet. Smart as a whip.'

We came to another a park, where a woman was pushing a kid on a swing. The girl was screaming, 'Higher, Mummy, higher.' Pop stood and looked at them for so long I wondered that maybe this was all that he did on his walks, came to the park and watched people. He finally turned his back on them and looked at his watch.

'Come on. We don't want to be late.'

We crossed to the other side of the park, to a wooden building that looked a bit like a church, except there was no cross on top. A woman and two men were standing out front of the hall smoking. The woman came over and said hello to Pop.

'Pauline, this is my grandson, Jesse.'

When she smiled at me I could see a scar on the side of her neck; it was raised and looked like it had been badly stitched together.

'Want to come into the hall,' Pop asked, 'or wait in the park? You can watch from the doorway if you want. They won't mind.'

I followed him into the hall. People were standing around an urn of steaming water, drinking tea and eating biscuits. I sat with Pop on a wooden bench near the back of the hall. The men were around his age but I reckoned the women mostly were younger. I couldn't work out what was going on. I just hoped it wasn't some sort of dating meeting for lonely people, and I'd be embarrassed for him.

A snowy-haired man, who'd been sitting on one of the front benches, stood up, clapped his hands together a couple of times and asked the people who were still standing down the back to finish their tea and come and sit down. When everyone was seated Pauline got to her feet. She coughed a couple of times as the room went quiet, and she walked slowly to the front.

'My name's Pauline,' she said, 'and I am an alcoholic.'

After the meeting, as we walked back home, I asked Pop why he went to the meetings as often as he did.

'Would they kick you out if you didn't turn up every day?'

'No. Nobody can kick you out unless you're drinking and rowdy. You can come and go as you feel like it.'

'And you feel like it every day?'

'That's right. Every day.'

I remembered what Jon Dempsey had said to Gwen the day before he left the farmhouse.

'So you're on the wagon, Pop?'

'Yeah.' He laughed. 'I have been for years. You had a drink yourself yet?'

I'd snuck some beer from Gwen. And one night, when I was about nine or ten, I'd mixed half a bottle of vodka with some lemonade and drank all of it. I threw up all the next day and felt real sick. It wasn't a story I wanted to tell Pop.

'No, I haven't. I'm only thirteen.'

'Don't matter. My old man gave me my first taste of grog before I could walk, my ma told me years later. He used to soak my dummy in it. I must have got a taste for it because I was knocking his beer off when I was younger than you.

'Dad knew the drink was no good for him but he couldn't stay away from it. It killed him. He died in the street before he was fifty. If I hadn't stopped drinking when I did, it would have killed me too. We can't handle it, our family. We've got a weakness. I'd been a social drinker until your grandmother died. But once she was gone I hit it harder than the old man ever had.'

He stopped and put a hand on my shoulder. 'I could give you the best advice I know, to stay away from it. But you've got to make that decision for yourself. No one else can do it for you.'

When we turned the corner into our street, he said, 'Gwendolyn had lost her own mother, who she adored, and I didn't lift a finger to take care of her. No wonder she went off the rails. I was no good as a father. No good.'

I thought he was a lot better than Gwen was.

'Pop, are you what they call a born-again Christian?'

'No, mate. I'm a born-again alcoholic.'

'Why do you read the Bible then?'

'You seen me, have you? You've got a sharp eye. It's like any book. There's something to learn from it. Some great stories in the Bible. Your sister, Rachel, she's got a name from the Bible, from the Old Testament. Rachel is a beautiful woman from the Bible. And that's what your sister will grow up to be, a beautiful woman.'

On New Year's Day Pop said it was about time I got my own bed.

'I don't know if we can fit it in that room. Might have to clean out the bungalow and paint it up. Would you like that?'

I could tell from the look on his face that he knew I would.

'And school. We'll have to start thinking about school, for both of you.'

When Gwen turned up on the doorstep a week later it was like seeing a ghost. Pop had been in the kitchen when the phone went. I heard him raise his voice a couple of times, and I knew it could only be her. After he hung up he told us to take Maxie for a walk. I'd only just got back with the dog and told him so.

'Well, take him again. The two of you.'

When we got back to the house after the walk I saw our case standing in the hallway. I went into the kitchen. Pop was doing Rachel's job, setting the table. He looked over at me but didn't speak. Rachel marched into the kitchen carrying her doll.

'My bed is all folded up. Why's that? And where's Comfort? He likes to be on my pillow, Pop. You know that.'

He was moving a sizzling frypan from the stove to the table. He stabbed at a sausage with a fork and threw it onto her plate.

'Sit down and eat your tea. Please.'

While we were eating I started telling him a funny story about Maxie chasing another dog around and around the oval.

'They were going faster and faster in circles, like those tigers in that story that turn to butter. You know that story, Pop?'

He wasn't listening to my story, and didn't answer or look up from his plate.

We were quietly sipping tea when the doorbell rang, followed by a knock.

Pop looked up at the clock on the wall and down at his empty cup. 'Jesse, get that.'

I knew who it was and didn't want to answer it.

'Jesse, the door!'

'I don't want to,' I said, shaking my head.

Rachel didn't have a clue what was going on, and went to jump up from the table. 'I'll get it, Pop.'

He grabbed her by the arm and told her to sit back down. 'Jesse. Go. Please.'

Gwen was standing on the doorstep. The light over her head made a dark shadow on her face. She looked creepy. As she opened her arms I moved back, out of reach.

'Hey ya, babe. You packed? Where's your sister? I rang and told him to have you ready.'

She took a step into the hallway and stopped suddenly, like she'd hit a wall.

'Come on. We gotta split. I've got a ride waiting.'

I could hear a car idling in the street. When I got back to the kitchen, Pop was standing at the sink with his back to me.

'It's Gwen,' I said. 'She says we have to go with her. Is that true?'

I thought Rachel might be excited to know Gwen had finally come for us, but she didn't say a word. She hopped down from her chair and walked over to the sink. She touched the back of Pop's hand with her own.

'Do we have to go?'

'Get the case, Jesse,' he said. 'I've packed everything. I put your binoculars between some clothes to keep them from getting knocked around.'

I heard a car horn and then Gwen, calling to someone to 'wait up'. Rachel asked him again, 'Do we have to go? I don't want to leave here.'

He picked up a plate from the sink and threw it in the dish strainer. It smashed to bits.

'Go on, girl. With your brother. Now.'

She looked at me, hoping I'd refuse. But I knew I couldn't. 'Do what Pop says. We have to go.'

He threw the tea towel on the table and walked out to the backyard, slamming the door behind him. I grabbed the case and went out the front door. Rachel trailed behind me. The boot of the car was open and Gwen was leaning against the passenger door. Her old friend Midnight Mary was behind the wheel.

Gwen nodded towards the boot. 'Throw the case in there.'

When she saw Rachel she ran at her, wrapped her arms around her and lifted her off the ground.

'Hey, look at my baby doll. My beautiful girl.'

Rachel tried wriggling herself free. Gwen put her down.

'Hey, come on, babe, I've been missing you.'

Rachel broke away from Gwen and hopped into the back seat of the car without saying a word. Mary looked over her shoulder at her.

'You'd think she'd be fucken grateful to see ya, Gwennie. I'd smack her arse if she were mine.'

Gwen stuck her head in the car. She noticed the rag doll in Rachel's lap. 'Where'd you get the doll, honey?'

'From Pop. For Christmas.'

Gwen snatched the doll from her and threw it out the window. Rachel looked at Gwen liked she never had before. Her face was full of hate. I shoved the case in the boot and got in next to Rachel. Mary blew some smoke in my face.

'How you been, handsome? Long time no see. You've grown. Good looking too. Getting any?' she cackled.

When Gwen spotted Pop coming out of the house she jumped in the car and wound up her window.

'Come on, Mare. Fucken hell.'

Pop ran onto the road, and stood in front of the car. I thought Mary might run him over. She did a wheelie away from the kerb, dodged around him and fishtailed down the street. When I looked back I could see Pop standing in the middle of the road between rising clouds of smoke. He looked as lonely as anyone could be.

Mary had moved just a few streets away from the old place above the tyre yard. That night Gwen and Rachel took the couch and I slept on the floor. It was a noisy place, with a train line outside the back window. The local trains stopped around midnight, but the diesels kept on coming, all night long.

Mary wasn't growing her own dope any more. She was buying it by the bagful from a bush grower who delivered to the door. She packaged it and sold it on the street. Gwen had been helping her out. They sat in the kitchen of a night filling matchboxes with deals. Mary was always at Gwen, ordering her not to shove too much into each box. And she was also pissed off that Gwen was smoking as much as she sold.

Of a morning they would jump in the car and head for a shopping centre down the road and their regular customers, mostly tradies and kids out of school, who shoplifted for their dope. Mary would take just about anything in payment – DVDs, cigarettes, perfumes and aftershave and clothes, which she sold on to another fella who ran a stall at the trash and treasure market at the local drive-in on Sundays.

Neither Rachel or me had spoken more than a couple of words to Gwen since we'd left Pop's. She didn't trust us and said we'd have to come along with her and Mary while they did their business.

'I don't want you two doing a runner on me. And if you're going to keep at me with the silent treatment, you can do it in the back of the car.'

Mary had her own plan for me.

'He could deliver for us. You know, like a pizza boy.'

'Na. Don't think so. Keep him out of it.'

'If he's in the car, he's already *in it*, love.'

Mary walked over, sat on the couch, put an arm around my shoulder and started playing with my hair. She had bad breath.

'He'd be good. What do ya reckon, Jesse? Help your mum out with an earner? What about it, Gwennie?'

Gwen didn't say yes, but she didn't say no either.

When it was time to leave for the shopping centre the next morning Mary threw me a plastic bag of stuffed matchboxes. 'Hold onto that for me.'

We drove to the shopping centre and parked outside a Kmart. Mary unwound the window and looked around before getting out of the car and walking off. I watched as she made a call on her mobile. Rachel tapped Gwen on the shoulder.

'Are we going to the shops?'

'Yeah, babe. In a minute.'

Pretty soon, a van drove up and parked a few rows away from us. Mary came back to the car and got in the back seat next to me.

'You see that van over there? The one with the ladders strapped to the roof?'

When I didn't answer she dug her fingernails in my arm.

'You see him? Pass me the bag.'

I passed her the plastic bag. She took out a matchbox, tied up with a red rubber band.

'You go over to the van and knock. He's expecting you. You wait until he gives you the money and you hand over the deal. You see any coppers, if they come near the van or try grabbing you for a chat, you take off.'

'Take off?'

'Yeah. Take off. Get those legs of yours moving and hop it.'

'Where to?'

'Through the shops. Brings you out to the other side, to another car park. There's a wire fence and the railway line. You follow the line back to the flat.'

She spotted the fear in my eyes and patted me on the hand.

'Don't worry. Nothing'll go wrong. Do this and you'll be helping your mum get in front. Won't he, Gwen?'

'Yeah, he will.' She shrugged and wouldn't look at me.

I put the matchbox in my front pocket, got out of the car and walked between the rows of parked cars until I was standing beside the van. The driver's door was open. A man in overalls was lying back in the seat, resting a muddy boot on the dash and listening to the radio. He had dirty blond dreadlocks. When he spotted me he sat up, rested his hands on the wheel and looked at me through his mirrored sunglasses.

'You with Mary?'

I was nervous, and my mouth was dry. I couldn't speak.

'You got the gear or what?'

The best I could do was nod my head.

'Good. Give it here.'

I reached in my pocket and pulled the matchbox out before I remembered what Mary had told me.

'I have to have the money. Mary said you have to pay me first.'

He stuck his head out of the side of the van and looked back at her car. 'I bet she did. The shifty bitch.'

He reached into his pocket and pulled our four twenty-dollar notes. He stuck his hand out the window and waved the money at me. I took it, buried it in my pocket and handed him the matchbox. As I did he gripped my hand, squeezed tight and wouldn't let go.

'You watch that bitch, kid. You get into strife doing this, she'll let you fucken swing. Good people have done time over her big mouth.'

I waited until he'd driven off and walked back to the car. Mary counted the money and put it in a cloth bag under the front seat. She pinched me on the cheek.

'Good work, kid. Look, we got another customer.'

'Customers for what?' Rachel called out from the back seat.

'For nothing, Rache,' Gwen said. She took some money out of her purse. 'Go into the shop there and get yourself an ice cream.'

One morning, about two weeks later, I was just about to hand over a deal to a fella sitting in his tow-truck when I spotted a police car in the reflection of a shop window. The copper was walking towards me. I threw the matchbox through the window of the tow-truck as I ran by. I ran by Mary too, who was in a café ordering coffees.

I kept on running, along the arcade and through the shopping centre. I raced out the other side, across the car park, jumped the wire fence and started following the railway line back to Mary's place, just like she'd told me to do. By the time I got there my chest was burning. I lay on the landing outside her flat and tried to get my breath back, too tired to move.

I was still there when Gwen arrived in Mary's car a half-hour later. She grabbed her bag in one hand and dragged Rachel out of the car with the other.

'Get up, Jesse.' She whacked me hard in the ribs with the toe of her shoe. 'We've got to split.'

'Where to?'

'Dunno yet. I haven't thought that far ahead, but we can't stay here. Don't matter if Mary opens her mouth or not, it won't be long before they turn this place over. We're going.'

'Where is she?'

'The Jacks got her. They'll turn up here soon enough. We're taking Mary's car.'

'Won't she miss it?'

'Maybe, but I don't reckon she'll need it for a while.'

The car, an old Commodore, didn't have a straight panel on it, it blew black smoke and the tyres were worn smooth as racing slicks. We threw our stuff in the boot, along with a black plastic bag stuffed full of marijuana.

We took the back streets until we reached the entrance to a freeway heading out of the city. Gwen turned onto the freeway, put her nose over the wheel and her foot flat to the floor. She didn't look back and didn't think about stopping until we were more than a couple of hours away, when we pulled into a place off the side of the freeway to go to the toilet and get something to eat.

Rachel and me shared a bowl of chips while Gwen went through a tattered notebook she kept in her bag. She flipped through the pages, back and forward a few times, before she found what she was after. She borrowed a pen from a girl behind the counter, wrote an address on her arm and threw the notebook in a bin.

'Let's rock 'n' roll.'

'But I haven't finished yet,' Rachel complained.

'Yes, you have.' Gwen could see that Rachel was about to answer her back and waved a finger in her face. 'Don't you say a word, girlie. Just do what I say.'

Gwen told us we were going to Adelaide, she had a friend there. I slept some of the way, but kept getting woken up by Rachel whining that she was still hungry and asking Gwen to stop again for food.

Gwen turned the radio up to drown her out, which made it impossible to sleep. I closed my eyes again and thought about how close I'd come to getting caught by the police. If they'd got me I'd have been put in a home for sure, I reckoned. Maybe a place like Jon Dempsey got beaten in. I opened one eye and looked over at Gwen. She was humming along to a tune from the radio and seemed happy enough. If I'd been caught by the coppers back at the shopping centre and got locked up it would have been her fault. Not that she'd care much about what happened to me.

She turned to Rachel. 'Look, babe. See the lights? That's Adelaide. We'll be there soon.'

Gwen hadn't been to Adelaide before and didn't know her

way around. She stopped at a shop, and came out with some instructions on a bit of paper. They didn't help much, because pretty soon we were driving around in circles.

'Where's this fucken house?' she moaned.

When she finally located the place she was looking for, a small red brick house with a vacant block of land on either side, she found out that her old friend, some woman she'd worked with years ago, had moved on. The man who opened the door had half a bottle of beer in one hand and was wearing only his underpants. He had so much hair on his body that at first I thought he was covered in dirt.

He looked Gwen up and down, and then smiled at Rachel.

'Yeah, Ronnie Mac shot through ages ago, but you can stay here if you want. You must be rooted. All that driving.'

Gwen said no thanks and put us back in the car.

She sat in the front and smoked a cigarette as she thought about how much shit we were in. The man in the house opened the curtains and looked out at us a couple of times.

'What are we going to do?' I asked.

'Dunno,' she snapped. She opened the window and threw out the cigarette butt. 'Got any bright ideas?'

'Well . . . we got that plastic bag in the boot.'

She nodded her head a couple of times and smiled at me. 'Jesse, sometimes you're a bit of a dill. Then other times you're a fucken genius.'

A few minutes later Gwen was handing the hairy man the bag of dope in exchange for some money, which she started counting on the way back to the car.

Rachel sat up. She couldn't take her eyes off the wad of notes in Gwen's hand.

'Did him like a dinner,' Gwen said, as she revved the engine and drove off.

We tried some motels along a strip next to a beach. Two of them were full and another was closed. Gwen turned into a car park on the beach and got out. She looked up at the sky and then along the beach.

'How about we sleep under the stars tonight? It'll be an adventure.'

'The beach?' Rachel screamed. 'I don't want to sleep on the beach. A killer might come.'

'You can stay in the car then. Me and Jesse are going to sleep on the sand, aren't we?' She nodded to me to follow her. 'If a killer does turn up, he'll go for the car first. Happens in the movies all the time. Suit yourself, Rache.'

There were other people on the beach. A group of teenagers sat around a fire, drinking and talking and watching a girl splash in the water. Rachel came running after us and we picked a spot and I built a mound to rest my head on, lay down on the sand and looked up at the night sky and twinkling stars. It would have been beautiful if it weren't for the trouble we were in. I didn't know what was going to happen next, but I was sure it would be something bad and felt sick worrying about it.

The next morning I washed my face and hands in the sea. People were out jogging along the beach and walking their dogs. When Gwen and Rachel woke we walked along the beach to a café and ordered breakfast. Gwen picked up a notice advertising 'fully serviced vans – weekly rates', got some change from the cashier and made a call at the pay phone by the toilets. She came back to the table and clapped her hands together. 'I've got us a place.'

THREE

Ray Crow stood out front of our van in a pair of black jeans, a dirty white t-shirt, a sweat-stained cowboy hat and a pair of black leather boots with silver buckles that jingled when he took a step. He looked like he'd walked out of cowboy movie. And he was the bad guy.

Gwen was so excited about her new fella she couldn't keep still. I knew she'd want me to be nice to him but she was wasting her time if she thought I'd suck up to a new boyfriend just to keep her happy. From the second I got in the back seat of Mary's car I'd thought of nothing but running away for good, even if it meant leaving Rachel. She was always falling behind and never stopped complaining. I felt bad but knew I couldn't take her with me and look after her properly.

Gwen nudged me in the back, pushed me towards Ray, and ruffled a hand through my hair.

'Ray. This is my little man, Jesse.'

He looked me up and down, like he would an enemy. 'Don't look like a man to me, big or little. How old are you, boy?'

'He's thirteen, going on fourteen,' Gwen answered for me. She was jumpy.

Ray shaped his right hand into a pistol and aimed the trigger finger between my eyes.

'Bang! Bang! Jesse, hey? Like Jesse James. The outlaw. Are you an outlaw?'

He relaxed his hand and offered it to me. I buried mine under my armpit. He squinted and looked me in the eyes.

'Where I'm from, not shaking a man's hand is an insult.'

'Yeah, well he's just a kid,' Gwen said, moving all over the place, like she had to take a piss.

Ray pushed the brim of his hat back on his head. He was about to say something more when he spotted Rachel standing in the doorway of the van. He smiled at her.

'Hello, darling.'

'Honey, come meet a friend of mine,' Gwen called.

Rachel hopped down from the van and ran and stood in front of Gwen. She put her hands on Rachel's shoulders.

'And this is my baby, Rachel.'

'I'm not a baby,' Rachel growled. 'I'm eight.'

Ray touched her cheek with the back of his hand. He left it there while he spoke to her in the quietest voice. 'Yeah. You're no baby. And you're so pretty.'

'Takes after me,' Gwen piped up, leaning forward so Ray could get a good look at her face.

It didn't take much to get her jealous.

'Maybe,' Ray answered, without looking at her. He couldn't take his eyes off Rachel.

★

Gwen had met Ray at a bar in the city, after she'd knocked off work at the nightclub she was at. He stayed in the crowded van with us one night. Rachel and me slept in single beds up one end of the van while he and Gwen shared her bed down the other end. It was used as the table during the day then made up with a rubber mattress and blankets and pillows at night. Sometimes, when Gwen got in late, she didn't bother fixing the bed and slept on the floor.

Sitting around the wobbly table the next morning, Ray, wearing just his smelly t-shirt and a pair of stained underpants, looked round the van, waved a spoon in the air like a magic wand and said a woman as good-looking as Gwen deserved a lot better than some 'wooden box wrapped in plastic'.

He tapped Rachel lightly on the end of her nose with the back of the spoon. 'And you, princess. You deserve a palace.'

Rachel turned red and jumped on her bed.

Ray got dressed, spat in his hands, ran them through his hair and eyed himself in the mirror. He told us to be ready to leave the van 'for all time' before he got back later in the day. I was sure he was just another bullshit artist who would get what he wanted from Gwen and then take off and never be seen again.

We packed up and were ready to go, but there was no sign of Ray. Gwen sat on the step of the van, smoking as she waited for him to come back. I lay on one of the bunks and Rachel sat on the other shuffling Gwen's tarot deck.

'Pick a card, Jesse.'

'Leave me alone.'

She stuck the deck under my chin and made me look at it. 'Go on. Take one and tell me what it means.'

I told her to knock it off but she wouldn't let up until I picked one. It was a heart with three swords stuck through it. Behind the heart were dark clouds, rain and lightning.

'What's it mean, Jesse? Is it a good luck card or bad luck?'

I took a closer look at it. It wasn't as scary as the card with the ten swords sticking out of the dead soldier, but for anyone who believed in the cards I reckoned it couldn't be much better.

'I dunno what it means. Don't care either.'

'Have a guess then. Play the game, Jesse.'

'You really want to know?' I snatched the card from her and held it up. 'Okay then. It means that this fella, Ray, is going to murder the three of us. See the three swords? That's you, Gwen and me. He's gonna kill us all. You happy now?'

Rachel ripped the card from me and buried it in the deck. 'Like you said, you don't know what they mean anyway. I'll ask Gwen.'

Ray didn't get back until dark. He said that he'd had some business to take care of. Gwen wanted to know what kind of business.

'Can't explain, babe. The details would bore the shit out of you.'

He'd booked us into a motel further along the beachfront from the caravan park. He had a brochure with him, with pictures of a swimming pool, a gym, room service and 'en suites'. As Gwen looked at the brochure, Ray put an arm around her shoulder, slid his hand down her dress and rubbed her on the back.

'I got two rooms. One for us and the other for these two.'

She hung her arms around his neck, pushed her body into his and kissed him on the mouth.

The motel had three floors and was square-shaped with a glass roof over the top. The roof was so dirty the light didn't come through too good. Our rooms were on the top floor and looked down on a swimming pool with banana lounges and fake palm trees around it. From my doorway I could see into the rooms off the balcony across from us. I stood there most mornings to get a good look at what was going on. People came and went and didn't stay long, mostly young women with older men. It took me about a minute to work out they were prostitutes with their customers. The women were mostly friendly, smiled and said hello when I passed them on the stairs. The men looked the other way or down at their feet.

The rooms had TV with regular channels and cable. The bar fridge was loaded up with beer, chocolate bars and little bottles of spirits, and the beds vibrated when you pushed a button on the side. Ray said we could order anything we wanted just by picking up the phone on the table between our beds and hitting the '9' button. I hit it every chance I got.

The first night at the motel Rachel and me sat up in bed and picked out a horror movie from one of the cable channels. It was rated R but there was no one around to stop us from watching. It was full of teenage kids getting tortured and chopped up by zombies. Rachel missed most of the movie. She was so frightened she stuck her head under the blankets. About halfway through I picked up the phone and ordered Rachel's favourite, nachos with double sour cream. Ten minutes later a waitress knocked at the door with the order.

Gwen and Ray had been out drinking and got in late, long after the movie was over and I'd turned off the TV, covered

Rachel with a blanket and put out the lights. The wall between the two rooms was as thin as paper and they kept me awake most of the night partying. I could tell by the sound of her voice, she was just about singing, that she was pretty drunk. I could also hear the clinking of glasses, music playing on the radio, and Ray screaming 'trick or treat, baby, trick or treat?' about every five minutes, like it was Halloween.

The next morning a garbage truck picking up rubbish in the car park out back of the motel woke me. Rachel was dead to the world. I got out of bed and put my ear to the wall. It was quiet next door. I picked up my jeans and t-shirt from the floor, and went onto the balcony. Down in the swimming pool one of the banana lounges was at the bottom of the deep end. Some fella carrying a bamboo pole was balancing himself on the edge of the pool and trying to fish the chair out. He had no hope of hooking a catch.

He noticed me looking and called out, 'Hey, kid. Come down here and give us a hand.'

'What for?' I called back.

'Get your arse down here and I'll tell you.'

He was old, maybe fifty or more. His gut sat over the top of his work pants and he was sweating and puffing like he'd run around the block at full speed and followed up with fifty push-ups.

'Will you fucken look at that?' he hissed, as he speared the pole into the pool, trying to stick the chair. 'The drunken cunts do this every weekend. Throw the furniture in the pool. They piss in it. Use it for a fucken ashtray. See those long necks on the bottom. I'll never get them out. Can't swim to save myself. Last week it was one of the palm trees. Cunts.'

He pulled out his wallet and showed me a five-dollar note. 'What do they call you?'

'Jesse.'

'Jesse, how do ya feel about ripping those jeans off, jumping in the pool and dragging that chair out for me? And then maybe you could duck-dive for the bottles. I've got to clean this shit up before the boss lobs for the morning shift. I've been going all night and I'm fucked. I was just about to knock off when I spotted the wreckage.'

He spat into the pool.

'I can get you a fresh towel from the shower room to dry yourself off.'

The wallet was full of notes. I looked up to the third floor balcony.

'I'll get in trouble if my mum or dad catch me in the pool. And my dad wakes up early.' I coughed a couple of times. 'And I've got a cold. I've had it all week. Mum says I can't go for a swim until I'm better. And anyway, like you said, it's been pissed in. Maybe it's not safe.'

He spat again.

'Well I'm fucked then. I'll never get out of here.'

'I'll do it for ten dollars.'

'You trying to con me, kid? Well, don't. I been around.'

I'd already taken my t-shirt off. 'I'm not trying anything. If you don't want me to do it . . .'

'You're an up-and-coming conman, for sure. But I got no choice. You've got a deal.' He offered his hand. 'Cyril.'

The water was warm. I waded across to the banana lounge and dragged it to the edge of the pool. Cyril lifted it out.

'Good job, kid. Now the bottles.'

I dived for the empty beer bottles. I stuck one in my underpants and grabbed the other two, one in each hand. I surfaced
and handed them to Cyril. As I got out of the pool one of the
doors to a room above us slammed shut. I looked up and spotted a short, baldy man in a dark suit. He walked as quickly as
he could without running, along the balcony towards the fire
exit. Cyril nodded.

'See that?'

'See what?'

'The old boy. He's a minister at the church down the road.
Comes in every week, same time, early in the morning when
he thinks no one's watching, books the same room. Under the
name of Mr Bell. A little while after, one of the working girls
turns up. Same girl every week. Waltzing Matilda, she goes
by. Wears an akubra hat, I fucken swear.'

He laughed so much he had to wait a bit until he could go
on with the story. 'One of the housemaids, Beryl, she tells me
that after he's left of a morning and she goes in to clean the
room, nothing's been touched. Not the bed. The bar. Nothing. Except . . .' He looked over his shoulder, like someone
might be listening. 'Except, just at the end of the bed there's
this sunken bit where he's sat his arse.' He lifted his eyebrows.
'And you know what that means, my friend?'

'What?'

'She sucks him off. "Rings old Mr Bell's bell", as Beryl
puts it. He sits on the end of the bed and gets a head job. Must
think it keeps him half holy or something. Jesus Christ, what a
trick. He goes to all the trouble to get her up here and pay for
it. He might as well fuck her. Wouldn't you think?'

I didn't know what to say. 'I really dunno.'

'No, you wouldn't. You're too young.'

He took out his wallet and pulled out the five he'd shown me earlier. 'Here. You done a good job. Put that in your pocket.'

'You said ten.'

'Well now it's five. Sorry, kid. It's all I can afford.'

I'd earned the money and didn't want him ripping me off. 'I want my ten.'

'What are you gonna do, throw the furniture back in the pool?'

I hadn't thought so, but it was a good idea. 'I just want the ten you promised me.'

'Arrgh, fuck. This world's gonna suck me drier than the minister's prick.' He shoved the five back into his wallet and pulled out a ten. 'Take it. But you see any shit in the pool when you're in here swimming, you get rid of it for me and there's another five for you. Deal?'

'Deal.'

As I walked back upstairs I thought it would be a good idea to throw a banana lounge in the pool now and then, and make myself some money. I passed a woman on her way down. She was holding a pair of high heels in her hand, the top buttons of here dress were undone, and an akubra hat sat back on her head. She winked at me and put a finger to her lips as she walked by.

Gwen and Ray woke late that morning. We had breakfast in the dining room next to the pool. Some of the other guests were already having lunch. Gwen couldn't stop laughing long enough to shove food in her mouth. She was still high, and had a love bite on her neck. She nibbled at Ray's ear while he tucked into his bacon and eggs. He acted like she wasn't there. She finally got bored with him and pulled her tarot cards out of her pocket, shuffled them and started laying them out on the table. He put his knife and fork down.

'I've seen this before. Russian bird I knew from a mining camp out in the desert. Made a quid with the cards of a day. On her back of a night. Pick out a card for me, babe. Tell my future.'

'Don't work that way, Ray. This isn't a pick-a-card trick. I have to lay them out and tell your story.'

'I don't have time for my story. Anyway, I already know it. I'm gonna kick on, big time. Let me pick one. I'll go with that.'

She picked the cards up from the table and shuffled them again. He picked one and threw it down on the table. It was The Hanged Man, lynched to a tree, swinging upside down by his feet. Ray wiped grease from his mouth with the back of his hand and looked at the card. He wasn't happy.

'What the fuck does it mean?'

'Like I said, it don't matter on its own. It means nothing.'

I crossed my fingers under the table and wished as hard as I could that it meant just what it looked like.

Ray whispered something to Gwen. As they got up to leave, he handed me a fifty-dollar note and told me to take Rachel and buy the two of us bathers so we could have a swim. I bought myself a pair of striped board shorts and Rachel picked out a pink swimsuit with tiny diamonds sewn into them. With the money we had left I let her buy some lip gloss and hair ties and got a pair of goggles for me.

We hung around the pool for the rest of the afternoon, shoving as much food into our mouths as we could without being sick. I went in for a swim but Rachel said she was tired-out and lay down on a banana lounge. I told her to get off her bum and come in. Not that she could really swim. When she did go in the water she just splashed around and kicked a lot.

The next morning Ray was nowhere to be seen. When Rachel asked where he'd gone Gwen said he had a job on and had taken off early.

'He's got a big pay day coming up,' she sang, wagging her head from side to side. She closed her eyes and ran her fingertips across her lips. 'I got something to tell you both. Something you're gonna love. Ray's asked me to marry him and I've said yes.'

She told us they'd come up with the idea when she'd read that Adelaide was called the city of churches. Later in the day they were going to take a drive around the city and decide on which church to be married in. She could see I was giving her a dirty look.

'Ray's gonna be your stepfather, Jesse, so get used to it. I'm gonna have someone to look after me for a change. And help me with you two. He's a good catch for us.'

She held Rachel by the hand and talked about how she would be the flower girl at the wedding. 'You'll have a pink satin dress, little miss, you love pink, and fresh flowers all through your hair.'

I wasn't going be left out. It would be my job to give her away, she said. She reached across the table and tried touching my bottom lip.

'I'm gonna get you a suit, Jesse, a pinstriped suit. You can have a flower in your lapel, a carnation, and a silk tie. You'll look like a real man then.'

'Wouldn't I have to be an adult, twenty-one or something, to give you away?'

'Maybe. Maybe not. If you can't do it we'll get someone else and I'll find another job for you. You can be the usher or something. Ray's got friends all over the city. One of them can give me away.'

I didn't want Ray Crow being a stepfather to Rachel and me, but I wasn't too worried that it might happen. Gwen had sprung wedding plans on us before and nothing had come of them. I didn't expect it would be long before things soured between her and Ray and one of them would shoot through.

They went hard at it over the next week, out on the town, partying and banging around in the next room at all hours of the night. We left them to sleep during the day and caught the bus into the city. Gwen didn't know where we were and didn't care as long as we were back at the motel by night-time. While we were exploring the streets we came across an op shop. I bought a backpack for a dollar to put our stuff in: the bathers, goggles, and two fluffy white towels we'd borrowed from the motel. We caught the bus back from town in the late afternoon and went for a swim in the sea. And when we'd finished we bought hot chips and sat under the pier eating them until it was close to dark.

'Are we on a holiday?' Rachel asked me one afternoon as we were throwing soggy chips to the seagulls fighting each other for them on the beach.

'Suppose so. Gwen always said she'd take us on one. It's not Disneyland, but it's pretty good. Be better if Ray wasn't around. I don't trust him.'

'If Ray wasn't with us, we'd be in the caravan with no money.'

'I don't care. There's something bad about him. You stay away from him.'

'Bad, how?'

'I'm not sure yet, but I just know he is.'

On the first day we wandered through the city we found a cinema in one the shopping malls. There were enough films showing to watch a different one every day. But Rachel fell in love with the movie we saw on the first morning and begged me to take her again the next day.

The story was in England in olden times. It was about a girl who has to go and live with her relatives in an old house in the country because her dad is in the war against the Germans and where they live in London is being bombed every night. The girl's mother can't go to the country with her because she promised the dad she would leave a light in the window and wait at home for him to come back from the war. The girl has a terrible time in the country because she is lonely and cries herself to sleep every night. In the end she gets back with her mother. A grenade has blinded her dad and when he comes home from the war he doesn't know his wife until she calls his name over and over at the train station where he's waiting for her. They lived happily ever after, of course. It was just the sort of movie Rachel loved. I didn't like it much on the first day, or the second. And by the third day, I'd had enough.

We ate hamburgers, pizzas and, one day, a Chinese meal in a sit-down café. We also took photos of people standing in the street or sitting on the bus, with a throw-away camera that Ray had given me. He made a big deal of handing it to me in front of Gwen and said it was a present from him. And maybe it was but I knew he hadn't paid a cent for it. I'd seen him steal it from a supermarket around the corner from the motel. Rachel said we had to take a photo of every dog we passed in the street. The camera had thirty-six shots and we used most of them up in a couple of days. When we got down to the last shots Rachel asked that we not take any more.

'I want to keep them for best,' she said.

'For best? What about when we see another cute pup on the beach? I bet you'll want to take a picture then.'

'No I won't. I want to keep them for, you know, a special . . . special . . .'

'Occasion. A special occasion, Rachel.'

'Yep. A special occasion.'

We walked by a shop that printed photos and stopped for a look. In the window were t-shirts and cups and even jigsaw puzzles that you could make out of photos. And different size photos, from ones you could stick in your wallet to posters that would cover half a wall.

On the bus going back to the motel Rachel asked, 'Do you think you could you get one of those posters made for me, from one of the pictures we've taken? With the money you have? I'll pay you back. When we get our own place, not a caravan or a motel, a house, I can put the picture up on the wall. Gwen says that when her and Ray are married I'll have my own room. And no matter what the colour is when we move there, she will paint it pink for me.'

She looked out the window at a row of houses we were rushing by. 'And a dog. Gwen's going to buy me a dog.'

She was the happiest I'd seen her in a while, so it wasn't the time to remind her that Gwen was bullshitting to her again.

On our next bus ride into the city I told Rachel I wanted to find another movie. 'I've had enough of the girl and her sad mum. Let's see something different.'

We went to a café next to a bus stop, ordered milkshakes and went through a newspaper we found on one of the tables. When she brought our drinks over the waitress asked what we were looking for. She was the oldest waitress I'd ever seen. Her face was all wrinkled and her hair was snow white.

'We're going to a movie,' Rachel said. 'But we don't know which one yet.'

'Well, I saw a great movie when I knocked off from here yesterday, at the old picture theatre just round the corner from here. Shows old black and white movies.'

'My brother don't like black and white.'

The waitress looked at me as she spoke to Rachel. 'Oh, I think he'd like this one. The two kids in it, a boy and a girl, they're not far off your age.'

'What's it about?' I asked.

'Why don't you take a look and find out for yourselves.'

She gave us directions to the theatre and we walked there in five minutes. Rachel waited out the front while I bought us tickets to see *To Kill a Mockingbird*.

Like she said, the movie was in black and white and I didn't think I'd like it, but I did. I liked the boy and girl, Jem and Scout, and how they played with each other and their friend Dill and the trouble they got into. But most of all, I loved the father, Atticus. He looked after his kids and he never got angry, even when he had to use a gun to shoot a crazy dog. He reminded me a little bit of Pop. Rachel loved the movie too and talked about it all the way back on the bus. Her favourite was Scout.

'I liked it when she found the presents in the hole in the tree that the man next door who wouldn't come out of the house had left there for her.'

She was still raving on about the film when we got to our stop. 'Jesse, did you see how they called their dad by his first name?'

'What about it?'

'Well, it's like us and Gwen, isn't it?'

'I don't think it's anything like that.'

We were about to go into the fish and chip shop when I saw Ray, standing in a phone box on the street. He could have easily used the mobile he carried or the phone in the motel room, so I wondered what he was doing there. He had a knife in his hand and was scratching something into the wood while he spoke. I disappeared into the shop before he saw us.

We sat underneath the pier again to eat our hot chips. Rachel coughed a couple of times, the way she did when she wanted to ask me something.

'What bit did you like best of all, Jesse?'

I didn't want to upset her and tell her that I liked it when Atticus shot the mad dog, so I said, 'All of it. I liked everything in the film,' which was true.

She dropped a chip, picked it up and brushed some sand away. 'Can you guess which bit I liked best?'

'Nup.'

'Do you want me to tell you then?'

'Course.'

'I like Scout when she doesn't want to wear a dress on her first day at school and she fights the boy in the schoolyard. I think she's brave.'

'Do you think you could be like her?'

'Like how do you mean?'

'Be brave, like when she stands up to that creep who wants to hurt her when she's coming home in the dark.'

'But the man from next door, Boo, he saves her and Jem.'

'He does. But she was brave walking through the woods in the dark. She knew the baddie was coming for them. Could you be like her, if you had to?'

She frowned and thought about what I'd said. 'I can try to be.'

The next morning Ray got Gwen up early. She looked miserable sitting at the breakfast table. He couldn't take his eyes off a woman sitting at the next table wearing short shorts and a singlet. Gwen tried getting his attention by leaning across the table and talking about some dress she'd seen in a shop window that she wanted him to buy for her. He grunted a couple of times and kept looking at the blonde. When she got sick of being ignored she jumped up from the table and went upstairs. Ray moved across to Gwen's chair and finished off her breakfast. He looked across at Rachel.

'Come here and chat to Ray.' He slapped his knee. When Rachel didn't move he spoke a little louder. 'Come on, sweetie.'

Gwen had left her cigarettes on the table, almost a full packet. Ray was too busy giving his attention to Rachel to spot me picking them up and putting them in my pocket. When she didn't move Ray shifted his chair next to Rachel's, put his hands on her shoulders and massaged them as he whistled a tune he never let up on; the only song he seemed to know.

I stood up and pushed my chair into the table, as hard as I could, spilling his coffee over him.

'Hey, watch what you're doing, awkward arse,' he yelled.

'Rachel. We got to be going.'

'What's the hurry, outlaw? We've plenty of time. Your mother's probably gone back to bed. I kept the old girl up late.'

'Rachel. We can't miss the bus or we'll be late for the movies. I wanna see the new one,' I lied.

'What's it called?'

'Can't remember. It's starts today. Come on.'

'Can we see the mockingbird again instead?'

'Sure. Let's go.'

As I walked away from the table, she wriggled free of Ray and chased after me. Up in our room I sat Rachel on the bed.

'You're not to do that again.'

'Do what?'

'With Ray. Get close to him.'

'I can't help it. He grabbed my neck and it hurt.'

'Just stay clear of him.'

'How am I gonna do that?'

I didn't really know what to tell her.

We went to the movies again that day and they went out as usual that night. I sat on the bed while Rachel acted out some of the scenes from *To Kill a Mockingbird*. She forgot some bits but made others up, which was fine by me. We watched some TV but none of it was as good as the movie.

I was woken by a knock at our door later that night. It was Gwen. She was drunk and couldn't talk properly and held onto the door handle to keep herself from falling down.

'Give us a smoke, will ya, Jesse? I left a pack on the brekkie table.' She stuck her jaw out. 'You take them?'

I lied and added, 'Maybe one of the waitresses picked them up. Or Ray. He's probably got them.'

'You don't have them? My ciggies?'

When I told her again, she waved her hands around in front of her face, like she was trying to shoo a fly away and staggered back to her room. I was just getting back into bed when I heard a thud from her room. She must have fallen over. I felt a little bad for stealing her cigarettes, so I wriggled under the bed and took three cigarettes from the pack I'd hidden in one of my shoes.

When she didn't answer her door I went into the room. She was alone. The bar fridge door was hanging open and Gwen was lying on the floor. She had an opened bottle of beer in one hand and a chocolate bar in the other. She was tearing at the wrapper with her teeth.

I showed her the cigarettes. 'I forgot these. Ray left them on the table in our room the other day. Where's he gone?'

She bit at the chocolate bar, right through the wrapper.

'Don't care. Ray can fucken fuck hisself.'

She grabbed at the bedspread and pulled herself to her feet. As she snatched the cigarettes from my hand she fell backwards onto the bed and bounced up and down like she was on a trampoline. She started laughing, stuck a cigarette in her mouth and raised both arms in the air

'Hey, Jesse baby. Help your mummy here, will ya?'

She tugged at her clothes. The buttons on her shirt popped off and shot across the room. She had a lace bra underneath that Ray had bought her. She lifted her legs from the bed and kicked her feet in the air until her high heels slipped off.

'Take my dress off for me, Jesse.'

The cigarette in her mouth had broken in half.

'Please.'

I walked out of the room to the sound of her calling my name over and over again.

The next morning there was just the two of us for breakfast. Rachel said I should have knocked on their door so we could eat together, 'Me, you, and Gwen and Ray.'

'Ray's not there. He didn't come back last night. And don't you listen? I told you to stay away from him.'

'Well, what about Gwen? I bet she'll be angry when she comes down and we're all finished.'

'Bad luck for her. If she wants to get pissed and sleep in, it's her fault if she misses out.'

'Don't say pee, Jesse.'

'Didn't. I said piss.'

'That's what I mean. But I'm not going to say it. I might go upstairs and wake her up.'

'Please yourself. But I'm warning you, you know what she's like if she doesn't get her sleep. It's more important to her than having breakfast with us. Anyway, I don't care if she never wakes up.'

'Don't say that. If we didn't have Gwen, who would look after us?'

I could have hit her right then.

'Our pop. He was looking after us real good before she come back. And you know it. You wanted to stay with him as much as I did. Jon did a better job of looking after us than she does, and she made him go away. She doesn't care about us. Never has. I could do better than she ever has.'

She jumped off her chair and ran from the dining room.

'Where you going, Rachel? Finish your breakfast.'

'To get Gwen.'

I leaned across to the table next to ours and picked up a glossy book with a picture of a bus on the front. I opened it. It had the prices and maps of bus trips from Adelaide to anywhere in the country. The price of a one-way ticket to Melbourne was only twenty-nine dollars, half the adult price. I stuck the book in my pocket.

Rachel came back to the dining room. I knew she wouldn't have got far, trying to get Gwen out of bed. She sat quietly, twirling a spoon in the half-full container of yoghurt she'd left.

'So, is she on her way down? Or doing her aerobics?'

I heard the jingle of Ray's boots and looked up. He was wearing his cowboy hat and carrying a large picnic basket with the price tag dangling from the handle. He sat the basket on the table and put a hand on Rachel's bare neck as he spoke to me.

'Where is she? Your mother?'

'Dunno.'

'I said, where is she?'

'I dunno.'

He sat down next to me as he stroked Rachel's shoulder. He stuck the middle finger of his other hand under my chin, pushed upward and lifted it until we were looking into each other's eyes.

'I don't know what it is with you, Jesse. For some reason you don't like me. Haven't I been good to you two? I thought we'd be good pals by now.'

I would have liked to tell him that I didn't trust him as far as I could throw him. But I said nothing, seeing as he was digging a grubby fingernail into my skin. He pushed his chair back, picked up a rind of bacon from my plate and chewed on it. It looked like a rat's tail, dangling from his mouth.

'Now, you do me a favour, Jesse, and go upstairs and get your mother's arse moving,' he ordered, then turned to Rachel. 'Because we're going for a drive. And a picnic lunch. Would you like that, princess?'

She nodded and smiled, then noticed me giving her a dirty look. She dropped her head.

I stood up. 'Let's go, Rachel.' When she didn't move I pulled her chair away from the table. 'Now.'

We ran into Gwen on the stairway. Her hair was all over the place and she was half asleep. I told her Ray was downstairs waiting for her. Her eyes lit up. She started fixing her hair, using her fingers for a comb.

'Where is he?'

'Eating breakfast. Says we're going on a picnic.'

'A picnic? Where to?'

'Didn't say,' I said as I climbed the stairs, leaving her there. 'Come on, Rachel. With me.'

I stopped outside our room and looked down at the pool. There was a bottle lying on the bottom, in a corner at the shallow end. Cyril would have missed it, or maybe couldn't fish it out.

I lay on my bed and pulled out the book to read the time-table. There was a bus leaving for Melbourne that afternoon. I could be on it and gone.

I read about some of the other places I could catch a bus to, if I had more money, while Rachel sat in front of the mirror, brushing her hair and putting on lip gloss. She put on a pair of sunglasses she'd found down the side of her seat at the movies the day before. She kept smiling at herself in the mirror and pouting her lips.

When I heard Gwen outside on the landing I stuck the timetable under my pillow. She pushed open the door.

'Off the bed, Jesse, and get moving. Ray's gonna meet us out the back. I don't want to keep him waiting.'

I didn't budge, even when she yelled at me for the third time to get going.

'I thought I might stay here,' I said.

Rachel stopped brushing her hair. 'But, Jesse, I want you to come with us.'

'There's nothing stopping you from going. I can stay here on my own.'

'But I want you to come with me,' she pleaded.

'Yeah, *I want you to come with me*,' Gwen copied her, in a baby voice. She walked around to the side of the bed. 'You're not staying here, sport. I don't trust you. You're cooking something up. Now, get up. You're coming with us. It'll be our first family outing with Ray.'

'Family?'

'Yeah, family. Soon as Ray and me are married that's what we'll be. A family.'

Ray drove up to the motel in the biggest car I'd ever seen. It took up two spaces in the car park. It was covered in red dust and most of the panels were dented. It was a Chevvie Camaro, an 'American car', he said, as he stood on the foot-path admiring it while we waited for Gwen and Rachel to come downstairs.

'No cheap Jap shit. And no anti-pollution gear to fuck her up. She was built when cars meant something.'

He dangled the keys in his hand.

'Listen to this. I bet you haven't heard a motor that grunts like this.'

He was carrying on like a kid trying to be my best friend. He jumped in the driver's seat, turned the key in the ignition and put his foot to the floor. I could hear two sounds. One was loud enough to rattle the windows in the motel laundry across from the car park, while the other was so deep it sounded like it was coming from underground.

He left the car idling, got out and rested both hands on the warm bonnet. 'If this car was a woman, she'd fuck you to death.'

He winked and flicked out his tongue like a slimy lizard. 'You behave, Jesse, and I'll let you ride her. Break yourself in.'

When Gwen saw the car she was just as excited as Ray. 'This yours? I didn't know you had a car.'

'Not exactly. I'm owed money, so I'm holding onto it.'

'You should keep it. I like it.'

She ran a finger across the bonnet, held it up and showed us the dirt-red spot on her fingertip. 'It could use a wash, Ray.'

'Na. Last car I cleaned up was knocked off the same day, out front of where I was staying. It was an omen. I'll leave this one the way she is. She's a dirty-looking bitch. It's what she's got underneath that matters.'

He threw her the keys. 'You like her. You can drive.'

Gwen drove while Ray pulled a piece of paper out of his shirt pocket, opened the glove box and searched around until he found a pen. He wrote on the piece of paper, mumbled to himself and did some finger counting. The picnic basket was sitting on the back seat between Rachel and me. When I was sure he wasn't looking, he was busy concentrating on his mental arithmetic, I lifted the lid on the basket. It was empty.

Every couple of minutes Gwen would ask him where we were heading. He waved her on and said, 'Keep driving. I'll tell you when to turn off.'

We drove out of the city and into the country. We passed farms, places that made wine and a small town so old I thought I was in a movie set. Rachel said it looked pretty and asked if we could stop but Ray said we had to keep going.

'We'll stop at a place I know up ahead and get some food.'

It was a hot morning and Gwen's love for the Camaro was already over.

'It's a long way to go for a picnic, Ray. We could have sat on the beach across from the motel and the kids could have had a swim. You could at least let me know where we're heading.'

'Stop your whingeing. It's not much further. An hour. An hour and a half, max.'

'An hour and a half? Fuck that. Rachel wants something to drink and I need a piss. We're not waiting an hour and a half.'

We stopped at the next town. It had about half a dozen houses and a general store. Gwen drove around the back of the store and parked under a tree across from a tin shack with a hand-painted sign nailed to a door: 'Toilet – Ladies & Gents'.

Ray handed me the picnic basket and some money. 'You take your sis into the shop and stock up.'

'What should I get?'

'Picnic food, I guess.'

We filled the basket with packets of potato chips, soft drinks, chocolate bars and some made-up sandwiches. I was watching Ray through the window. He was talking to someone on the pay phone out the front of the store.

We were still filling the basket when he came in. He lifted the lid to see what we'd bought. 'Look at all this shit. Junk food's no good for you. You two need to take better care of your bodies.'

I reckoned Ray smoked about forty cigarettes a day. And he got whacked with Gwen most nights, on the drink and real junk. He was no health freak.

'It's not all bad stuff,' I said. 'I got us some sandwiches. And orange juice for all of us.'

I reached into the basket and pulled out one of the bottles. 'See. One hundred per cent, it says. It's good for you.'

Ray grabbed the basket and money from me and walked over to the counter.

'You got any fruit, love?'

The girl behind the counter, who looked no older than me, was reading a fashion magazine. She was pretty and had an earring in her nose and a bolt through her eyebrow. She didn't bother looking at us until Ray asked her a second time.

She pointed towards the back of the shop. 'Had a few bananas yesterday. On the shelf next to the bread. That's all we got. If there's any left.'

Ray muttered 'fucken bananas' under his breath, and handed the girl the basket.

'Lot of stuff in here.' She smiled at Rachel as she put the prices through the till. 'You must be hungry?'

'I am,' Rachel said. 'We're going to have a picnic.'

'A picnic? Round here? That'll be a first.'

When we got out of the store Rachel asked me if I'd seen the girl's ring through her nose.

'It would be hard to miss it, Rache. It's right in the middle of her face.'

'Did you like it?'

'It's just a ring. It must give her the shits when she has a cold and has to blow her nose.'

'Did you like her? She was pretty. I think you liked her, Jesse.'

'What would you know?'

'Lots. I saw you look at her and you liked her.'

'Get in the car.'

'You liked her.'

We drove on until Ray ordered Gwen to take a turn-off, onto a dirt track. She took the corner too fast and had to hit the brakes to stop from slamming into a fence post. The back wheels of the Camaro drifted across the road and the car turned a full circle before we stopped in a cloud of dust.

Ray's hat flew off his head and out the window. He punched Gwen in the arm.

'What the fuck you trying to do? Get us killed?'

'Knock it off. It was an accident.' She jumped out of the car, slammed the door and ran around to the passenger side. 'You fucken drive.'

'Don't worry. I'm going to.'

He pointed though the windscreen at his hat, caught in the wind, tumbling along the road. 'But not before you grab that.'

The track was full of potholes and the Camaro shuddered and shook. It turned again and headed towards the sea. Before I knew what was going on we were driving on sand. It was smooth and flat. I looked out the side window. It was the weirdest colour.

'Look at the pink sand, Rachel. Your favourite colour.'

'It's not sand,' Ray said. 'It's salt.'

'Yeah, right,' Gwen said.

'Serious. Same stuff that you put on your tomato sandwiches, before they've cleaned it up. My old man used to work here. Mined it. Hard work, it was. They used to shovel it by hand. Broke his back, doing that.'

'You come from round here?' Gwen asked.

'Yeah. Lived out here for a bit when I was a kid. Back in that small town. It was a fucken hole.'

'So, why we out here for a picnic? If it's such a hole.'

He tipped his hat back on his head. 'I want to take a last look round. Won't be back again. I'm just sentimental, I guess.'

'You headed somewhere, Ray?'

He leaned across the car and put a hand on her thigh. 'I am, babe. And so are you. On our honeymoon.'

We pulled in alongside an open shed of old machinery. The roof and walls of the shed and the machines were a rust-red colour. Ray jumped out of the car, grabbed the picnic basket and leaned against the bonnet. He pointed to a wooden pier in the distance.

'Let's head over there.'

Perched along the pier were hundreds, maybe thousands, of birds. They were big and ugly and made an awful noise.

Ray took Rachel by the hand. 'You like birds? I bet you do, honey.'

'Some. But not big ones like those. They look scary. I like puppies best.'

Walking over to the pier the salt scrunched under my feet and the hot sun beat down on my head. When we got close the birds started screeching louder. At first it was just one or two of them, until they all joined in and the noise was deafening. Ray picked up a rusted bolt from the ground and hurled at them. It crashed against the pier wall. The birds took off and, for a few seconds, blocked out the sun. They flew over our heads and landed on the roof of the shed.

Ray slipped his shirt off and laid it down for a tablecloth. He took the food out of the basket and placed it on the shirt.

'Here you go, kids. Dig in.'

The pier was covered in bird shit and it smelled bad. Gwen sniffed the air. 'Great spot you picked, Ray.'

He laughed, took the top off a bottle of soft drink and had a long swig.

I looked at Ray's body as we ate. He had a round scar on his side, under his ribs. It looked a bit like the scars on my shoulder except the skin was a darker colour to that around it, and it was sunken. Gwen was looking too. She leaned across and touched it. The tip of her finger fitted the hole.

'I been meaning to ask you, Ray. How'd you get this? Never seen a scar so round and neat. It's kinda cute.'

'Cute? Weren't cute when I got it. A .38 put that hole in me.'

She quickly pulled her finger away like she'd burned it on a hot iron.

'What's a .38?' Rachel asked.

'You tell her, Jesse. You're a smart kid. I bet you know.'

I did know but didn't want to say. He was watching me closely. I was sure it was some sort of test, but didn't know what would be the smart answer. I wished that Jon Dempsey was around so I could ask him. He'd know how to deal with someone like Ray Crow.

'I dunno what it is.'

'I just bet you do.'

With no warning he ripped his shirt from the ground and slung it over his shoulder. Food and drink went everywhere.

'Jesus, what are you doing?' Gwen screamed. 'We haven't finished.'

'Yes we have. Grab what's left and put it back in the basket. We have to go.'

When we got back to the car Gwen headed for the bushes. 'I need another piss.'

She walked off into the scrub and Rachel trailed behind her.

Ray came up to me and fingered the scar in his side. 'You know how I got this. Why didn't you say?'

'Cause it's none of my business.'

He seemed impressed.

'Good boy. Keep your mouth shut when you have to. Would you like me to tell you how I got a bullet in my side here?'

'Like I said, it's not my business.'

'Go on. Take a guess.'

I thought that maybe the police had shot him in a robbery but didn't want to say.

'I really dunno.'

He put his shirt back on and tucked it in his jeans. 'I got myself into trouble and was taught a hard lesson. Learned something out of that, to keep my trap shut.'

He put an arm around my shoulder and squeezed, a lot harder than he needed to.

'You're luckier than me. You're a smart kid, Jesse. I reckon you already know that. And you didn't have to get shot to learn.'

'Where we going now?' Gwen asked.

We'd headed back along the dirt road to the highway and Ray had taken another turn-off and crossed a railway line. Now we were driving towards some low hills in the distance.

'I've got to call in just along here a bit. Have to pick up a mate.'

'Pick up a –'

'Hey, it don't need explaining. He's coming back with us. We've got some work on.'

'What work?'

'Enough!' Ray shouted at her as he thumped the steering wheel with his fist. 'Fucken enough.'

The road was rough but it didn't stop Ray from driving faster. He gripped the wheel and stared through the windscreen. He didn't slow until he saw two rusted milk cans guarding a track leading into a farm. He turned in and headed for a house in the distance.

The house was unpainted fibro, the walls covered in a grey mould and the tin roof so rusted it was dirt-brown. Behind the house we pulled up alongside a car graveyard: thirty or maybe forty wrecks parked in the weeds and long grass. Some of the cars had no doors. Others had missing side panels and bonnets. And a couple sat on low brick stacks with their wheels missing. One car was parked on its own next to the back veranda of the house. It looked expensive and almost brand new, except for a damaged front panel. And it had been cut clean in half.

As soon as Ray got out of the car we heard loud barking. When two large dogs ran out from behind a shed and charged at him, he jumped back in the car and locked the door. The dogs were covered in mud and dust and grease and shit. One of them ran around the car snarling. Gwen wound up her window just as the other dog jumped at her and butted the glass with its head. Its face was covered in scabs and old cuts and, when it opened its jaws, I could see it had a mouthful of broken teeth. Rachel jumped down from the seat onto the floor and squeezed herself behind the driver's seat.

Gwen screamed at Ray to do something, but he was just as frightened as the rest of us and couldn't move.

The dogs went quiet all of a sudden. I looked across the yard and saw an old man hobbling towards the car. He was dragging a leather whip behind him. His skin was black and his bare arms looked like charcoaled tree branches.

He stopped and spoke quietly to the dogs, 'Get off, you fellas, get off.'

When they didn't move he threw his arm back and cracked the whip across the back of the dog at Gwen's window. It jumped in the air and slammed itself against the car door. Rachel screamed and the dog circling the car took off from where it had come from, yelping in pain, like it had been whipped too.

The old man gave the second dog a couple more cracks before it gave up. It dropped down from the car, looked at the old man and opened the side of its mouth and snarled. Yellow froth dripped from its cracked tongue. The old man raised the whip in the air to be sure the dog got a good look at it.

'You get off, old fella. Or you can have some more of this, here. You don't wanna try me, boy.'

The dog slowly backed off and waddled away. Ray wouldn't get out of the car until both dogs were well out of sight. When he did, he and the old man gave each other a hug and slapped each other on the back and laughed.

'Jesus Christ, Magic. Fuck. He should keep them locked up. They'll end up tearing someone to pieces.'

The old man chuckled as he ran the whip through his hand. 'Oh, they've already done that, Ray boy. Killed plenty. That's why we keep the buggas. You was shitting your pants there,' he said, laughing. He nodded towards the road beyond the farm. 'We been letting them fellas run loose. Had a bit of trouble lately.'

'He never said a word of it to me. Spoke to him on the phone yesterday.'

'Not the stuff ya talk about on the phone. You know better than that, yaself. We been sellin a cut-and-shut two weeks gone. Flash car. Import. Don't work out for the fella buyin. Wants his money back. Boss says no and that fella's not happy. Not one bit. Says him and his crew be payin us a visit. An they will, soon enough.'

'They serious?'

'Oh yeah. Serious. But you know what he's like. Serious too, with money. We sold it fair and square and they take a risk. That's the business. Always been the way. He won't be givin them boys a thing without some trouble to go with it.'

Ray looked over at the house. 'He inside?'

'Yeah. Got a mighty sore head. Finished cookin last night. Had a big night. Run up a card game for the lads off the farms. Pay day out here. They come over for the game.'

'He win?'

'Maybe. Maybe not. He never tell me. Cunnin bugga with money. You know that, good as me, Ray.'

Ray walked around to the passenger-side window and tapped on the glass. Gwen wound down her window.

'Jump out. I want you to meet a mate of mine.'

'This old Abo bloke?' Gwen sneered. 'I don't want to meet him.'

Ray stuck his head through the window. 'Keep it down. Magic's a top bloke. Good as any white man. It's my mate inside I want you to meet.'

He opened the door. 'Get out.'

Gwen followed Ray into the house. It was steaming in the car. I took a good look around for the dogs before hopping out, but stayed next to the car, with the door open, ready to jump in if they came back. I heard a pig grunting off in the distance, then a painful cry, and then nothing.

Rachel wouldn't get out. She jumped on the front seat and stuck her head out the window to get a good look at the old man. He watched us just as closely as he spat on a piece of rag he took from his back pocket, and passed the leather whip through it. When he'd finished cleaning he pocketed the rag again and looped the whip around his neck. He walked over to me.

'What's your name, young fella?'

I looked at his leather-worn face, into his eyes, a pair of dark marbles surrounded by dull yellow.

'Jesse,' I croaked, spitting out a mouthful of dust.

'Jesse. That's a good name right there. I knew a Jesse fella one time. We was on the mission together. Skinny little fella. Smaller than you is now. He could look after himself, that boy. Fight like his life was in it. He went out west, across the desert. Fightin in the ring, on the road, in the tents. That poor fella, he died, fightin the grog.'

He came closer, lifted a hand and placed it on my head. I was too scared to move or open my mouth.

'He was like you, I think? Yella Fella. You a Yella Fella?'

'Yella Fella?'

'Yeah. Bit of that fella, this fella, and then another fella, all mixed together.'

He cocked his ear, as if he'd heard something behind him. He patted my head a couple of times and slowly took the whip from around his neck and gripped the handle as he looked over at Rachel.

'And you are, missie?'

He rested against the car and offered her his hand. 'Don't you be afraid of old Magic. I'm a harmless fella.'

'Her name is Rachel. And it was the dogs that frightened her, not you.'

'Well, don't worry about them mongrel fellas. They come back, old Magic will deal with them proper.'

He turned back to Rachel. 'And that's a mighty name too. A Bible name. I remember that from mission days. Good book, that one.'

'My pop,' I said, 'he told me that too, that Rachel is from the Bible. The Old Testament.'

'Old Testament. You right with that, boy. Your old pop must be a smart fella.'

Magic had the softest voice. He sounded more like a woman than a man. And he was real friendly.

'Why do they call you "Magic"?' I asked. 'Is that like black magic? The Dreamtime?'

He laughed out loud. 'What do you think I am, boy? A voodoo fella? Bullshit, all that Dreamtime. You don't be thinkin about that. No. It's like this. Rachel girl, you be good and come on out. You get out of the car and I'll show you some proper magic. Come on, now.'

I opened the door for her and she slowly got out of the car. Magic reached into his pocket and took out a twenty-cent piece. He placed it in the palm of his hand so we could get a good look at it. He closed his hand, lifted it to his mouth and blew on the back of it. When he opened his hand again the coin was gone. He showed us his other hand. It was empty too.

'Wow,' Rachel said, laughing. 'How'd you do that?'

He reached behind her ear with his hand, opened it and showed her the same coin. 'Can't tell you that one, girl. It wouldn't be no magic, then. But here. You take this one and you keep it for your own good luck one day.'

As Rachel was about to take the coin from his hand I heard the bark of the dogs. They ran out from behind the shed. The bigger dog, the one with the scabby mouth was heading straight for Rachel. She dropped to her knees and cowered next to the back wheel of the car.

I was sure she would be attacked. As the dog was about to pounce on her Magic stepped between them. The dog jumped at him. He raised his knee, just high enough. The dog crashed into it and collapsed at his feet. It was stunned and couldn't move, like all the life had been knocked out of it. The second dog turned and headed back to where it had come from.

As the dog lay on its side sucking for air, Magic walked slowly around it, stomping on the dog with the heel of his boot. He kicked it in its ribs and along its back. When the dog tried lifting its head off the dirt, Magic said, almost feeling sorry for the animal, 'Don't you try gettin to your feet, not yet, old boy.'

He stepped back and took a last swing at it with the toe of his boot. Its body shook and blood ran from the side of its mouth. Magic gave it a gentle tap in the stomach with the toe of his boot.

'Come on, get off, fella. Get off.'

The dog got slowly to its feet, took a step and fell. In the end it got up and staggered away, towards a cut-down drum filled with water. Rachel jumped up and climbed back into the car.

Magic smiled at me. 'Don't worry yourself about him. He's a dumb bugga. Take him a long time to learn, that's all.'

He looked down at his boot, took the rag out of his pocket and wiped away the blood and spit.

'I tell you, any fella, don't matter who he is, man or a dog. Anyone out there in the bush too. You whip him hard enough he can do anythin you want him to. Just about.'

He threw his shoulders back. 'Magic, he learn quick as the wind, a long time back. They give me a good whippin when I was a lad, and I learn good.'

I heard a door slam, looked across the yard and saw Gwen walking from the house. She didn't look happy. Ray was next to her, carrying a large bag over his shoulder. I could see a man behind him, pulling on a denim shirt. He was taller and thinner than Ray and had long greasy hair and pale skin the colour of milk.

He spotted the dog dragging itself over to the water drum. 'Hey, Magic, what's up with Pup?'

'Oh, he's just worn out. Runnin round like crazy after these kids. Got too excited, the fella.'

'Excited? He looks fucked to me.'

He was a step away from me when I saw the mark on his cheek, just below his eye. It was tattoo. The teardrop tattoo. I looked down at the ground as he walked straight by me like I wasn't there and followed Ray to the back of the car. Ray opened the boot and threw the bag in. I could hear them talking, real quiet.

Ray slammed the boot down and walked to the driver's side of the car. 'Kids. This is Limbo. Limbo. The kids.'

Limbo didn't bother looking at us. Ray ordered Gwen into the back seat with us. As she was getting in he patted her on the arse. She pushed his hand away.

'Fuck off, will ya.'

Ray looked over at Limbo and laughed. 'Fuck off yourself.'

Limbo got in next to Ray and turned to Gwen as we were about to drive off. 'Sorry about this. Putting you and your kids out. Ray and me have a job on. We'd arranged this before you come on the scene.'

She said nothing and stared at the back of Ray's head. Limbo looked at me, and then Rachel. She pointed at his cheek. I was sure she was about to say something and I dug an elbow into her side. She pushed against me.

'Don't, Jesse.'

She tapped Limbo on the arm. 'You've got a crying mark on your face. Are you sad?'

Limbo touched the tear and pulled the skin down, over his cheekbone. He had a bloodshot eye.

'Yeah. I've been sad. Lot of times. The world's full of sadness.'

Gwen wrapped an arm around Rachel and pulled her closer.

Limbo stuck his head out of the car and said to Magic, 'Any trouble you call Pickett in town. He knows how to get hold of me.'

'Won't be no trouble, Lim,' he said, looking at me. 'Hey wait up, boss. I got something for the boy.'

He walked around to my side of the car and offered me the twenty-cent piece. 'It's gonna be dark, later on, sometime soon, boy. Clouds gonna come. Rain and thunder. You got to take care. This is help for you.'

Before I could take the coin Gwen butted in. 'Sorry. He don't take money from strangers. I taught him that.'

'We not strangers.' Magic smiled. 'We old friends.'

★

It was dark by the time we saw the lights of Adelaide again. Gwen was restless and asked Ray to pull into a takeaway off the highway.

While Ray was all for it Limbo was against the idea. He coughed as he spoke and it was hard to make out what he was saying.

'We don't need to stop and eat, Ray. This can wait.'

Ray looked at Gwen in the rear-view mirror. 'What about it, babe? We keep driving?'

'I said I was hungry,' she insisted. 'So are the kids.'

Ray hit the indicator and turned off the highway. Limbo huffed and puffed.

'Who's running the show here, bro?'

'Cool it. Man's got to eat and we got plenty of time.'

Gwen jumped out of the car, slammed the door and headed for the café with Rachel. Limbo leaned against the bonnet and lit a cigarette.

'Jesus Christ, Ray. We gotta front up on time for the meet, or it could fuck up on us. And here you are taking orders from your woman. You cunt-struck or something?'

Ray looked over at me. 'Keep it down, Lim.'

'No, I fucken won't. I cooked the gear, I'm having a say.'

Ray took a step towards him and glared until Limbo lowered his eyes to the ground.

'Good. You've had your say, now come on, it's my shout.'

The café was called The Devil's Kitchen. We ate in silence. Gwen looked up at Limbo from her plate of hamburger and chips every minute or so, like she was about to say something nasty him. Her mouth had got her into a lot of trouble over the years. I was praying she could keep it shut. Limbo didn't eat a thing. He sulked and looked at the bottom of an empty drink can. I took a quick peek at the tattoo on his cheek and wondered what he might have done in prison to earn it.

When they'd finished eating Gwen and Rachel bought ice creams and headed back outside. I was stuck between Ray and the wall and couldn't get out of the booth without asking and I didn't think that would be a good idea, right then. Limbo took a ring from one of his fingers, a plain silver band, and spun it across the table. Ray drank black coffee as he watched him.

'Hey, Jesse. How do you reckon my old mate here got his name? Limbo. It's not his real name, of course. Why do you reckon they call him that?'

I didn't know and told him so.

'Don't matter. Take a guess.'

I shrugged my shoulders.

'Fuck it, Jesse. Do you have to be so miserable all the time? Limbo and me are trying to be your mates here. Take a guess.'

'Cause he got sent there one time? To limbo, like in the Bible?'

'Hey, that's not bad. You're close.'

Ray drained the last of his coffee.

'You want to tell him, Lim, where you were sent?'

Limbo snatched the spinning piece of silver from the table and stuck it back on his finger.

'This kid don't like me. Don't like you either, Ray. You tell him, if you like. I don't give a fuck. Don't have time for guessing games. This is fucken kids' stuff.'

Ray tapped out a drumbeat on the tabletop with his knuckles and told me the story of how Limbo got his name. It was after he'd been arrested, charged and remanded for armed robbery.

'In the history of the South Australian prison system no one spent more time on remand, waiting for his case to come up, than this boy. How long were you on the yard waiting, Lim? Two years?'

'Two years and three fucken months.'

'You get it, Jesse. More than two years in limbo before his day in court. That's how he got his name.'

Limbo lit up another cigarette. 'And when I finally got my day in court they gave me another six years to go with it.'

'So you got out?' I asked.

'What do you mean? Course I got out. I'm here.'

'Then it's not right, calling you Limbo. It should be Purgatory, your name.'

'Purgatory?'

'Yeah. Purgatory is where you go after you die, and you stay there until somebody says enough prayers for you to go to heaven. It's dark and cold there and you can be there for a long time. People pray for your soul so you can get out. Limbo is different. It's a place for babies that die before they are baptised. They die with sin on their soul, but it's not their fault because they're too little to have done anything wrong. You never get out of Limbo. That's different.'

Ray whistled. 'Like a life sentence, without parole. That's fucken deep, for a kid your age. Who taught you that shit?'

'My pop. He goes to a church where they give out these books, picture stories. I looked at them.'

'This pop you stayed with, he Gwen's old man?'

'Yep.'

'And where's he live. Where'd you stay with him?'

'In Victoria. Melbourne.'

'You know anyone else over there?'

'Not really. There's a friend of Gwen's, but no one else. Pop's is the only place we know.'

Ray scoffed. 'No wonder she's a barrel of laughs, with an old man like that.'

He slapped Limbo on the back. 'You're lucky you didn't end up in Purgatory. You got no fucken soul, and even if you did, there'd be no one praying to get you out.'

A worker in a dirty apron came over to the table. He smiled at Limbo. He had a glass ashtray in his hand.

'Hey ya, mate. You can't smoke in here. Let me take it for you and butt it out.'

Ray and Limbo laughed out loud, as if the man had told them a joke. He tried again.

'It's not on my account. It's the Health Department that makes the rules. If I let you to smoke inside the café and they come by, I could be in trouble.'

Limbo looked around the café. A teenage couple were sitting at another booth kissing and hugging, while a road worker was perched on a stool at the counter.

'Well, mate. Unless they're undercover I reckon we'll get away with it.'

He took a drag on the cigarette and blew the smoke in the man's face. 'Now fuck off and let me finish this in peace.'

The man knew better than to ask again and retreated behind the counter. Limbo finished his cigarette, butted it on the tabletop and stood up.

'We paid, Ray?'

'Na. I reckon it's on the house.'

★

Back at the motel Gwen put on a pair of tight jeans and a singlet top and went down to the bar on her own. She wasn't happy. Ray had taken off with Limbo and wouldn't say when he was coming back. I ordered a bowl of chips from room service, lay on the bed and turned on the TV. I flicked through about thirty channels before I found something to watch. It was a movie about a boy who could fly. I'd seen it before, but it was a good one. I rested my head on the pillow and sat the bowl on my chest.

I woke up in the middle of the night with Ray standing over the bed. Limbo was behind him, eating one of my cold chips. Ray had a bag over his shoulder. It was red and looked new, not the same one he'd had earlier.

'You seen Gwen? She's not in her the room.'

'She went downstairs, maybe.'

He handed the bag to Limbo. 'Look after this. I'll be back up in a minute.'

At little while later I heard Gwen and Ray arguing. I got out of bed, put my ear to the wall and listened. Ray was calling her all sorts of names and screaming about someone he'd seen her sitting with at the bar. Gwen yelled back at him. I heard something smash against the wall. The fighting was loud enough to wake Rachel.

'What's going on, Jesse?'

'Nothing. They're having a party. You know what they're like.'

'It doesn't sound like a party to me. I can hear Gwen crying.'

'That's a song playing. I want you to close your eyes and go back to sleep.'

I got back into bed and turned onto my stomach. I was more or less asleep when Rachel tapped me on the shoulder.

'Jesse, can I get into bed with you?'

I threw the blanket back and let her climb in next to me. I turned my back on her. She tapped me on the shoulder again.

'Can I hold onto you?'

'Yeah. But keep still.'

In the morning we found Gwen on top of her bed with her body tucked into a ball. She was wearing only her underpants and a bra and had bruises all over her. I could see a dark patch above one breast about the size of a fist. Streaks of mascara ran down her cheeks and her lipstick was smudged across her face. An ashtray was turned upside down on the bed and the floor was covered in more cigarette butts, empty glasses, a whiskey bottle and some of her clothes, which had been torn apart. A clock radio was smashed to pieces on the floor.

I could feel Rachel's breath on my neck. I told her to go back to our room and stay there until I came for her.

When she didn't move I yelled at her. 'Get out of here!'

She ran past me, jumped onto the bed next to Gwen and put her arms around her neck. Gwen wrapped her hands around Rachel's face and smothered her with kisses until her cheeks were painted with lipstick. Gwen leaned across to the bedside table, picked up a half-full glass, sniffed it and took a long swig, then sunk back into the mattress. She tried pushing Rachel away.

'Move your arse, little sister. What time is it, Jesse? We've gotta get out of here.'

When she tried sitting up, she caught her breath a couple of times and hunched over in pain. 'This is killing me, Jesse. You got to help me up. I think I've broken a rib or something where the bastard kicked me.'

She put her feet on the floor and tried lifting her arms. 'Help me up.'

She hung her arms around my neck and held on tight as she could while I lifted her to her feet. She fell forward and head butted me, not too hard. Her breath stunk of grog and cigarettes. I looked into her eyes and then the bruises underneath them and a cut above one eye. She looked away from me. I reckoned she was about to cry. I wasn't too sure how I felt about her right then. But I knew I'd do anything I had to to hurt Ray, kill him even.

She fell to her knees and crawled across the floor, grabbing her clothes as she went. When she got to the dressing table she pulled herself up and looked at herself in the mirror.

'I'm a piece of shit.'

She picked up a hairbrush and raked it through her hair. 'What time is it, Jesse?'

'After twelve.'

She grabbed at her breasts and rearranged them in her bra. 'We're going back to Melbourne.'

'Does Ray know we're leaving?'

She pointed at her battered face. 'Look what he fucken did to me. You think I'm gonna tell him? We won't be here when he gets back.'

She picked up a denim dress off the floor. As she tried putting it on she fell back on the bed. 'I'll need a hand, Jesse. Anything here that's mine, on the floor, in the bathroom, the wardrobe, throw it on top of the bed. I'll pack it up. Then go back to your room and pack up your stuff. Quick.'

I walked to the sink and filled a glass with water. 'Want any, Rachel?'

'Jesus, fuck me, Jesse. Move! Don't you get it? *You*, of all people. He kicked the shit out of me last night and his mad mate Limbo nearly killed some poor bloke sitting at the bar minding his own business. They're psychos. We have to get away from here before he gets back.'

Rachel sat on the bed while I picked up some of Gwen's things from the floor. She didn't like what she'd heard, and had started a conversation with Comfort.

Gwen finally got the dress on. She stood up, breathed in and zipped it up. 'He'll be back later tonight. Maybe early morning. I heard them talking. They had another drive to do, some pick-up.'

She got down on her hands and knees, and pulled out her purse from between the mattress and the bed-base. She opened it, rifled through it and then tipped it upside down on the bed. All that fell out was a five-dollar note and some coins.

'Great. We're rich.'

She threw the purse on the bed, went into the bathroom and closed the door.

'You going to help, Rachel, or what?' I asked.

'I'm tired out.'

'Yeah, so am I. Bad luck. Go back to our room and get all your stuff out of the drawers.'

'No.'

She was being a pain in the arse. I dragged her off the bed and pushed her out of the room. 'I said do it. Didn't you hear what she said about Ray? Do you want him coming after us? Go.'

I was pulling some of Gwen's clothes from their hangers when I noticed in the bottom corner of the wardrobe, stuffed behind some pillows, the red sports bag that Ray had with him the night before. It felt heavy when I picked it up. I put the bag on the bed and opened it. There was money inside, lots of it, in rolls. There was also a plastic bag with a gun inside and some loose bullets. The gun was silver and had a wooden handle. I heard the toilet flush. I zipped the bag and put it back where I'd found it.

'Jesse, load up from the mini-bar here, in your room and whatever else you can grab. And go in the bathroom. Grab the soaps and shampoos and those nice white face washers. Blankets. Anything that might come in handy.'

'Face washers?'

'Yeah. And the towels. We have no money, grab whatever you can.'

I packed our case and shifted it to Gwen's room. She hung a 'Do Not Disturb' sign from the doorknob and we went down to the dining room for something to eat.

'I thought we were in a hurry,' I said as we walked down the stairs.

'We are, but not in too much to get a decent feed into us. We mightn't be eating for a while.'

We ordered roast chicken, baked potatoes and onion rings. When lunch was over Gwen winked at the waiter and told him to be sure to put a big tip on the tab for himself.

She took us out to the Commodore and emptied the boot of rubbish and drove it to a parking bay alongside the fire escape. She ordered Rachel to sit in the back of the car and wait for us.

'I don't wanna.' She didn't want to be left alone.

'Well, you have to.'

'What about my things? What about Comfort?'

'Jesse's packed it all. Wait there.'

Upstairs, I picked up two pillowcases of stuff we'd knocked off. Gwen grabbed her bag and another pillowcase.

'You'll have to come back for yours and Rache's suitcase.'

When I did, I went straight to the wardrobe and grabbed the sports bag. I then threw our suitcase on the bed and unzipped it. It was packed tight with dirty clothes, my backpack, the binoculars and Rachel's old teddy. I took Comfort out and laid him on the bed. I hung the binoculars around my neck, threw out some of the dirty clothes and shoved the sports bag inside. I was about to close the door behind me when I remembered Comfort. I tucked him under my arm and slammed the door behind me.

Gwen had a large packet of toilet rolls under one arm and a cardboard box in the other.

'What's in the box?'

'Bottles of water and packets of biscuits. This will have to do until we get back to Melbourne.'

As we drove out of Adelaide I thought about the bag of money in the boot. By the time Ray and Limbo got back to the motel we'd be in Melbourne. I rested my head against the seat and watched through the window. We drove through the near-empty streets. Slowly there were less and less houses until all I could see was some trees and grass and the road ahead.

FOUR

The road baked in the heat. The air conditioning was grumbling so loud I could hardly hear the radio, even though it was up full blast. Gwen chain-smoked and stared out the rear-view mirror, checking behind us more than she watched the road up ahead. When she wasn't smoking she was biting on her fingernails. If she'd known what I'd put in the boot, she'd have been chewing her fingers to the bone.

We were two hours gone from Adelaide, not far from the Victorian border, when Gwen pulled off the highway into a store. There were bags of manure and soil stacked out the front, racks of gas bottles and one petrol pump. I hadn't counted on stopping, and it made me nervous. As soon as Ray and Limbo found out about their money they'd be searching for us.

'Why we pulling in here? Shouldn't we keep driving before it gets dark?'

'Got no choice, Jesse. We've run out of petrol.'

She parked next to the pump, turned the engine off, sat for a few minutes and tapped her broken nails on the steering wheel. I knew what she was thinking without having to ask.

'Have you got any money on you, Jesse? Even a few dollars?'

'I've got nothing,' I lied.

'Well, there's less than ten in my purse, and I'm not parting with that. Looks like we'll have to bike it. You fill up while I sit here, ready for the run. You know what to do. Hurry before someone comes out to help us.'

We'd done plenty of biking over the years and only came close to getting caught one time when Gwen left me standing at the bowser and took off down the road. I was lucky that the kid behind the counter didn't seem to care what we were up to. I'd run after the car and jumped back in before he'd moved his arse.

Having done it before didn't make me feel any better, but I was ready to do just about anything to get us back on the road.

'Okay. But don't you leave without me.'

Rachel unwound her window. 'Where you going, Jesse? Can you get me an ice – ?'

'No, he can't,' Gwen interrupted.

'Maybe I'll go for myself, then.'

'No you won't. Don't you move. Jesse has something important to do.'

I waved and smiled at the man sitting behind the counter in the shop. He had no hair and looked pretty old and overweight. I felt a bit better. He'd be slow off the mark. He waved and went back to the newspaper he was reading. I kept an eye on him as I filled up. Petrol splashed all over my jeans when the tank was full. As soon as I put the nozzle back in its holster he looked up at me. I waved again, opened the door and jumped in the front seat just as Gwen put her foot on the accelerator.

Nothing happened. She'd stalled the car.

'Fuck,' she screamed.

The old man scratched his head like he wasn't sure what was going on. When he worked it out he jumped down from his seat, reached under the counter and picked something up in his hand. He was quicker than I thought he'd be.

'Gwen, he's coming. He's coming.'

He ran out of the store, waving around a small baseball bat. I leaned across Gwen and pushed the button down, locking her door. I quickly did the same to Rachel's and my door. She took one look at the crazy man running toward us, and covered her eyes with her hands.

He grabbed Gwen's doorhandle and tried ripping it open with one hand as he showed her the bat with the other. 'Open up. You've fifty bucks' worth in that tank.' She kept on pumping the accelerator and turning the key. When he worked out he couldn't get the door open he took the bat in both hands and swung it at the side window. The window didn't break but the bat split in two. He threw the two shattered bits onto the ground.

'Open the door, you thieving bitch.'

He picked up a long metal pole leaning against the bowser and ran around to the other side of the car. Rachel took a peek just as he speared her window with the pole. She ducked as the pole shattered the window, showering her with glass. 'Go, go,' she screamed. 'He's going to get us.' He ran to the front of the car and took aim at Gwen's head as the motor kicked into life. She slammed her foot down and would have run right over the top of him if he hadn't jumped out of the way.

We screeched out of the driveway and back onto the highway. I turned to see the man running after us with the pole held above his head. He tried chucking it at us like a javelin thrower, but he didn't have the strength. The pole skidded along the road, sending out sparks.

It was late in the day when we crossed into Victoria. Gwen pulled off the road again and stuck a towel in the door, covering Rachel's broken window. She cleared out as much of the broken glass as she could, and had to pick some out of Rachel's clothes and hair.

'Was he a bad man?' Rachel asked, as Gwen sat her on her lap and combed through her hair with her fingers, looking for glass.

Gwen looked at her like she was stupid. 'Na. He was your guardian angel. What do you reckon that thing he was waving around was? A magic wand or something?'

When we got going again I saw a few sheep and a cow along the road and some old farm machinery tangled with weeds that looked like it hadn't moved in years. Every now and then the car sputtered and slowed a bit. Even with Gwen's foot to the floor the speedo was going backwards. I looked out of the back window now and then, worried the Camaro might be on our tail. I suddenly realised that taking the money had been a mistake. Between Ray and Limbo I was sure they'd do whatever they had to, to get it back. But there was nothing I could do about it now. If I dumped the bag and they lost the money anyway, they'd be even madder and would skin me if they caught up to us.

Rachel was lying across the back seat, half asleep. Every now and then she'd open her eyes and get her fingers to dance in front of her eyes. I looked down at the scar across the top of my thumb and thought about the day in the kitchen when I'd promised her that sharing our blood would keep us together. If Ray and Limbo did come after us, I'd have a tough time dragging her with me if I got the chance to run.

The country we were driving through was flat as an iron and bone dry. The sky was big, blue and empty, except for a flaming ball of sun, low in the sky. It had tracked us all day like a satellite, and it looked about ready to explode. I got thirsty just looking at it but didn't think it'd be a good idea to ask Gwen to stop and get some water from the boot in case the car conked out.

As the car got slower and slower the massive trucks that hurled by threw us from side to side. Everything we passed on the side of the road – a stunted tree, an animal in a field, even the buildings – looked as good as dead, whipped by the dust and wind.

To take my mind off Ray and Limbo I started counting the roadkill: rabbits, kangaroos, wombats and maybe a fox. It was hard to be sure. Some of the bodies were so flat they'd spread across the road like a jam sandwich. We passed a hawk, or maybe an eagle even, on the side of the road, hunched over a carcass, tearing into it with its claws and sharp beak. I also saw dead birds that seemed to have dropped out of the sky. As we drove by a broken wing would lift in the breeze.

Rachel could hear me counting. She rubbed her eyes and sat up. 'What are you doing?'

'Look.'

I pointed to a lump of fur up ahead of us. A car was travelling towards us in the opposite direction so Gwen had no chance to swerve and miss the dead animal. She drove straight over the top of it.

'That's four kangaroos,' I counted, as Gwen swore to herself and the force shook the car.

Rachel slapped me on the shoulder. 'You're horrible. All those animals are dead and you don't care.'

'I care. Jesus, Rache, I didn't run over them. But it's my job to look after the body count.'

Gwen told me to stop teasing her.

'I'm not. I can't help it if the road's full of dead animals. If she don't like it she can keep her eyes shut.'

I leaned over the seat and looked at the speedo. We were down to thirty on a single-lane stretch of the highway. There were a lot of cars and trucks coming towards us, and a long line of traffic tailing us with no chance of overtaking. Drivers had started tooting their horns. When a car did get to pass, the driver would pull a face, or stick a finger in the air. Gwen was now grinding her teeth and sweating like a pig. She looked from the side to the rear-view mirror, not sure what to do.

'Hey, Jesse, do you reckon we should pull over and let these cars by?'

It was a bad idea. We'd be a sitting duck for anyone following us.

'If we stop we mightn't get the car started again. I think we should keep going.'

'What about if I keep the motor running. Maybe that'll work?'

'I still don't like it.'

'Well, we're hardly going anyway.'

She spotted a sign up ahead – 'Scenic Route' – pointing to a side road. 'We're taking this turn-off.'

'You sure?'

'I'm not sure of anything. But I don't want these bastards up my arse abusing me all the way back to Melbourne.'

The road we turned onto was empty in both directions, which was lucky for us, as the car was crawling along like a snail. It didn't look too 'scenic' to me. At first the land was just as flat and dry as it had been back on the highway. But as we drove on, the country started to change. There were a few more trees here and there and some low humps we drove over, as the land got hilly. As each hump got a little steeper the car found it harder to clear the next rise. It coughed and choked and almost came to a stop near the top of a hill before picking up enough speed to clear it.

I could see a few houses and other buildings at the bottom of the hill. The car went quiet; the motor had cut out altogether but we were still moving. Gwen turned the key in the ignition and pumped the accelerator. Nothing happened. She looked at the dashboard and thumped it with a fist.

'Shit. Shit. The petrol gauge is on empty. Already? How can that be?'

The car picked up speed and raced down the hill. We crossed a wooden bridge over a dry creek and drifted into the main street of a town. As the car slowed again Gwen eased it off the road and put a foot on the brake. I wound down my window. We'd come to a stop outside an old stone building with wide steps leading to a pair of heavy wooden doors. A cannon was mounted on a slab of stone in front of the building, with the names of dead soldiers written on the slab in gold lettering.

Gwen was making a strange noise. I couldn't make out if she was crying or laughing. Or maybe both at the same time. She took a few breaths and ran her hands through her hair.

'Let's see what we got here. Come on. Out of the car.'

She stood on the footpath, looked up and down the street and pointed with her chin. 'Looks like there might be a servo on the corner up there. Could be a mechanic around. Maybe we should walk up there. What do you reckon, Jess?'

As far as Gwen knew we had no money for repairs. I was thinking about sneaking a roll out of the bag in the boot when Rachel sat down in the gutter and arced up.

'I'm not going to walk all the way up there. I'm hot. I want to stay here.'

Gwen opened her mouth, about to yell at her, then stopped herself, took a breath a spoke quietly. 'Please yourself, girlie. But don't you move from here.'

She took out three bottles of water from the boot and handed one to me. I ripped the top off and skolled most of the bottle, even though the water was warm.

She took the top off another bottle and passed it to Rachel. 'Like I said. Don't move an inch.'

The shops we passed along the street, a general store, a butcher shop and a dressmaker, were closed. Some of the shopfronts were boarded up and deserted. The service station was empty too, and the petrol pumps were chained and padlocked and covered in cobwebs. Gwen walked over to the workshop behind the pumps and put her hand against a dusty window. She looked through the glass and knocked a couple of times.

When nobody answered she took a step back and turned a full circle. Her denim dress was drenched in sweat. She threw her hands in the air.

'What is this place? A ghost town?'

'Looks like it.'

She sat down on a step out front of the workshop and took a drink from her water bottle. She poured some water into her hand and splashed it on her face. I walked out to the footpath and looked back at the car. Rachel hadn't moved. The road leading into the town was empty. I stood and watched Gwen for a bit as she lifted the bottom of her dress and wiped her face with it.

'Do you reckon Ray'll come looking for you?'

'Come after me? Why would he?'

'I don't know. He might be pissed off at you for not telling him you were leaving.'

'Oh, he'll be fucken angry, all right. We racked up a nice bill at the motel and they'll know we nicked stuff from the rooms. He'll have to pay for that as well.'

She laughed just thinking about it.

'But he won't come after me. Him and that Limbo, they had something cooking that'll keep them busy for a while. He won't give me a second thought. I've seen the last of Ray Crow.'

'Help yas?'

A man was standing in the doorway of the workshop, wiping his hands with a dirty cloth. He put it in his side pocket and stuck a cap on his head. He was wearing a boilersuit unbuttoned to the waist that showed off a belly streaked with grease. The boiler suit was caked in a mix of oil, metal flakes and dirt.

Gwen got to her feet and tried fixing her hair, as if it might make her more presentable.

'We've had a breakdown. Our car's back on the street there. Could you have a look at it?'

When he answered I couldn't understand much of what he said. His lips hardly moved, like a ventriloquist. He took out a handkerchief from his back pocket, unwrapped a set of false teeth, top and bottom. He stuck them in his mouth. His bright smile stood out against his grubby whiskered face.

'That's better. You say you broke down?'

He listened closely as Gwen told him what had gone wrong with the car. He smiled again, keen to show off his teeth, and pointed to the bruise on the side of Gwen's face. 'Looks like you've had an accident too. Your face has been knocked about.'

'Don't worry about me, I just want you to look at the car.'

He shrugged his shoulders. 'Okay, I'd better have a look at it then.' He offered a hand to Gwen. 'Gussie. Gus Rizzo.'

As we walked back to the car I asked him where everyone was.

'This town's gone. Has been for years. We haven't had proper rain in more than ten years. There's no water and no work. The youngsters have all taken off for the smoke and the farmers that haven't gone to the wall or blown their heads off don't have much to come into town for.'

Rachel had moved from the gutter to the shaded steps of the building. Gus touched his hat when Gwen introduced him to her.

When he couldn't get the car started he lifted the bonnet and talked to himself as he fiddled around with different parts of the engine. We stood back and waited until he lifted his head. He was holding a piece of hose in his hand. There wasn't much left of it.

'See this? You've got no petrol getting to the motor. Car won't get far without petrol. There's your problem. The fuel line's stuffed. Something's blocked it and split the webbing. What petrol you had in the tank has been pissing out all over the road.'

He put the length of hose to his eye and tried looking through it. 'Can't see daylight. Going by this I reckon your tank is full of shit. Can't be sure of it but someone might have sweetened it for you. Couple of pound of sugar. Someone who didn't want you getting far.'

He twirled the hose between a finger and thumb.

'Can you fix it?' Gwen asked.

'Sure I can. I can replace the length of fuel line for you. I don't have the same part but I can put something together that'll do the job. But, if your tank has been stuffed with, and I'd say it has, won't be long before the line blocks again. Or it'll play up some place else. The carbie, most likely. The only way to fix it proper is to drain the tank and clean it out. And a couple of other things on top of that. Can't do that in a day.'

Gwen muttered 'fuck' under her breath.

'Exactly,' Gus added.

'Can you do enough to get us going again?'

'Yeah sure. But I can't guarantee how far you'll get. That's all.'

'Could we make it to Melbourne?'

He took his hat off, scratched his head, put it back on again and scratched his belly. 'Maybe. Maybe not.'

He saw her face drop. 'But you never know,' he said, smiling. 'No harm in trying. At least I'll get you back on the road. Let me go back to the shop and grab some tools. You happy with that?'

When Gwen answered that she had no money I almost blurted out, 'We do.' Gus saved me from dobbing myself in.

'You'd fit in here, love. No one's got a cracker. Can't remember the last time I was paid for a job.'

He stroked his belly again. 'Round here, we usually barter.'

'What's that?'

'You know, I get paid with something of like value. We'll work something out.'

As Gus walked slowly back to his workshop Gwen pulled me aside.

'Jesse. Why don't you get Rachel and yourself another drink and take her for a walk?'

Rachel overheard us and called out, 'I don't want to walk.'

'Yes you do. Go on, Jesse. Take her.'

'Take her where?'

'I don't know. Find somewhere.'

Gus was soon heading back, swinging a toolbox in one hand and lugging a jerry can in the other. A hedged wall ran along the side of the road across from us, broken by metal gates with long metal spikes sitting on the top. I grabbed hold of Rachel's hand and dragged her to her feet.

'We're going for a walk.'

'No I'm not. Where to?'

'Over the road there. I reckon there might be a secret garden behind those gates.'

She looked across the road, interested and sussing me at the same time. 'How do you know? I bet there's nothing there.'

'Might not be. But do you reckon someone would go to all the trouble to plant a hedge that long and put those big gates up if there was nothing behind them? I don't think someone would do that for nothing. Are you coming or not?'

I gave her time to think about it.

'You coming, Gwen?' she asked.

'No. I'm going to stay here and give this fella a hand.'

We crossed the road and walked alongside the hedge until we reached the gates. They were shut but not bolted. When I pushed against them, they cried out. I turned to Rachel.

'Let's take a look inside.'

She leaned on the gate and stuck her head between the bars. We could see a few trees, dry patches of grass, and some flowers growing beside the pathway leading away from the gates. I noticed statues and headstones in the distance. It was a cemetery. When I walked through the gate Rachel didn't budge.

'Are you coming?'

'Don't know yet. I'm still thinking. It looks like a scary place.'

'Well, don't think for too long or you'll be on your own. I'm going in – you can stay here, or go back to Gwen. But I don't reckon she'll be too happy if you do.'

'I'm coming,' she whimpered, and ran after me.

She grabbed my hand and squeezed it tight as we walked along the pathway to the first row of graves. Lanes ran between the graves as far as we could see.

'This is just like a city,' she said. 'An old city. Do you think so, Jesse?'

She was right. It looked just like a city. I read the headstones as we walked. Stuff about the dead people in the ground, like how long they'd lived, how they died, who their parents and brothers and sisters were, and, on some headstones, where they'd gone after they'd died. Like Joseph John Ross, who lived until he was eighty-eight and was now 'waiting at Heaven's gate'.

For as long as I could remember I'd never believed in a heaven or hell and didn't think that Joseph John Ross, or me, or Rachel, or anyone else was going anywhere after we died except in the ground or all burned up. When a kid at the foster home had asked me if I believed in God, and I said no and told him what I reckoned happened to people after they died, he bawled like a baby. I knew it should have scared me too, but it never had.

Rachel picked up a bunch of fake flowers from the ground in front of Mr Ross's grave. They were made of cloth and had faded to a dirty red colour.

'Do these belong here, to this grave, do you think, Jesse?'

'Don't know,' I said, taking a look around.

There were flowers on other graves and more scattered between graves. There was even a bunch of flowers stuck in the branch of a tree.

'They could have blown here from any grave in the cemetery. They don't belong to anyone.'

'Can I keep them, then? If we don't know who they belong to?'

I looked down at the miserable bunch she was holding. 'If you like. I don't care.'

Some of the dead had been in the ground for more than one hundred years. I thought about what they might look like down there, with all the flesh off them, and no air, and all the dirt on top of their coffins, trapping them. There were no fresh flowers on any of the graves and the low iron picket fences around some of them had almost rusted away. Some of the headstones had toppled over like fallen buildings and were broken in pieces. Most of the stone statues standing over the graves were also broken. We walked by angels with busted wings or missing arms and legs. I stopped in front of one of the angels. He was offering me an open hand. The fingers on the hand were missing and his face had tiny holes all over it, as if he had a disease. A large statue of Jesus Christ stood over the next grave. He had the same marks on his face and had a finger pointing to the place where his heart should have been.

But his heart was missing. It had been chiselled out of his chest and stolen.

Rachel was standing a few graves down from me wiping the face of a small statue with her t-shirt. It was a girl with a pair of large wings sprouting out of her back. She wore a dress and her hands were held together in prayer. She looked sad. Rachel stepped onto the stone slab over the grave and stood next to the angel.

'I like this one. She looks like me. Don't you think so, Jesse?'

I didn't think so but said that she did anyway, which made Rachel happy. We stopped at another grave off on its own, under a tall ghost gum. The roots of the tree had grown under the grave, lifting one corner and collapsing another. It looked more like a boat stranded in a dry lake, and the marble slab on top of the grave had moved, opening a dark hole.

I lay on the slab. As I looked down into the hole I felt a cool breeze on my face. I could see a spider web through the darkness. It had trapped a dead bird. I got Rachel to pass me a piece of wire lying on the ground next to the grave. I poked at the web with it and told her to stick her head in the hole too and take a look.

'See that? That's what happens when you die and get buried in the ground. Spiders and bugs eat you. And big slippery worms burrow their way into your skull. They slip in through the holes where your nose was and come out your mouth.'

'Stop it, Jesse.' She punched me in the arm. 'Don't you say that. I want to go back now. You give me the creeps. Are you coming?'

I was still busy poking at the spider web.

'Nup. I'm gonna stir up the devil.'

She punched me again. 'Why are you trying to scare me? You'll pay for this. It's scary for the dead people too. I'm not staying here.'

'Please yourself,' I answered with my head stuck in the hole.

I was sure I heard an echo deep within the grave and kept poking at the bird until I'd freed it from the web and it fell deeper into the grave. I heard footsteps behind me. I knew Rachel wouldn't have had the guts to walk back through the cemetery on her own.

'Are you a brave young man? Or maybe just a silly one?'

I looked up to see a long thin scarecrow blocking the sun, sending a shadow across the grave. I jumped up, stepped back, and tripped and fell over a large tree root. The scarecrow laughed. It was a thin old woman with stick arms and legs and straw-coloured hair under a hat. She was wearing a moth-eaten black dress underneath a man's suit coat. She lifted a bony finger and pointed towards a stone bowl sitting on the end of the grave.

'Do you see that, boy? Do you know what that is? In the urn? Look.'

The bowl was full of dirty water, and had trapped hundreds of insects and spiders. The old woman looked up to the sky. Its colour had changed from a clear blue to streaks of orange and red without me noticing.

'Has not been a lick of rain over this place in months, possibly more, but see that? Verter water, that's what you're looking at, boy. It's stronger than holy water and it will spirit her to the other side. Spirit all of those who are worthy.'

She read the inscription on the headstone: 'Miss Annie House. She's being well cared for. House. I've always liked to think about that when I walk by this way. It's comforting to think that she is resting in a house. Don't you think so?'

It was a weird question and I didn't know how to answer it. She coughed and buttoned her coat as if she'd been bitten by the cold. The sun was almost down but it was still hot.

'Let me give you some advice, young man. I would not be poking around in there too deeply, if I were you.'

She looked down at the piece of wire I was holding. It started vibrating as my hand shook. I threw it on the ground just as something sprung from the hole in the grave and flashed by me. I screamed out and felt a shiver through my body as something brushed against the side of my leg. The old woman laughed out loud. I turned to see a small red fox sprinting along the lane. It disappeared into a thorny bush up ahead of us.

When I looked back the old woman had turned away from me and disappeared behind a headstone.

I searched up and down the lanes of the cemetery for Rachel but couldn't find her. I was almost back at the gates when I heard her calling my name. I yelled back and followed her voice, along a line of trees, through a patch of weeds and a pile of garden rubbish. She had made her way to another section of the cemetery. It was clean and tidy and the graves were mostly new. They were marked with brass plates set in slabs of concrete. Some had fresh flowers on them.

Rachel was kneeling on the ground reading names and dates and holding the bunch of faded flowers in her hand.

'What are you doing there?'

She laughed at me. 'Jesse. You're all white in the face, and your hair is sticking up in the air. Did you see a ghost or something?'

'Don't be stupid. I didn't see anything.'

She was sitting in front of the grave of two children, a boy and a girl. Stuffed animal toys had been placed around their names. The toys were covered in dirt, parts of their noses and ears had been eaten away and their insides were tumbling out. Rachel picked up one of the toys. It had an eye missing.

'Is this a donkey, Jesse? Do you think?'

'Don't know. Maybe. Or it could be a dinosaur. Or a dog.'

'Can I take this one with me? I'd like to clean it and fix it up. Maybe Gwen could sew a new eye for me.'

I looked down at the sorry-looking animal. 'You can take it if you want to, Rachel. But I'd sneak it, if I were you. I wouldn't be asking Gwen to fix it up. She'll probably throw it out of the car window when she sees how dirty it is. And if you do take it, you have to leave something for those kids.'

She held up the flowers. 'What about these?'

'Would you want someone putting that ratty bunch of flowers on your grave if you were dead?'

Rachel dropped the flowers and looked around for something she could leave in exchange. She ran across the dry ground to a large pine, picked up pine cones from under the tree until both arms were full, and laid them at the side of the grave in the shape of a heart.

'This is a boy and a girl, a brother and a sister, just like us, Jesse. But we're alive.'

'Yep. We're alive.'

'Jesse, when we get old, and when we die, do you reckon we'll be together forever, like this?'

'Rachel, we don't have time to be talking about that sort of stuff. We've got to be going. That Gus fella must have fixed the car by now. Gwen'll be waiting for us.'

She picked up the stuffed toy, lifted her t-shirt and shoved it down the front of her jeans. 'Is this a good place to hide it, Jesse?' She smiled and grabbed the bunch of flowers.

'Well, it looks like you've got an alien about to explode from your guts, like in that movie we saw that time. Is that the look you're going for? We've got to go, Rache. Or we're in trouble.'

The car had been shifted from the street to the servo. Gwen was sitting in the back seat of the car and Gus was hitching up his dirty overalls. I could tell that they'd been up to something, but didn't want to think too much about it. Rachel stopped at the open back window of the car and offered Gwen the flowers.

'I picked these for you.'

Gwen turned her nose up. 'Where'd you get them?'

'At the cemetery. It's behind the garden wall there.'

'You stole those from a grave?'

Rachel looked over at me, worried. I stuck my head in the other side of the car. 'No, she didn't steal them. They were blowing along the ground. I picked them up and gave them to her. They don't belong to anyone.'

'It don't matter where you found them. They're from the cemetery and that's bad karma.'

Gwen was always going on about karma, good and bad. Just like our luck, we only got the bad.

'You put those flowers in this car and we'll end up in a smash. It could kill us all. Now chuck them away.'

Rachel dropped her bottom lip. 'Chuck them away?'

'That's what I said.'

Gus was wiping his hands with his dirty hanky. 'Oh, don't you go throwing them away, young lady. I'll take my chance with them. Things couldn't get any worse around here. I'll put them in a vase in my office.'

Rachel smiled and offered him the flowers. 'You don't need a vase because you don't have to water them. They're not real.'

'Even better then.'

Gwen got out of the back of the car and jumped into the driver's seat. Gus leaned against the door.

'Keep heading this way you'll drive through another town, Connelly. It's even smaller than this place, if you can believe it. After that you meet up with the highway again. A few clicks down the road and you're on your way. You've got a full tank and I've topped the jerry up for you. It's in the boot.'

He waved to Rachel and me. 'Good luck, kids.'

'Will we need it?' Gwen laughed, nervously.

'Oh yeah, you will. If the fuel line blocks up on you again, you can forget about making it back to Melbourne. The more petrol you use up, the closer you get to the shit in the bottom of the tank. So it can only get worse. Sorry, love.'

He looked along the road. It was just about dark. 'But, when luck's all you've got, well, you go with it till it runs out. That's what I've always done. It's all the advice I can offer you.'

He tapped the roof of the car, said goodbye, and headed back along the footpath swinging the toolbox by his side.

'He a nice fella?' I asked Gwen, as we drove past him.

'Don't know if he's nice. But he's harmless. Can't expect a lot more than that from a bloke.'

The large trees on both sides of the road crowded in on us. It was hard to make out the road, even with the high beam on. Gwen crouched over the steering wheel and just about stuck her face against the windscreen. At least the car was running okay. By the time we got to the next town, which must have been Connelly, it was pitch black. Gwen braked hard when she spotted something up ahead. She asked if I could see anything. I couldn't, not at first, but then I saw something moving. It was a horse, standing in the middle of the road. As we pulled up, it lowered its head and looked through the window at us. It had a dark head with a white band running from the top of its forehead to the tip of its nose. Gwen unwound her window to get a better look.

'Fuck. This is spooky. Hey, horse. Get off the road.'

'A horse,' Rachel squealed. 'Can I get out and pat it?'

'No, you can't. Stay where you are.'

She tooted the horn but it still wouldn't move. 'What do you reckon I should do, Jesse?'

'Dunno.'

'Is that all you can say? Dunno? It's the only answer I ever get out of you.'

'What do you want me to say? I've never seen a horse on the road before.'

She had to blast the horn a few times more before the horse finally trotted off.

After we passed the horse I saw a single light shining from the front veranda of a house. It was so close to the road that, had I stuck my arm out the window of the car, I could have touched the front fence. An old man wrapped in a blanket was sitting on the veranda in a rocking chair under the light. He had thin white hair down to his shoulders and his face was a deathly grey colour. He looked more like a ghost than a man.

'Did you see that?' I asked Gwen.

'See what? The horse?'

'No, the man.'

'What man?'

'Don't matter.'

By the time I turned and looked again the house had faded into the dark.

We were soon back on the highway. A road sign said we were three hundred and sixty kilometres out of Melbourne.

Gwen was sitting just on eighty. I could add up well enough to know that if the car kept running we'd be there in less than five hours.

I had no idea what Gwen had planned for us when we got back to Melbourne. Or if she had a plan at all. But I knew that once we were back in the city we'd become invisible. It was the way it had always been for us. Gwen was always warning us about the police and welfare, and to stay away from anyone asking too many questions. We'd always got about on our own, wandering the streets, searching out new adventures, and no one had asked us a single question. It was like we weren't there at all.

If it was just Rachel and me I'd head straight for Pop's place. We wouldn't be doing that with Gwen. She hated him as much as I reckon he hated her. He'd never said so, but I'm pretty sure he did. If we could just get away from Gwen I'd head there.

I felt tired and rested my head against the back of the seat and closed my eyes. I could feel the road through my body as I listened closely to the sound of the motor. It sputtered a little now and then, but didn't seem to lose any speed. I started to relax for the first time since we'd left the motel. Gwen must have felt okay too. I could hear her humming a tune from the radio as I drifted off.

I had a dream about Rachel and me. We were back at the farmhouse outside Melbourne, sitting in the yard, thinking about Jon and how much we missed him. It was night and she was showing off her bloodied thumb and begging me to promise that I'd take care of her and never leave her on her own. And I did promise, over and over again, but it didn't stop her from getting upset. She ran out of the yard screaming, with me running after her. I followed her round to the front of the house and out the gate. She ran onto the road at the same time that a huge truck, a road train, was coming. Its lights were a dirty yellow colour and shaped like diamonds. As I reached out to grab hold of Rachel we both crashed to the road. I heard the truck brake hard and looked up as it was about to run over the top of us.

I woke with a fright. Rachel was holding onto me as tight as she could. She had her face buried in my chest and was crying. I pushed her away and told her to sit up.

'Why you crying?'

'Because I had a bad dream.'

'So did I. What happened in yours?'

'I can't remember. I just know it was scary. I'm afraid, Jesse.'

'Well, don't be. We'll be home soon.'

She put her arms around me. 'Where's home?'

I wanted to say Pop's, but didn't, in case Gwen was listening. 'We'll work that out when we get there. Now go back to sleep.'

She rested her head against my chest and was asleep again within a couple of minutes.

When we rounded the next bend I saw an outline of what looked like a giant tree on the side of the highway. As we drove by it got bigger. It was a strange shape for a tree. The trunk was too fat and as I looked up it seemed to have ears. I shook my head to be sure I wasn't dreaming again. It was a giant koala, taller than the tallest gum trees around it. I looked over at Gwen, to see if she'd noticed it, but she hadn't taken her eyes off the road.

The car started bucking again, followed by exhaust farts and shotgun backfiring. I knew straightaway that we were in trouble. Gwen pumped the accelerator as hard as she could. The car roared back to life for a few seconds, before it slowed then stopped and rolled backwards.

She grabbed the handbrake, rested her head on the steering wheel and swore to herself. She stuck her head out the window just as a truck roared by and jolted the car. She turned around, looked down at Rachel sound asleep, and then at me.

'We can't stay here. It's dangerous. We'll end up with a truck buried up our arse. Got any ideas?'

'Maybe I could get out and push while you steer? It looks like there's a downhill bit up ahead. Maybe we could roll for a bit, like we did getting into that other town?'

'Push this on your own? Not a hope.'

She punched herself in the side of the head a couple of times, which couldn't help her sorting things out, but I knew better than to say so.

She laughed. 'When'd you last pray?'

'When we were at Pop's house. We prayed before we ate our tea. And he prayed every night.'

'Bullshit. Your grandfather prayed? Every night?'

'Yep. On his hands and knees.'

'Well, fuck me.'

She laughed again, more like a giggle that Rachel might make. 'Well, let's pray that this old girl has some spunk left in her.'

She turned the key in the ignition and put her foot down. The explosion from the exhaust was loud enough to wake Rachel. She sat up, startled, and searched around the car. She didn't know where she was. Gwen was revving the guts out of the motor but we were getting nowhere.

'The handbrake,' I yelled, when I worked out what was wrong. 'You've still got the handbrake on.'

As soon as she let go of the handbrake the car jumped forward and sped along the highway, grunting and farting some more as we went. I could see lights in the distance.

'There's something over there.'

Gwen squinted as she looked through the windscreen. 'Looks like a town. Keep your eyes open for a road sign or something.'

We rounded a bend and saw the turn-off to the town. We were about to take it when the Commodore died for the last time, quietly. The motor creaked like a bag of old bones. We were down to less than ten ks an hour and slowing. Gwen flicked the high beam on and off a couple of times. She spotted a break in the road and steered the car off the highway onto a gravel track. We followed it into an open yard surrounded by a wire fence. We pulled up alongside a battered shipping container just as the motor let out a final breath and crawled to a stop.

Gwen rested her head on the seat and stared up at the roof.

'Why we stopping here?' Rachel asked. 'I don't think I like it here.'

I jabbed her in the ribs to get her to shut up.

Gwen opened the door and walked across the yard. I got out too, leaving Rachel lying across the back seat. A full moon broke through the clouds, low in the sky between a wheat silo and a tin shed. I could see a railway line, signal lights and a narrow platform. Gwen asked if I knew where we might be.

'A wheat depot, maybe?'

She walked over to the shipping container and tried the door. It was padlocked.

'Well, we can't do nothing tonight. We'll have to sleep in the car and see what we can come up with in the morning. We've got that stuff from the motel. Help me with it.'

'Maybe we could pour some of the petrol from the jerry can into the tank,' I said. 'It might get us going again.'

'No. That fella, Gus, had filled the tank again. The way it must have been pissing out, half a jerry can wouldn't get us much further than back on the highway.'

She opened the back door of the car and threw a blanket over Rachel. I got in next to her. I'd grabbed three packets of sweet biscuits from the boot and a bottle of water for each of us. Gwen took one of the waters but didn't bother with the biscuits, so Rachel and me divided the third packet between us.

I ate my biscuits as I tried working out where Ray and Limbo might be. They'd have got back to the motel and would know the money was gone, and that we'd taken it. They'd come looking, for sure. I just hoped they wouldn't know where to find us.

Gwen lay across the front seat of the car and moved her arse around the gear stick, trying to get comfortable. I stuck a pillow in the corner and rested my head against it, while Rachel stretched out along the back seat and stuck her dirty feet in my lap. Normally I'd have told her to get them off but it would have been a bad time to start fighting with her.

She coughed and sneezed. She'd always hated sleeping on the side of the road and whenever she got anxious over something she was fidgety. She pulled more than her share of the blanket over herself and started whimpering. Gwen ignored her by pulling her blanket over her own head. Rachel cried a little louder to get her attention, so Gwen called across the seat at her to be quiet. When she wouldn't stop, Gwen sat up, threw her blanket on the floor and climbed into the back seat with us. She was angry. I thought she was about to whack Rachel in the face. Instead, she squeezed in between us and put an arm around her.

'What's wrong, little sister?'

'I'm frightened.'

'Hey, don't be. You saw that sign for the town, didn't you?'

'Nope. I didn't see anything.'

'Well, there is a town there, and I bet there's a pub in the main street. Every town has a pub, even the little ones. Tomorrow morning I'll walk in and get some work behind the bar. We'll be out of here in a couple of days. You'll see.'

'And what will we do? While you're at the pub?' Rachel asked.

Gwen looked out through the windscreen before she answered.

'I don't know. You'll be here with Jesse. He'll look after you. Won't you, Jess? Jesse?'

I was too tired to answer.

Early the next morning the sounds of a bird calling and tap-tapping woke me up. I opened one eye and saw a black bird perched on the bonnet of the car, pecking at the paint. It tilted its head to the side and looked at me. I sat up. It lifted its wings in the air, flapped a couple of times, and disappeared above the car.

My body was all stiff as I got out. The sky was clear and the morning was cool. I hobbled across the dirt in bare feet, to the back of the shipping container. A cloud of steam lifted into the air as I took a long piss. Gwen was sitting up awake when I got back to the car. She had the door open and was sucking the life out of a cigarette butt. She must have scavenged it from the ashtray. She looked through the windscreen at me as I walked around to her side of the car. Smoke hissed between the gap in her front teeth as she spoke.

'We've stuffed up this time, haven't we, Jesse?'

We? I shrugged my shoulders and didn't answer.

Rachel rolled around inside her blanket a couple of times, sat up and rubbed the sleep from her eyes. When Gwen told her she'd have to piss behind the container like I had, Rachel looked at her like it was the most disgusting idea she'd ever heard, which made no sense to me, as both of us had been forced to take a piss, and more, in plenty of places worse than we were in now.

'I'm not going over there behind that box.'

'Yes you are, Rachel. You'll go to the toilet wherever I tell you to.'

Rachel filled her cheeks with air and let out what sounded like a fat man's fart. 'Well, I'm only going to pee then. That's all I'm gonna do.'

Gwen held up her butt, took a final long hard drag and flicked it onto the gravel. 'Jesus, Rachel. Piss or don't piss. See if I fucken care.'

Rachel must have had to go in a hurry. She jumped out, slammed the door and ran behind the container. Gwen went to the boot and opened her case. She waved me away.

'Shoo, Jesse. Don't be perving on me. I'm getting changed here. I'm gonna walk into town and see what I can find.'

I lay on the bonnet of the car and caught some warm sun as I waited. I heard the boot close and her footsteps on the gravel. I looked up. She was wearing what she called her 'lucky dress'. It was sleeveless and a red colour with a low neckline. I'd seen her in it a lot of times, but I can't remember much luck coming with it.

I slid off the bonnet and walked down to the highway. The turn-off to the town was ahead in the distance. I looked back at her. She was fixing her hair in one of the side mirrors. It wouldn't have surprised me at all if she'd walked away and never come back. She called me back to the car.

'If anyone comes snooping around, you tell them we've broken down and that your father'll be back soon. He's gone to borrow some tools from a mechanic in town.'

'My father?'

'Yeah. Your father. Fucken play along, will ya? I don't want anyone thinking there's just a woman here with her two kids. There could be all sorts of creeps around.'

It didn't look like there was anyone around, for miles.

She gave Rachel the same warning.

'What about the toilet? What if I have to . . .'

Gwen didn't seem to hear the question. She was too busy doing her lipstick in the mirror. When she'd finished she puckered her lips, stood up and jabbed the air with the lipstick as she spoke. She wanted to be sure that Rachel got the message.

'Use your brains. Go where you have to. There's plenty of toilet roll in the boot. Just don't go too far from the car. And be sure your brother's with you.'

She turned to me. 'Get her a toilet roll and something to eat.'

I went to the back of the car and searched through the boot while Gwen grabbed her bag from the passenger seat.

She was about to walk off when Rachel called out, 'Wait. Please, Gwen. Can I take a picture of you?'

She was holding the camera in her hands. She walked towards Gwen, stopped a few steps in front of her. 'Smile.'

Gwen had never been able to resist getting her photo taken. She threw the bag over her shoulder with one hand, rested the other on her hip and pouted her lips like a model in a magazine. She held the pose until Rachel had snapped the picture. Before I knew what she was doing she grabbed hold of me and wrapped one arm tightly around my waist and planted a lipstick kiss on my cheek.

'Take this one, of me with my toy boy.'

Rachel snapped the photo before I had time to wriggle free by pushing her away.

'Take it easy, will you?' she complained. 'Come on, Rache. Another one of me.'

Rachel was busy looking at the camera. 'No. I can't. There's only two pictures left. I have to save them.'

Gwen didn't look too happy that Rachel might want to take a picture of someone other than her. 'Save them for what? A birthday party or something?'

'I don't have birthday parties,' Rachel fired back.

'Suit yourself then. I'm off. I'll see you two later.'

Gwen dropped the bag to her side, turned and walked away without bothering to say goodbye. I thought Rachel might chase after her, but she looked almost happy to see her go. She hopped into the front seat of the car and pretended to be driving.

'Hey, Jesse. Where would you like to go? I'll take you any-where in the world.'

'Alaska. I've always wanted to go there.'

'Why?'

I looked across the highway, at the orange ball of sun lifting in the sky. 'Cause it's just about as far away from here as you can get. And because it's going to be stinking hot again. In Alaska just about everything is frozen solid. In Alaska if you stand too long in the one spot your blood freezes and you die.'

'You're dumb sometimes, Jesse. Picking a place where you freeze to death.'

'But I wouldn't. I'd wear a fur coat and these pants and hats they have that are made out of seals and polar bears. And I'd live in an ice house, an igloo.'

She turned the steering wheel hard left. 'I wouldn't want to wear a polar bear. Or a seal. They're cute. I'm going to Eng-land instead. To see the Queen. Like in that nursery rhyme.'

I left the driving to her and walked back out to the road. I watched closely as the red triangle of Gwen's dress got smaller. It stopped for a bit and floated in the steam coming off the road. While I couldn't make out her face, I was pretty sure she'd turned around and looked back at me. The triangle moved forward again and, bit by bit, it vanished.

Once she was out of sight I went back to the car and told Rachel she could pretend that she was driving the car back to Melbourne while I took a look around the yard. She let go of the wheel.

'I've run out of petrol and can't get to England. It's too far. Anyway, Gwen said we weren't to go away. You have to stay here with me.'

'I don't care what she said. She's not here. And you don't have to come if you don't want to. I'm taking a look around on my own.'

'Good. I don't want to come.'

'And I don't care.'

I'd taken only a few steps when I heard the car door creak open, followed by Rachel's footsteps scraping through the gravel. 'I thought you said you weren't coming?'

She had the toilet roll in her hand. 'I have to come because I need to go, Jesse. Real bad.'

Part of me wanted to keep fighting with her. At least it gave us something to do. She looked sad, like she might cry any minute. 'Okay. Come on. We'll find a place for you to go.'

We walked along the boundary fence on the far side of the yard. I didn't want her going off into the bush. I remembered when I was in school one time the teacher had drawn a bare arse on the blackboard. All the kids laughed, until he drew a snake with a long forked tongue biting the arse. He warned us not to go off for a shit in the bush without taking a good look around.

I told Rachel the story as we followed the fence, which was probably a mistake because she looked terrified.

'I don't know where you can go, Rachel. Back behind the container looks like the only spot.'

She shook her head. 'Nope. I don't want to go there. Somebody might see me.'

'From where?'

'From the road,' she said, pointing.

'The road? Couldn't see you from there even if they had the binoculars.'

I tried the door to the shed next to the silo. We'd struck our first piece of good luck since leaving Adelaide. The door opened and there was a toilet in the corner. Rachel stood in the doorway as I walked over and looked into the bowl. What was left of a long-dead rat sat in the bottom.

'Is it okay to go, Jesse?'

I had to get rid of the rat before Rachel saw it and started screaming. 'Yeah. It's great. But just stay there for a bit. I'll just make sure it's clean. I don't want you getting any germs.'

I pressed the button. After a few flushes the rat was gone and the bowl was clean enough. I took the toilet roll from Rachel and wiped down the seat with a few sheets. She was looking up at the corner of the roof, at a large spider web.

'I don't want to go here. Look at that.'

'At what? It's just an old web. There's not even a spider living in it.'

'He might be hiding. I'm not going.'

'Okay then. If you won't go here or behind the container you can go on the side of the road. Or maybe in the middle of the bush and have a snake bite you. Is that what you want? If you get bitten I won't be sucking the poison out. Not down there. And then you'll die. We'll have to carry your body back to that town we stopped at before. And we'll have to bury you with all the worms and spiders. More spiders back there than one old fella up in the corner of a shit house.'

Maybe it was because she was frightened over what I'd teased her about, or she was hungry, I'm not sure. But she started bawling and wouldn't stop until I promised I'd stay with her while she sat on the bowl. I also had to promise that I'd look out for any spiders that might come down from the roof.

When she was done, I got her to scrub her hands as best she could under the tap on the wall, which wasn't easy seeing as the water was almost black with dirt. We walked to the fence line then, behind the silo. There was a hole it, just big enough to climb through. I looked back at the car.

'Wait here for me.'

I got the sports bag out of the case and went back to the shed to search around. A row of plastic drums were piled along one wall. They each had a large skull and crossbones printed on the front along with the word 'POISON'. I tried taking the lid off one of the drums but it wouldn't budge. I picked up a rusty screwdriver from the top of a workbench, stuck it under the lid and pushed down as hard as I could until the lid popped open. The drum was full of white powder. After emptying it behind the shed, I squeezed the bag inside, closed it again and put it back with the others. I walked back to the hole in the fence.

'You coming?'

Rachel had her eye on the shed. 'What was in that bag?'

'Just some of my stuff.'

'Your stuff? Why'd you put it in there?'

'In case anyone comes while we're away. I don't want then knocking it off.'

'What about my stuff? They could steal my things too.'

'You don't have anything worth stealing. You coming or not?'

'You don't either. Except the binoculars.'

'That's what you think.'

I hopped through the fence. As she climbed through after me, she caught a pocket of her jeans on a loose wire and ripped it. She pulled her t-shirt down, trying to cover the tear.

We walked through the paddocks behind the yard. There was a lot of junk lying around, bits and pieces of machinery, a water tank that had fallen over and rolled down a hill, and beer cans with what I was pretty sure were bullet holes through them. I picked one up, shook it and listened to the rattle of the bullet inside. Lying next to a dry dam, below the silo, was a bloated flyblown sheep with its insides torn out. It reminded me of a story I'd seen on TV about a drought, with pictures of hundreds of dead sheep being pushed into a ditch by a machine.

I picked up a couple of bullet shells from the ground near the sheep. It had been blasted to death rather than died of thirst. Rachel couldn't put up with the bad smell and ran back up the hill to the yard. I put the shells in my pocket and followed her through the hole in the fence. She said she was hot and thirsty and headed back to the car.

I couldn't think of anything better to do so I picked up some stones from the railway track and started pitching them at a 'Beware of Trains' sign on the platform. It took me three throws before I hit it, and only a couple more before I was bored.

I walked to the end of the platform where I could see a dirt track below me that followed the railway. I looked back at the car. Rachel was pulling a blanket from the back seat. I jumped down from the platform and followed the track. It ran between the railway and a row of trees. I'd walked for only a few minutes when the railway came to an end at a large open shed. It was empty. The walking track went on, along the side of the shed then it ended too, at a fence topped with barbed wire. I looked through the fence and could see a building with a pointed roof. I climbed a tree next to the fence, and moved my way through the branches until I had a good view.

I could hardly believe that I was looking at one of the pyramids from Egypt. A large statue of a lion was guarding its entrance. I could see the tops of other buildings in the distance. I got down from the tree and followed the fence to a gate, and a sign hanging from it that read 'Welcome to Carson's World in Miniature'. Through the fence I could see other wonders of the world.

I ran back along the track as fast as I could, calling Rachel's name. When I reached her she was sitting on the blanket, resting against the car and laying the tarot cards out in front of her. She picked up one of the cards.

'See this, Jesse? The Queen of Swords. She's mine. I like her crown and the sword she's carrying. If I had a sword I wouldn't be afraid of anyone.'

'Forget about the cards, Rache. I've got something better to show you. You said you wanted to drive all the way England. How would you like to see the Eiffel Tower on the way?'

'You're being stupid, Jesse.'

'Do you want to see it or not? It's true.'

'You're tricking me.'

'No, I'm not. Promise.'

'Can I bring the camera and take a picture?'

Carson's World in Miniature was overgrown with weeds and most of buildings were falling down. We visited a Dutch windmill, the Leaning Tower of Pisa, which was not leaning as bad as the Eiffel Tower was, and the Great Pyramids, although there was just the one I'd seen earlier from up in the tree Rachel didn't think any of them were worth one of shots she had left in the camera.

'What's wrong with this place?' she asked, as she sat in one of the seats of a small Ferris wheel, going nowhere. 'Maybe they had an earthquake here?'

'I don't think they have earthquakes round here. Looks like people gave up on it and left. It's an abandoned world, like in science fiction.'

'Where's Australia then?'

'What do you mean? We're in it.'

'But they should have made something special here. Of Australia.'

'Well, they didn't.'

I was wrong. They had made something special.

As we walked on, across the world, and were passing an African village with a couple of grass huts and another that had been burned to the ground, Rachel noticed something on a mound of dry grass up ahead.

'What's that?'

I wasn't sure, but it looked like a giant dog turd.

'Beats me.'

As we got closer we could see writing on the turd. The word 'Uluru' had been crossed out and replaced with 'Ayers Rock' and a Nazi swastika. It took me only two steps to climb to the top of the rock and look down on 'The Canals of Venice' on the other side. Venice was made up of a giant statue of a nude man with his dick missing, standing in a dam next to an oarless wooden boat floating in the water.

I walked down to the dam and stood at the water's edge. The surface was covered in a green scum.

'Let's have a swim.'

Rachel bent down and put her hand in the water. 'No. It's too cold. And the water looks dirty.'

'So what? I'm hot. I'm going in.'

I stripped down to my underpants and walked in until the water was above my knees. It was cold. I screamed out, 'One-two-three', took a deep breath and dived. When I stood up the water was around my chest. My arms and shoulders had turned green. I could hear a deep rumbling sound, way off in the distance. It made me nervous. 'Can you hear that, Rache?'

She listened. 'No, I can't hear nothing. What is it, Jesse?'

'Nothing,' I answered, as the sound faded. 'Forget it.'

Rachel took off her jeans and t-shirt, folded them neatly into a pile and laid them on a rock. She sat her camera on the pile of clothes, and splashed around in the shallows in her undies and singlet while I swam out to the middle of the dam, to where the boat was. I tried to climb aboard but couldn't pull myself up, so took hold of a rope threaded through a ring at one end, and dragged the boat into the shallows and up onto the bank. It tired me out. I lay on the bank while Rachel got into the boat and pretended to be a pirate.

Between swims I skipped pebbles across the water. Rachel kept herself busy scoring for me. It was her job to count the number of skips of each stone I threw in my attempt to break what I'd announced as the 'World Freshwater Tor-skipping Record'.

'What's a tor, Jesse?' she asked, scratching the tip of her nose.

'The tor is a killer marble. An assassin. When you're play-ing marbles it's the one you have to capture to win the game.

180

If you don't hunt it down and kill it, the tor will take you out. It's like the king in a game of chess.'

She looked at the stone gripped between my fingers. 'A marble is round,' she said. 'The ones you're throwing are flat. They can't be tors.'

'They are. At least this one is. When I break the world record, it will be this stone that does it for me.'

'But it won't be yours. That stone you've got will be at the bottom of the dam somewhere. You won't get it back. Even if you dive for it.'

'Well, Rachel, when you want something bad enough, there's always a price to pay. The tor will sacrifice its own life for its master. That's one of the rules of the game. And I'm the master,' I said, puffing my chest out.

'But who are you playing against?'

I looked across the water to the naked statue. 'Dickless, there. He's the champion from Rome.'

I threw my arm back, pitched the stone and watched as it skimmed the surface.

'Seven . . . eight . . . nine . . . ten . . . That's a new record, Jesse,' she squealed and clapped her hands together. She picked up the camera and pointed it at me. 'Let me take a picture of the champion then.'

I turned side-on to the camera and flexed my muscles. My arm was sore from all the throwing. I sat next to her and poked at the bed of mud under my feet with the sharp end of a twig as my body dried in the sun. My skin was covered in silt and scum. Rachel had mud caked between her toes.

'You'd better clean those feet before Gwen gets back. She won't want you putting that mud all over the back seat of the car.'

'But the car's already dirty. It always is.'

'Maybe. But I reckon we'll have to sleep in it again tonight and I don't want dirt and mud in my blanket.'

'How long will we be here for?'

'Dunno. Depends if she finds any work in that town.'

Rachel wiggled her toes. One or two clumps of mud fell to the ground. She took the twig from me and started drawing something in the mud. It looked like a house.

'When will she, when will . . . Mum be back?'

She had mouthed the word deliberately. Mum. I hadn't heard her say it in ages. I shrugged my shoulders.

'I dunno. Soon I hope. Maybe she'll have something decent for us to eat.'

My stomach rumbled at the thought of proper food. 'We should get back. She might be waiting for us.' I dragged my foot through the mud and tapped her on the side of the leg. 'And don't call her Mum, Rachel. You know she don't like it.'

'But she is my mum. And she's your mum too. Sometimes I think you're smart, Jesse. And sometimes you're silly.'

She looked at me and laughed. 'You look silly right now. You've turned green as a frog.'

I watched as she finished drawing her house. It had a dog in the yard and some flowers in the garden. She was now onto a stick-figure girl standing outside the house.

'I know she's our mum, but don't waste your time calling her that.'

'But why can't I call her Mum? Other kids are allowed to do that. It's not hurting anyone.'

'Maybe not. But she don't like it. It makes her feel old, she says. Makes her angry too. So don't you call her nothing but

Gwen, or you'll be the one who ends up hurt. She's in a shitty mood already, with no smokes and no money. I don't want her starting on us when she gets back.'

Rachel wouldn't look at me and busied herself with another drawing while whispering 'Mum, Mum, Mum' under her breath. She'd drawn another person standing next to the house. She tossed the stick to the ground and stood up.

'Jesse. There's just one shot left in the camera. Can you please take a photo of me?'

She sat on the end of the boat with her arms folded across her muddy t-shirt while I took the picture.

There was no sign of Gwen at the car. We ate four packets of biscuits each, which left just two packets, and shared the last bottle of water. My favourite biscuits were Scotch Fingers and Rachel loved the Monte Carlos. She broke her biscuits in half and licked the icing away with her tongue while I bit straight through mine. It was the way we'd always done it.

When she'd finished eating she took the blanket and pillow from the back seat of the car. She spread the blanket on the ground, on the shady side of the shipping container, and lay down with her pillow and Comfort by her side.

'The blanket'll get dirty there, Rache. Make sure you shake it before it goes back in the car.'

'And Jesse, you make sure you put your clothes back on. If somebody comes and sees you walking round with just your underpants on and green hair we'll be in trouble.'

There was nobody around to get into trouble from but I put my clothes on anyway. By the time I'd dressed she was lying flat out on the blanket, asleep, with her arms stretched out. I'd only just taken the last swig of water and was already thirsty. The only water we'd come across had been the dirty tap water in the shed. I headed back to the shed with some empty bottles.

I tried the tap again and let the water run for a bit. It was just as dirty as it'd been earlier. The water in the bottom of the toilet bowl was clear. I flushed it a couple of times, dunked the empty bottle and held it under until it was full. I sniffed at the bottle a couple of times before I took a sip. It was cold and didn't taste too bad, so I filled another two empty bottles and stood them in the shade outside the shed door.

I looked over at the stack of plastic drums. I was about to open the one with the sports bag in it and changed my mind. I went back to the car, grabbed my binoculars and walked down to the road. The blacktop was shimmering and dust was blowing around, but there was no sign of Gwen. I headed back to the shed.

I took the sports bag out of the plastic drum and picked up my bottles of water. I unzipped the bag on the bonnet of the car and took the gun out, still in its plastic bag. I laid it on the bonnet with the bundles of money, and started counting. There were twenty-five bundles, all the same size, each one tied with a rubber band.

I undid one of the bundles and slowly counted out forty fifty-dollar notes, some worn, some new – two thousand dollars. I counted another two bundles. They added up to the same amount. I retied the bundles and laid them in a row on the bonnet of the car, fifty thousand dollars.

'What have you got there?' I hadn't heard Rachel sneak up behind me. She was staring at the money.

'It's treasure. It's going to get us out of here.'

'Where'd you find it?'

I didn't see much point in bullshitting to her. 'It belonged to Ray. He left it at the motel. So I took it.'

'That's a lot of money, Jesse. Won't he be missing it?'

'Yeah. I reckon he will.'

'What if he comes for us, with that other man, Limbo, with the crying face? I don't like him.'

I took the gun out of the bag and waved it about in the air, trying to put on a brave show. 'They left this too. If they come after us, I'll shoot them.'

'No, you won't. You don't know how to shoot a gun.'

'It wouldn't be hard, I don't reckon. I've seen guns fired lots of times. On TV.'

I pointed to where the bullets went. 'This bit's called a chamber, and they call this gun a revolver because the chamber spins around and around. I know that much.'

'How'd you learn that?'

'I saw it on *Ripley's Believe It or Not*. They slowed the camera down as much as they could to show how a quick-draw expert can take his gun out of the holster and shoot in just hundredths of a second. He did it with a gun just like this. A revolver.'

'Has it got bullets in it?'

I stopped waving the gun around. 'I hope not. But there's some bullets in the bag.'

I mucked around with the gun for a while before I worked out how to slide the chamber out. I put a bullet in each hole

185

and pushed the chamber back until I heard it click shut. I made sure to point the barrel down at the ground, for safety, like I'd seen on TV. I walked over to the silo, searching for something to aim at. Rachel trailed behind me.

'What are you going to shoot?'

'I don't know. Maybe that dead sheep in the paddock?'

'That would be horrible. The poor sheep.'

'He wouldn't feel it. He's already dead.'

'I don't care. I don't want you to. Don't, Jesse.'

I pointed at the 'Beware of Trains' sign hanging from a strand of wire above the railway track. It had a reflective red light in each corner.

'What about those? I bet I can knock one of those lights out.'

'Bet you can't.'

I stood with my legs apart and my shooting arm straight out in front of me. I aimed at the light in the bottom left corner of the sign and closed one eye. I was about to pull the trigger and stopped. My hand was shaking and I could feel my heart beating like a drum in my chest. I dropped the gun to my side. Rachel looked disappointed.

'Go on, Jesse. Shoot the light out.'

'Give me a sec. It's not easy, you know.'

I lifted my arm again and aimed. I tried pulling the trigger but nothing happened. I looked at the gun.

'It might be jammed. That happens sometimes.'

I found the safety catch by accident, released it and pointed the gun at the target again.

I don't know what was more frightening, the deafening sound of the bullet or the feeling that an invisible man had grabbed me by the arm and thrown it back over my shoulder. Rachel was staring wide-eyed at the gun. The smell of the gunpowder itched my nose and made my eyes water. I looked over at the target. I'd missed everything, both the light and the sign. I looked up at the sky, in case I'd hit a bird by accident.

I took aim again, and held my left hand over my right and pressed downwards as I pulled the trigger. I heard the blast and a ringing noise at the same time. The sign was swinging back and forward. I could see a small hole of light between two of the letters. At least I'd hit something.

'Got it.'

Rachel had both hands over her ears. 'Can you put it away now, Jesse?' she screamed. 'That's enough.'

I had only four bullets left in the chamber and didn't want to waste them on more target practice anyway. I put the gun and money back in the bag, and hid it in the drum again.

The sun had fallen below the silo. Its shadow stretched across the yard. Rachel's face was bright red and she was dripping with sweat. I offered her some water.

'Where'd you get it?'

'In the shed there. I ran the tap for a bit and it came clean.'

While she drank the water I paced up and down in front of the car trying to work out what we should do.

'Rache. I don't know if we can stay here another night. It might be best for us to go.'

'Go where? What about Gwen?'

'I dunno where. Some place where there's food. And Gwen mightn't come back anyway. Don't see any point in waiting for her.'

'Yes, she will. I'm not going anywhere without her.'

'You will if I tell you to.'

'I won't.'

'Fucken will,' I screamed as loud as I could.

She threw the bottle at me, hard as she could. It hit me square in the face and hurt like hell. Straightaway I could taste blood in my mouth. I ran at her and tackled her to the ground before she had a chance to get away. I slammed her body into the dirt. She covered her face with her hands.

'Don't hit me. Please don't hit me, Jesse.'

I pinned my knees against her shoulders so she couldn't move. I grabbed hold of her t-shirt. It ripped down the middle.

'You stay here as long as you like then. You'll starve to death before Gwen comes back for you. She don't give a fuck about us. Me or you. Never has.'

I pushed my face against hers. 'You stay here if you like. And when they come and find you, Ray and Limbo, they'll skin you, Rachel. They'll take a knife and skin you like a rabbit.'

'Please, Jesse, don't say that. Don't. They won't come.'

I stood up and kicked the dirt. 'We can't be sure of that. I'm getting out of here, whether you're coming or not. I'm sick of dragging you around and having to look after you. And if Gwen comes back, let's see if she can take care of you on her own.'

I left her lying on the ground, cowering and covered in dust. I threw our suitcase on the ground and took out my backpack. I stuffed it with the only jacket I had, the last two packets of biscuits and the two full bottles of water. I could hear Rachel crying but stopped myself from looking around as I zipped up the backpack. I suddenly wanted to cry myself. I put my head down and wiped my eyes to stop the tears from running.

'Jesse.'

I looked over my shoulder. Rachel was holding a pink woollen jumper in one hand and a raincoat in the other.

'Can you put this stuff in your bag?'

Her face was streaked with dirt and dried tears and her nose was running with snot. She even had dirt in her ears and her hair. She shook the raincoat to get my attention.

'But before we go, Jesse, can we have one more go at the cards? Maybe they can tell us what to do?'

'And after we read the card, will you come then?'

'Promise, I will.'

I picked a tarot card with a picture of a castle being struck by lightning. It was on fire and people were tumbling out of the windows. The word 'Tower' was written across the bottom.

While the card meant nothing to me, Rachel was convinced it had something to do with the silo.

'Jesse, you could take a last last look for Gwen by climbing to the top.'

It wasn't a bad idea. Through my binoculars I'd have a view of the road leading to the town, as well as the highway.

A metal staircase wrapped itself around the outside of the silo. It was a big climb. I tightened the backpack straps, hung the binoculars around my neck and put a foot on the bottom step. The stairs shook from side to side and banged against the silo's concrete wall.

'Do you reckon it's safe?' Rachel asked, as she grabbed the rail with both hands.

'Probably not,' I called back.

I moved quickly around the outside of the silo. Rachel called out, 'Jesse, hang on, will ya? Hang on,' as she tried keeping up with me. I looked back but couldn't see her, so I had to backtrack. She was hugging the railing with both arms.

'You don't have to come with me, Rachel. Wait at the bottom. I won't be long.'

'But I want to come.'

'Well, you'd better get moving then.'

I sat on the step and waited for her to catch up. She was breathing heavy. Her camera was sticking out of her jeans pocket.

'What's the camera for?'

'I don't want to lose it. It's got important pictures in it. If I leave it down there someone might steal it.'

I waited until she'd got her breath back and we started climbing again. As we went higher I told her that if Scout were with us now she wouldn't be scared of heights.

'You don't know that, Jesse. You're just guessing.'

'No, I'm not. I reckon she'd be racing up there ahead of us.'

'I don't believe you.'

Maybe she didn't. But she did start climbing a little quicker and tried to look less worried. Pretty soon we'd reached the top and were standing inside a wire-framed box.

'Hey, Jesse. This is like a giant birdcage. If we just had some wings we could fly away.'

'Wish we could. We'd get home quicker.'

She pointed to a streak of cloud above us. 'It's beautiful up here. We're close to the sky.'

I looked through a rotting gap in the timber floor, down to the ground, maybe eighty or a hundred feet down. The strip of highway that had got us here cut through the scrub, back to where the car had stalled on the rise the night before. In the opposite direction a narrow road left the highway and headed in the direction of the town Gwen had walked to. Behind us, over the back of the railway shed were the Great Pyramid, the Eiffel Tower and the Canals of Venice. I lifted my binoculars and searched the streets of the town. I could see an old woman sitting alone on a bench and there were people moving about, but no sign of Gwen or her red dress.

'Is she there?'

'Na. Can't see her.'

Rachel pulled the camera out of her pocket and held it as gently in her hands as she would have held a small kitten.

'I've got us in here. Me and you, Jesse. Forever.'

'Good for you. I'd shove it back in your pocket if I were you. If you drop it, it'll smash into thousands of pieces. It's a long way down.'

She looked through the hole in the wooden floor. The colour faded from her face. She threw herself against me and held on as tight as she could. I wasn't sure if it was the staircase shaking or her body.

'Let go of me, Rache, or you'll get us both killed.'

She took half a step back but kept one hand wrapped tight around my wrist.

'Jesse? Are we still blood brother and sister?' she asked. 'Like you said we were, when we cut ourselves?'

'Of course we are. Like I told you a million times already, it can never be undone. Our blood is mixed together and it moves around our bodies. Forever.'

'What about if one of us was hurt and was cut and lost a lot of blood?'

'It wouldn't make any difference. As long as we had some blood.'

'What about if I lost all my blood, in a car smash or something like that?'

'Well, then you'd be dead, Rachel. So it wouldn't matter.'

'Tell me about that day again, Jesse. When we cut ourselves.'

She was frozen to the spot with fear. The sun was sinking below the treetops. There wasn't a lot of daylight left.

'I'll tell you the story, but only if you promise to climb down with me as soon as I finish. Do you promise?'

'I promise,' she said, as she looked through the cage and down at the ground.

So I told the story again, as quickly as I could. Although she knew it word for word she acted as if she was hearing it for the first time: screwing her face up in pain when I talked about slicing the top of her thumb, and smiling when I said we'd never be half and half again.

As I retold the story I watched a large bird off in the distance, gliding through the sky. It might have been a falcon, or maybe an eagle. It stalled above the silo and flew into the air by moving its wings just a fraction. It flew towards mountains in the distance. They were almost hidden in mist and dark clouds that were moving our way.

'Is that the end, Jesse?' Rachel asked, when I reminded her of how our thumbs had got stuck together with blood.

'Yeah. That's the end. We have to go back down now.'

She looked towards the town in the distance. 'Jesse, do you think she'll come back?'

'Probably,' I said, although I wasn't sure. 'You know how she gets the wanders. Whatever happens, she'll find her way back in the end. She always does.'

'But if she doen't? If we never see her again, what will happen to us?'

'Nothing will happen to us.'

'Wouldn't we get broken up? Like the time she was sick and you were put in the home?' Her voice cracked as she spoke.

'No, we wouldn't get broken up. Never. We'd go away. If they tried to separate us, we'd go where no one could find us.'

'Where?'

I had no idea. Right then it didn't matter anyway. I heard a terrible sound, deep and low and heading our way. I told Rachel to be quiet while I listened. There was no mistaking what it was, but I wasn't sure how far off it was or the direction it was coming from. I listened again, lifting the binoculars, and searched the road leading away from the town. I picked up a trail of dust and the flash of a car speeding along the road, coming our way. It was the Camaro. I pulled Rachel by the arm and forced her down on the platform.

'I need you to lie here and keep real quiet.'

The Camaro drove into the yard and slowly circled it. I could see Ray and Limbo in the front. There was no sign of Gwen. The car pulled up between the Commodore and the container.

They opened the doors of the Commodore and searched inside. While Ray sat in the front passenger seat, Limbo went through the boot. He threw the cases and the jerry can on the ground and started chucking everything else behind him. The blankets, toilet rolls and rubbish flew across the yard. He emptied Gwen's case and then ours. When he couldn't find anything, he picked her case up and hurled it across the yard.

Ray got out of the car and pulled something from his boot. It was his knife. He slashed the back of the passenger seat open and pulled out the stuffing. He moved around the outside of the car and did the same to all the seats. Pretty soon the yard was covered in large balls of white padding from the guts of the seats. Limbo searched under the seats of the Camaro and pulled out a short crowbar. He stuck it behind the padlock on the container and snapped it off. He had trouble getting the door open so he wedged the crowbar behind that as well. When he got it open he screamed out, 'Fucken empty', and threw the crowbar on the ground.

By the time they'd finished searching, the yard looked like a cyclone had gone through the place.

Ray put the knife back in his boot and took a long slow look around. His eyes stopped at the shed. He lifted his head and looked up at the silo. I closed my eyes and held my breath. I could hear footsteps in the gravel, coming closer. I looked across at Rachel. Her eyes were looking directly into mine.

'Keep still, still,' I mouthed.

She couldn't work out what I was saying and frowned.

The footsteps stopped right under us. I peeped through the crack in the board. They were standing at the shed door. Ray opened it and walked inside.

'Where'd they go?' Rachel whispered. 'Are they coming up to get us?'

I put my finger across my lips to get her to shut up. If they did come for us we were gone, unless we jumped off the top. And then we'd kill ourselves anyway.

We could hear a lot of banging coming from inside the shed. Right then, I was praying they'd find the money and go and leave us alone. If I could be sure they wouldn't hurt us I'd have called out to Ray and told him where the money was myself. But he wasn't like that. He'd kill for his fifty thousand dollars. And maybe just for fun too. I heard the shed door open. I looked through the crack again. They'd come out empty-handed. Ray walked to the fence line behind the silo. He called Limbo over.

'Get her out and give her some water and we'll take off. They won't have got far.'

Limbo opened the boot of the Camaro, laughed out loud and lifted Gwen out. Her hands were tied and she had something in her mouth. Her red dress was drenched and she had a mark across her face where she'd been bleeding. Rachel had closed her eyes, which was good for both of us. I reckon if she'd looked down and seen the state Gwen was in she'd have screamed out for her.

Limbo propped Gwen against the side of the car and pulled a piece of dirty cloth from her mouth. He looked across to see where Ray was before he grabbed hold of one of Gwen's breasts and kissed her on the mouth. He took a plastic milk container from the boot, unscrewed it and lifted it to her mouth. She took a long drink then coughed and spat some water out. Limbo stood back and threw water over her face and laughed. Gwen tried wiping her face with her hands. She was sobbing.

'Who's making that noise?' Rachel whispered.

'Be quiet. No one.'

Ray picked up the jerry can and shook it. He opened the lid and sniffed at the can as he looked at Gwen. He stood in front of her and lifted the can above her head. She started shaking from side to side and fell to the ground, crying. Ray threw his head back and laughed at her. Right then I wished I had the revolver in my hands so I could aim it at Ray, and if I was lucky, blow his head off. He threw the keys to Limbo.

'Put her in the back and move it.'

Limbo grabbed Gwen by the arm, dragged her around to the side of the Camaro, and threw her in the back seat. He got into the car, circled the yard again and stopped at the edge of the road.

Ray grabbed a few pieces of the scattered clothes and seat stuffing and threw it in the Commodore. He splashed petrol from the can inside the car and over the roof and bonnet. He lit a ball of the seat stuffing with his cigarette lighter, stood back and threw it in the car. He jumped as the car burst into flames.

As it burned, Ray walked across the yard, leaned against the Camaro and talked to Limbo. He stuck his head in the back of the car a couple of times and spoke to Gwen, smiling all the while, like he was having a great time. When the car was well alight they sped off, in the direction of the highway.

I waited until I could hear no trace of the engine before ordering Rachel to get going.

She wasn't ready to move.

'Maybe they'll come back.'

'Maybe. But they took off in a hurry. Probably looking for us out on the highway. We've got to find some place to hide before they decide to come back.'

I grabbed her by the hand and started running down the stairs. She crashed into me and we tumbled over. I looked up at the sky. For a second I thought I'd fallen over the rail and was about to die. The binoculars fell from my neck. I turned and looked through a gap in the stairs just as they smashed to the ground below. Rachel was lying on top of me. She looked over my shoulder at the ground.

'I'm sorry, Jesse. Your Christmas present.'

'Too late for that now. Get off me.'

I reached the bottom of the silo and kicked the shed door open. The plastic drums had been knocked around like bowling pins. I picked up the one closest to me and shook it. It was empty. The next one was full of powder. I must have gone through almost every drum until I found mine. Rachel was running across the yard, towards the burning car.

'What are you doing?' I screamed out. 'You'll get blown up.'

The heat had not only stripped the paint from the car, but from one side of the shipping container too. The heat stopped Rachel in her tracks. She was about to run back to me when she spotted something in the corner of her eye. She ran and snatched something from the ground. It was Comfort. She hugged him to her chest as she ran back to me.

'I saved him!'

The burning car lit up the yard and the silo. I slung the sports bag over one shoulder.

'Follow me, Rachel. And keep up.'

'How are we going to get away?'

'Haven't worked that out yet. But we've got to hide until there's no more light.'

We ran back along the track we'd taken earlier in the day until we reached Carson's World in Miniature and slipped through the fence. We walked downhill until we reached the Dutch windmill.

'This might be a good place.'

The windmill had no door. I threw my backpack through a small window and then the sports bag. I gave Rachel a boost up by putting both hands against her bum and pushing as hard as I could. She fell through the window and crashed to the floor inside. The fall must have hurt. She wasn't making a sound. I hoped she hadn't knocked herself out.

'Are you all right in there?'

'I think so. It's dark and I can't see nothing.'

I boosted myself up, squeezed through the window and closed the wooden shutters. It was so dark I couldn't see her at all.

'You there, Jesse?'

'Yep. I'm here.'

FIVE

A clap of thunder shook the windmill, quickly followed by another. It was shorter, and sounded like a shotgun blast. I opened the shutter, just wide enough to take a look outside. It was pitch black. The wind was roaring through the trees and branches were crashing to the ground. I pulled the shutter and felt around the floor until I touched Rachel's leg. She was curled up in a ball on the floor. I shook her.

'Rachel. Time to move.'

She moaned, threw her arms back and slapped me in the face with her hand. I shook her again, a little harder.

'Rachel. You've gotta get up.'

I felt her sit up. I could hear her crawling across the floor, away from me.

'Where you going now?'

'Comfort. I can't find him.'

'Bad luck. We're leaving.'

'I'm not going any place without him. I saved him from blowing up and he's coming with us.'

I unzipped the sports bag and searched inside. I gripped the barrel of the revolver. Careful as I could to not touch the handle or trigger, I took it out of the bag and put it in the front section of the backpack. I took out the jackets, Rachel's jumper, the bottles of water and the last packets of biscuits and laid them on the floor. I slowly felt for and counted each roll of the money as I moved it from the sports bag to the backpack. As I was counting I thought about what we might do next. We'd have to stay off the road as best we could, but I knew the only place we could go from here was back to Pop's, if we were ever to be safe again. I just didn't know how we were going to get there with Ray searching for us along the highway. When I'd emptied the bag I put Rachel's jumper and the bottles in the backpack and zipped it up.

'I've got him,' Rachel called out.

'Lucky for you.'

Outside the windmill, I handed her a jacket. 'Put this on. I think it's gonna rain.'

I put my jacket on, zipped it up and hitched the pack to my back. I waited and listened for any dangerous sounds, but could hear nothing but the roaring wind. Clouds had blocked the moon, and I could hardly see Rachel standing in front of me, even though she was so close I could smell her breath. I heard another deep rumble in the distance. I twitched, thinking it was the Camaro again. But it was more thunder. A streak of lightning lit up the Great Pyramid and the Eiffel Tower. I decided to head in the opposite direction.

'We'll go this way.'

'I can't see. Which way is *this* way?'

'Just stay close and keep quiet.'

I listened as hard as I could as we walked on. I thought I heard a sound behind us. Maybe a snapping twig? I grabbed Rachel by the arm and ordered her to stand still.

'Quiet,' I whispered.

'Why? Is someone there?'

I didn't want to frighten her. 'No. I'm just checking where we are.'

I listened again, and could hear nothing but the thunder and roaring wind.

We soon reached the far side of the park. The wire fence had just about fallen over in the wind. We'd walked to the edge of a thick forest of trees. Rachel sniffed the air.

'Hey. It smells like the Christmas tree we had at Pop's.'

'If it is Christmas trees, there must be a lot of them. We'll climb through the fence here. Be careful not to trip.'

'I'm hungry, Jesse. Can I have another biscuit?'

'We've only got two packets left. You eat a pack now and it might be all you get for a while. You still want it?'

'What about all that money in the bag? We could buy lots of stuff with that. Anything we want to.'

'Maybe, if we can find somewhere to spend it. You still want the biscuits?'

'Yes, please.'

I unzipped the pack, found the biscuits and got her to sit down next to me. She talked as she munched on a biscuit.

'Where are we going to, Jesse?'

'We have to find a way to get to Melbourne. I don't know how, exactly, but I'm gonna get us back to Pop's. He'll take care of us.'

'What about Gwen? Was she in that car with the men? I think I heard her voice.'

'I didn't see her,' I lied. 'But maybe she could have been.'

'So what's your plan to get us to Pop's?' she asked, louder than she needed to.

I put my hand across her mouth. 'No more talk, Rache. Not a word. I can't plan with you yapping all the time.'

But I didn't have any plan. Maybe we could hitch a ride, but we'd have to be careful.

I took the gun out of the backpack. I felt for the safety catch. I wasn't sure if it was locked or not. I laid the gun on the ground and took out one of the bundles of money. I peeled off a hundred-dollar note and put it in my front pocket. The rest I rolled up, retied with the rubber band, and stuck down the front of my underpants.

The wind was getting stronger and colder. Rachel's teeth were chattering. I opened the backpack again and took out her woollen jumper.

'Put this on, under your jacket.'

I waited until she'd reorganised herself and took off my jacket.

'Here. Put this on over yours. It'll keep the wind out.'

'But won't you be cold?'

'Do what I say. Put it on. Let's go. And remember, no talking.'

We hurdled the fence into the forest and walked over soft ground between two long lines of trees. It took about another ten minutes before Rachel broke the silence, which was just about a record for her.

'Can I say something, Jesse?'

'As long as you keep your voice down.'

'Do you think this is sort of like those kids in the mockingbird film, near the end, and they're trying to get home in the dark?'

'Yeah, a little bit. But without the boogieman, I hope.'

'I hope too. Do you think all these trees go to people's houses for Christmas?'

'I don't know. That would be a lot of trees.'

'And millions of presents to go under them.'

She went quiet for a bit. I knew she would be thinking about something she just had to ask me.

'Jesse?'

'Yep.'

'Did you like it when we had Christmas at Pop's house, with the presents and the roast chicken and the tree?'

'Yeah. I liked it a lot. Just about more than I've liked anything, even sitting under that pier with the fish and chips back in Adelaide.'

'That was good. But I liked the Christmas better too. I would like us to stay with Pop until next Christmas, so we could get another tree. A big one. Just like these. We could decorate it. Have you ever decorated a Christmas tree?'

'Never.'

'Me either.'

I felt a drop of rain on my head, and a few steps on, another one, and then another. We'd come to the end of the forest, and were standing on a ridge overlooking a road. The rain was getting heavier. I shouldn't have given up my jacket so easily.

'What road is this, Jesse?'

'Not sure. Maybe the highway we were on last night. Stand under a tree or you'll get soaked.'

She wasn't paying me any attention. Something back along the highway had caught her eye.

'Hey, Jesse. See those lights shining up there, what do you think that place is?'

Three lights winked at us, through the trees on a bend. One red. One white. One blue. We crawled along the ridge, me first and then Rachel, until we were across the highway from the flashing lights. It was a truck stop. Rachel tapped me on the back.

'What sort of place is it?'

'A big servo.'

'Do you think they'd be open and have food there? I'm real hungry and we've got no biscuits left.'

The lights inside the shop were on. There were no trucks or cars parked out the front. I could see someone sitting inside, at a counter. The highway was empty. I pointed across the road.

'We'll cross here. See that dumpster?'

She crawled alongside me. 'What's a dumpster?'

'Jesus,' I snapped. 'That giant fucken rubbish bin. It's red and yellow.'

She dropped her head and whispered, 'Yes.'

I felt bad for yelling at her. 'I'm sorry.'

I patted her on the head. It was drenched. 'Sorry. I really am, Rachel.'

I took the backpack off. 'When we cross the road, you take the backpack with you and wait for me behind that bin while I go inside.'

'Why can't I come in with you?'

'In case they come by afterwards, Ray and Limbo, and ask if a boy and a girl have been in. I don't want them to know it's us. You get it?'

'I get it.'

'You can't ask any more questions, Rache. You have to trust me and do everything I say from now on. I'll go in and buy us some food. You hide behind the bin and stay there until I come for you. Whatever happens, you stay there. If I have to take off for any reason, if anyone comes after me, I'll hide until I can come back for you. As long as you stay put, I'll be back. Don't come out until you hear me whistle.'

'Can I ask one question?'

'You just did.'

'Well, another one?'

I folded my arms and waited. The rain had soaked through my top and was running down my back.

'If they have hot chips in there can you get me some?'

'Yeah.'

'And if not, can I have a hot dog?'

'Yeah. A hot dog. And chips.'

We slid down a muddy bank and crouched down while I listened for traffic. The wind had dropped and there wasn't a sound, and there were no headlights in either direction. I took Rachel by the hand and sprinted across the highway. We ran past the bowsers, ducked underneath the shop window and ran to the bin. I handed Rachel the backpack and told her to wedge herself between the bin and a brick wall. She couldn't fit. I took the backpack off her, threw it behind the bin and told her to crawl in after it.

I couldn't see her at all, but could hear her heavy breathing. I poked my head into the darkness.

'You stay as still and quiet as you can. I'll come and fetch you in a bit. Listen for my whistle. The one I make that sounds like a bird.'

I walked into the shop. A blast of warm air hit me in the face. A fat kid in a black and white striped beanie and pimples over his chin was sitting behind the counter. He looked up at me from a magazine. I'd brought a puddle of water and muddy footsteps inside with me. He looked through the window and out to the highway, like he was surprised it was raining.

'Hey. It's wet out there. You need some help?'

I didn't want him getting a good look at me and kept my head down. 'I'm getting some food. I can help myself.'

He went back to his magazine.

I picked up two packets of potato chips, some chocolate bars, a carton of orange juice, and a packet of mixed lollies. I headed to where the hot food was kept. There were no chips or hotdogs and the pie warmer had been turned off for the night. I took two pies out of the warmer, put them in the microwave sitting next to it, and blasted them. When I took them out they were so hot they nearly burned my hands. I kept my eyes on the floor as I walked to the counter.

'Is that the lot?'

'Yeah.'

'You want this stuff in a bag?'

'Yeah,' I said, noticing some picnic rugs in a big plastic tub. They were 'on special' at $29.99. I put one on the counter.

'I'll take this as well.'

He leaned forward so he could get a better look at me. 'Where you from? Not from round here. Where's your car?'

'We're down the road a bit,' I said, without looking up at him. 'Our car. It broke down. My old man's looking at it now. Sent me up here to get us something to eat while we're waiting.'

He put the food in a plastic bag and scanned the rug for a price. 'What's this for?'

'Just in case he can't get it fixed and we have to sleep in the back for the night.'

I took the hundred out of my pocket and handed it to him. He held it up to the light and checked it out.

'That's real money, all right. It came straight out of my dad's wallet.'

I don't know if he was just being a smart arse, but he took another long look at the note before he finally put it in the till and handed me the change.

'Try keeping yourself dry.'

I walked outside and opened the bag of food, pretending I was searching through it, while I looked back at the shop from the corner of my eye. He'd already started reading again. I slipped into the shadows, crawled to the bin and whistled to Rachel. When she didn't move I whistled again, a little louder. I crawled along the ground and stuck my head in the dark space. I could just make her out. She was sitting at the far end, looking at me.

'What are you doing, Rachel? Didn't you hear me whistle?'

'Yeah. I heard. But I thought it might be a trick. You could have been somebody else. I heard Ray whistle like that one time.'

I was about to reach in and grab the backpack when I heard a car engine. I squeezed in alongside her and listened as it drove in and pulled up outside the shop. It was the Camaro again. No mistake. I heard a car door slam, twice, footsteps and the jingling of Ray's cowboy boots. Then nothing. Everything went quiet again, except for the pounding of my heart and Rachel breathing in and out as heavy as a steam train.

I crawled along the ground to the end of the dumpster and stuck my head around the corner. The car was empty. If Gwen was in it, she had to be lying across the back seat. Or maybe they'd put her back in the boot. I could see the kid at the counter, but not much more. He was talking to somebody, most likely Ray. I crawled back to Rachel.

'We're stuck here. We'll have to wait till they go.'

I put my head between my knees, closed my eyes and tried to remember the words of one of Pop's prayers. I couldn't think of more than a few words, so I made the sign of the cross, like I'd seen him do and said 'Amen' under my breath.

I heard the Camaro gun back to life. The vibration shook the dumpster as they drove back onto the highway. I grabbed the backpack and handed Rachel the rug.

'You've got to carry something.'

We crawled out from behind the bin and ran back across the highway. When we tried climbing the same spot we'd slid down earlier, the ground was too wet and slippery for us to get back up. We either had to stay where we were or walk along the highway.

'We can't make it, Rache. We'll have to keep to the road for a bit, until we find another spot to climb. If a car comes by, we'll lie in the ditch here on the side of the road.'

'But it's full of water.'

'We can't get much wetter than we are already.'

We walked on and tried climbing up the bank at other places. They were just as steep. Each time I tried boosting Rachel up she slid back and crashed into me. I tried myself but couldn't make it either. I fell into the ditch, up to my arse in water. I was picking myself up when I thought I saw something move behind a tree across the highway. I put my finger to my mouth.

'Jesse, what is it?' Rache whispered.

'Nothing. Keep still.'

I heard the sound of another car engine, heading our way, on the opposite side of the road. I was pretty sure it wasn't the Camaro but got Rachel to crouch in the ditch anyway. The headlights of a van lit up the tree. I couldn't see anything moving. I must have spooked myself. A battered milk van passed us and turned into the truck stop.

'Come on, Rachel. We'll find another place to climb.'

I was almost enjoying splashing through the puddles when I saw another tree move, across the road a little further along. I walked on until we were directly across the highway from the tree, stopped again and took a closer look. Limbo suddenly stepped out from behind the tree. When he smiled at me through the rain and pointed a finger at us I wanted to scream out and run at the same time, but couldn't move.

Rachel was chanting 'Jesse, Jesse, Jesse' over and over again. 'Jesse, let's go.' I was stuck to the spot like glue. I had the loaded pack on my back and was also carrying the bag of food. If I dropped the lot maybe I could outrun Limbo. But I wasn't about to give up the money or leave Rachel on the side of the road, where he could grab her.

I heard the sound of another engine behind me, quickly getting louder. I looked back along the highway. A truck was rounding the bend, cutting through the sheet of rain. It was big and heavy and moving fast. It had dirty yellow eyes, just like the truck in the nightmare I'd had.

Limbo took a couple of steps onto the road. He ran his hands through his wet hair then rubbed them together. He looked like he was about to sprint across the highway after us.

I tried keeping calm. 'Rache. When I yell "run", you take off as fast as you can.'

She was watching Limbo just as closely as me. 'Where to, Jesse? I'm scared.'

'Straight ahead, until you find a place where you can run back into the bush.'

'And if he catches up to us?'

'He can't keep hold of both of us. I'll fight him and you run.'

'Not without you, I won't.'

'Be quiet and be ready to run!'

I looked over my shoulder. The truck was about to swallow us.

'Run, Rachel, run!'

As soon as I started running Limbo took off too. I broke into a sprint, and tried dragging Rachel with me, but she fell.

'Jesse . . . wait.'

I turned to pick her up just as Limbo bolted across the road. He was quick, like a hungry cat chasing a feed. He would have got us too, I reckon, if he hadn't slipped on the wet bitumen. The truck's horn howled. Limbo got to his knees, got in the headlights, just as the truck smashed into him and threw his body into the air. I heard a thump, and then a groan from Limbo's body as it was dumped on the side of the road up ahead.

The truck didn't brake at all. It didn't slow down or stop. As quick as it had shown up on the highway it vanished into the mist with the rain kicking off its heavy tyres.

I put my arms around Rachel's waist and got her to her feet. 'What happened?'

'It got him.'

'What did?'

'The truck.'

Limbo was in a ditch up ahead of us, lying on his back. His legs twitched for a bit and then he went still. I told Rachel to stay behind me. I walked on and looked down at him. His face had been smashed to pieces and I could hardly recognise him. The front of his head was split open like a watermelon, his nose had shifted to the side of his face and the teardrop tattoo under his eye was missing. A piece of metal from the truck was sticking out of his chest. I jumped back when he coughed and spewed some blood onto his face. It was the grossest thing I'd ever seen. Worse than any horror film. I didn't feel sorry for Limbo, but it didn't stop me shaking.

'Is he dead?' Rachel called out to me, without moving any closer. 'He sounds alive.'

'He'll be dead soon. Cover your eyes and don't look. It's real bad.'

She came and stood next to me. 'No. I want to see him. He's a bad man.' She took a quick look at him and covered her eyes. 'You're right. I don't want to see.'

I heard another car, looked up and spotted headlights on the opposite side of the highway.

'Let's go.'

We scrambled over some rocks behind us and ran into the bush. I looked back. The car pulled up across from Limbo's body. It was Ray.

'Keep running, Rache.'

I couldn't see where I was going but could feel myself moving downhill. Rachel's hand slipped from mine. I called to her over my shoulder to catch up but couldn't see her in the dark. My head smashed into a low tree branch, I slid further downhill and slammed against a rock. I could hear a buzzing in my ears as I fell into a deep hole.

The rain was pelting my face when I came to. Something warm ran down my cheek, onto my neck. I wiped my hand across it, stuck my fingers in my mouth and tasted blood. Rachel crawled on top of me and wrapped my face in her hands.

'You have to wake up, Jesse. I've got the food bag you dropped and I found us a cubbyhole.'

'A cubbyhole?'

She helped me up. The ground under my feet was spinning. She took hold of my hand and led me around the other side of the boulder I'd crashed into.

'See? There's a cave here. And it's dry.'

I couldn't stand in the cave without my head hitting the roof. I sat down, slipped off the backpack and took a long drink of water from one of the bottles inside. The cave mightn't have been the safest place to be, with Ray driving around looking for us, but I couldn't go any further. I was cold and exhausted. I pulled one arm out of my wet t-shirt sleeve and tried to work it off, over my head.

'We have to get our wet clothes off, Rache.'

'But I don't want to take my clothes off. What if somebody comes?'

'Don't be stupid. Nobody's coming. Anyway, if you don't take your clothes off you'll freeze and die.'

'Well, I'm not taking my undies off.'

'Are they wet?'

'They might be.'

'Please yourself.'

We laid our clothes on the cave floor to dry. I tore the plastic wrapping off the picnic rug and put it over us. I took the pies out of the bag. They were squashed from having been dropped but were still warm. We ate them, shared the bottle of orange juice and finished off the meal with some lollies.

Rachel was a little spooked. She tried to keep her mind off it by talking like mad. One minute she was telling me how she was going to decorate the Christmas tree next year at Pop's and the next her head fell on my shoulder as she nodded off. I sat with my back against the wall listening to noises outside the cave. It had stopped raining. Just before I fell asleep I heard a siren somewhere out on the highway.

That night I had a nightmare about Limbo. He was chasing me, not across the highway, or through the bush, but through the farmhouse we'd shared with Jon Dempsey. He had the whip that belonged to the blackfella, Magic, and he was coming for me, across the front yard, with his two vicious dogs behind him, barking and howling like crazy. I was trying to run as fast as I could but my legs wouldn't work properly and I was going up and down on the one spot.

I got to the front gate just as Limbo was about to grab me. Old Magic was sitting on the fence, holding his belly and laughing.

'Don't you worry, Yella Fella,' he said. 'A good beltin does you real good.'

I woke up early in the morning, my face pushed against the floor of the cave. I freed an arm from underneath me, shoved my hand down the front of my underpants and felt for the roll of notes. It was still there. I sat up and touched my forehead above my left eye. It felt swollen and crusted with dried blood. I looked across at Rachel. She was lying with her eyes wide open, looking up at the roof of the cave. I followed her eyes. There was a drawing of a fat-bellied man with a small head. Two small animals were standing next to him.

'See the picture?' she asked. 'What do you think it is?'

'I don't know. It looks old, though.'

She pointed at one of the animals. 'This one is a dog.'

'Maybe.'

'Your eye is all black, Jesse. And there's a cut on it. You better wash it. Or you'll get poisoned.'

I got Rachel to pour some water into my cupped hands, splashed it in my face and tried rubbing the dried blood away.

'Is it gone?'

'Not all of it. Let me do it.'

She poured more water onto the dirty singlet she had on, stood in front of me and dabbed at the swollen cut while I looked at her belly button.

'The black eye's still there, but it's cleaner.'

Our clothes weren't exactly dry but we put them on anyway. We spread the rug out on the cave floor, ate a packet of chips each and finished off the orange juice. Rachel looked up at the painting again while she was eating.

'Do you think it means something, the picture?'

'Yeah. It means we'd better take off or a man with a pair of crazy dogs is going to chase us.'

I put the leftover food in the backpack, rolled up the picnic rug, tied it and handed it to Rachel. She tucked it under her arm.

'Where we going?'

'We have to get back to the road and take a look. I'll make up my mind then.'

'Won't that get us into trouble? Because of . . .'

'We couldn't be in much worse trouble. Come on, let's go and take a look.'

We walked along a narrow dirt track, away from the cave. The climb was steep and tired us out. I looked across at Rachel every few steps, wondering when she'd start complaining. She only asked me to stop when she saw a sign on the side of the track. It told the story of the painting in the cave and how Aboriginal spirits had made the land. One of the spirits went into the sky and became an eagle, while another one turned himself and his family into the night stars to protect the earth, so the sign said.

Rachel read aloud as she ran a finger over the words. She was a better reader than me.

'I like this bit, Jesse. "Guests should obey his laws and know that they must always care for the children." That's us. We're gonna be taken care of.'

I looked up at the empty sky, hoping the eagle was up there somewhere, looking out for us.

As we got closer to the highway I could hear people talking. I crawled between the trees, on my guts, to get a better look. A police motorbike was blocking the road just ahead of where Limbo had been run down. Other police cars were parked further up the highway, and a line of orange cones blocked the road. Two of the coppers were writing stuff down and taking measurements with a long tape.

Rachel crawled alongside me. 'Who is it?'

'The police.'

'And Ray Crow? Can you see him?'

'Na. He'd be long gone. Wouldn't have hung around once the police turned up.'

'Good. We can go down there and tell them what happened. They'll help us.'

I felt the weight of the pack on my back. 'I'm not doing that. I don't want them taking this money off us. We're going to keep it. And I don't want them separating us. That'd be the first thing they'd do, Rachel. Send you to one place and me to another.'

'I'm tired out, Jesse. I want to stop walking.'

I rested my hand in the middle of her back. 'You can leave if you want to, but I'm staying here. You know that house you want, with the pink room and the puppy?'

'Yeah.'

'Well, we need this money if we're gonna do that. I'm not going down there to the police and giving this money up. You stay with me and I promise I'll get you back to Pop. We can share the money with him.'

'What about Gwen? We could save her from Ray.'

There was no saving Gwen, but Rachel hadn't worked it out just yet.

I crawled back to the line of trees. 'We'll go around them, on the track here, up to where we slid down the bank last night.'

We walked along the track, between the trees, until we were across the highway from the truck stop again.

'We're going to sit here for a bit.'

'What for?'

'I want to see who comes and goes.'

A bus driver was filling up at one of the bowsers. He went inside to pay for his petrol and drove off. I opened the backpack, took a drink and passed the bottle to Rachel. I had a good view down the highway to the roadblock. A police lady was directing the traffic around the cones. A car or a truck pulled into the truck stop every few minutes. Each time a driver went inside to pay for their petrol they left the keys in the ignition. If I'd known how to drive we'd have been gone by now.

A double-cab ute pulled in. It was beaten up and even dirtier than Mary's old Commodore. The tray was tied down with a tarp and the bumper bar and back window were covered in stickers. I could make out a picture of a tree on one sticker and some sort of fish on the other. The driver got out and started filling up. He had long hair down his back and a beard and was wearing a red checked shirt. The passenger seat was empty. I could see someone in the back seat but couldn't tell if it was a man or a woman. I waited until he'd walked into the shop to pay for his petrol.

'Okay. This fella might be the one. Let's go.'

'The one for what?'

I shook her by the shoulder, not hard, just enough to be sure she was paying attention.

'Remember what I said last night when we were walking. No more questions. Sometimes you have to think fast and act fast. Jon told me that, one time. You got to trust me, Rachel, and do what I say.'

As we crossed the highway I looked along the road to where the police were working. They were too busy to notice us. I walked towards the ute just as the bearded man came out of the shop. He looked at me and smiled, sort of friendly, opened the door of the ute, jumped in the driver's seat and was about to close it when I called out to him, 'Excuse me. Mister. We need help.'

The back window rolled down. A woman stuck her head out, looked at me and then at Rachel. She had long hair too, tied in plaits and decorated with beads.

'You kids okay?'

'Not really.'

I told them we needed to get back to Melbourne.

'Where's your family?' the man asked. 'Your mum and dad?'

'We don't have a dad and our mum is in Melbourne. We came up here to stay with our Pop and now he's sick and we have to go back home.'

'And your mother can't come and get you?'

I wasn't sure what to say next. I didn't want them getting suspicious and driving off. We'd be stuck at the truck stop, and the police would find us.

'She can't do it. She don't drive, and –' I swallowed some spit – 'and she's got no money, anyway.'

'I know what that's like,' he said, and smiled. 'Never had much myself.'

He looked at the woman and shrugged his shoulders. 'I don't know. We're not exactly going to Melbourne and we shouldn't be picking up kids. I'm sure there's some law against it. There's a law against just about everything these days.'

Rachel stepped in front of me and spoke to the woman. 'Please, can you give us a ride? We need to get home. Bad. And we won't break any laws. We promise.'

The woman nodded her head at the man. 'Sure we can, honey. Hop in.'

He told us that he couldn't take us all the way to Melbourne, and that he'd be making a detour.

'Before you get in, you need to know that this is a round trip. I've got two deliveries left, in the back here. And then we're heading home. We live out the back of Werribee. That's as far as I can take you.'

I jumped in the front seat and Rachel got in the back with the woman. He pointed to the backpack.

'Maybe you'd be more comfortable with that off your back.'

I gripped the straps of the pack. 'I'm comfortable enough. I'll leave it.'

'Please yourself.'

He introduced himself as Pete and his wife as Sharon. Rachel clapped her hands together when she saw a baby strapped into a baby seat between her and the woman. The baby's name was Indigo.

'I like that name,' Rachel said.

'It's a colour,' Sharon told her.

'What colour is that? I've got colouring pencils and I've never heard of it.'

'If I told you it's like the deepest blue in the sea, I'd only be half right. You can't pin that colour down. That's how beautiful it is. Just like this little girl.'

Rachel was in love with the baby. She picked up a rattle from the seat and shook it in front of her eyes. And she asked Sharon lots of questions. Like how much did the baby weigh? What foods did she like to eat? And had she spoken her first word?

I'd never heard her so chatty. She couldn't stop talking, and as I listened I thought she sounded older all of a sudden. And, better that that, she sounded happy.

We drove away from the truck stop and headed in the opposite direction to the roadblock, which suited me fine. Pete looked in his rear-view mirror.

'Bad accident back there. The bloke in the shop was just telling me that some poor guy was knocked down and killed last night. A hit and run. I don't know how anyone could leave someone on the roadside to die like that.'

Sharon told him to stop talking about something so gruesome. 'You'll scare these poor kids.'

As we headed along the highway I looked back a few times to see if we were being followed. Pete and Sharon seemed like nice people and I didn't want them getting tangled up with Ray. I felt a lot better when we turned off the highway. We drove by small farms with hand-painted signs out front, selling fruit and vegetables, garden plants and even 'pure alpaca wool' at one farm gate.

'What's an alpaca?' I asked Pete.

'Not sure myself. It's similar to a llama, I think.'

I didn't know what a llama was either. 'Do you know much about llamas?'

'Na. I'm a ferret breeder, myself. That's what I've got in the back here, ferrets. I'm delivering them to my customers.'

At least I knew what a ferret was. When I'd been at school one time there was a kid who had a ferret for a pet that he brought for 'show and tell' one day. As soon as he took it out of the box a girl sitting in front of him started screaming. The ferret looked nervous. It wriggled out of the boy's arms, jumped down from his desk and ran out of the classroom, and was never seen again.

'What do they do with the ferrets, your customers?'

'Some hunt rabbits. They're a big problem out here. A pair of ferrets can clean out a burrow in minutes. But that's not all they're used for. The ferret's a smart animal. The farmer I'm delivering to now, he runs electrical wiring through plastic piping under his chook pens. It's for the heating, to keep the birds warm. Now and then a rat gets into the pipes, chews through a wire and blows a fuse. Cooks itself in the process, of course. Well, for that farmer to lay new wiring, he has a hell of a job. So, he sends one of my ferrets down there with the new wiring strapped to his collar. Works every time. Goes in one end of the pipe, navigates the maze and comes out the other.'

'How do they get the rabbits from the burrows?' Rachel asked. 'You said they cleaned them out?'

'They kill them,' he laughed. 'That's if the rabbits don't bolt first.'

She looked horrified and went back to playing with the baby.

'You make a lot of money, breeding ferrets?' I asked.

'Enough to get by on.'

He was staring at my swollen eye. 'What happened there? That cut looks no good. You should get to the hospital. You might need stiches.'

I touched the side of my head. 'I fell over when we were walking last night, in the dark. I slipped in some mud. I'll get it fixed up when we get home.'

We pulled in at a farmhouse gate. I got out with Pete and helped him take the tarp off the back of the ute. It was stacked with wire cages. They were empty except for two cages that had two ferrets in each. Pete grabbed the handle of one of the cages. The ferrets inside were long and skinny and light brown in colour, except for a ring of white fur around the nose.

'Give us a hand, if you like.'

I followed him to the front of the house. He rang the bell and a woman came to the door. She had an apron on over the top of a purple tracksuit and was wearing a hat. I could see that her hair underneath it was cut short, like it'd been shaved and was starting to grow back. Pete introduced me as a 'fellow traveller'. She stuck a finger through the cage. One of the ferrets bared its teeth. I thought it was going to bite her. It sniffed her finger, turned on its side and nuzzled into her.

'They're beauties,' she said. 'This one'll be a bit of a sook, though.

She pulled a purse from the front of her apron and paid him.

'How you feeling?' Pete asked. 'You look well.'

'I'm okay. A bit tired and up and down. But I'm fine.'

When he told her that his wife and baby had come along for the ride she got excited and walked down the driveway. Rachel was sitting on the tray of the ute while Sharon brushed and plaited her hair. When she saw the woman, Sharon jumped down and wrapped her arms around her. When they finally stopped hugging I saw they both had tears in their eyes.

Sharon lifted baby Indigo out of the seat and handed her to her friend. The woman buried her face in the baby's neck and took a deep sniff.

'Life,' she said. 'Doesn't it smell good?'

She handed the baby back to Sharon and wiped her eyes on her apron.

'She's a beauty. You look tireder than me, love. Why don't you come in for a cuppa?'

'Oh, I'm tired, all right,' Sharon said, yawning. 'Buggered. But I have to get the baby home and fed.'

'You get off then. You drive safe, Pete. And don't you two forget me when you need a babysitter.'

'Long way to come to drop off a baby.' Sharon laughed.

'Good. She can stay for the weekend.'

Sharon hugged the woman again and told her to 'take care'. 'We'll talk on the phone.'

Pete's last delivery was about half an hour's drive along the same road. He pulled in beside a locked gate.

'I'll do this one on my own. He's a grumpy old bastard.'

He was back in the ute within a few minutes. As we headed for Werribee, Sharon finished Rachel's hair and I listened to Pete's stories about the years he'd spent on the road before he met his wife. He'd travelled all over Australia and across the world, hitchhiking from place to place, stopping whenever he felt like it, and moving on when the urge took him.

'Why'd you travel around so much?'

'Because I liked being on my own. Sure, I met a lot of interesting people along the way. There'd always be someone to talk to and stay with for a while. But while I was on the road, I spent most of that time alone. And that's the way I liked it.'

I told him that I liked being on my own too, but had never had the chance to travel.

'I've got to look after my sister. But when I'm older I'm gonna go off some place by myself.'

'You can tell me to mind my own business if you want to but let me give you some advice. Don't go travelling for too long. I think I went a little crazy by the end of my time away. When I met Sharon, she was on the road too, I wanted nothing more than to come back here and settle down. A home and family, that's what matters most of all. You know what it's like, I bet.'

'Yeah,' I answered, although I didn't really know at all.

'How long have you had the ferret business?' I asked.

'Oh, just a couple of years. When we come back from overseas we worked together for a year, running a winery for some city lawyer. We saved enough to buy ourselves a bush block out the other side of Melbourne. It was cheap. "No Power – No Water", as they say. But it was a great spot. A creek running down the back. Plenty of trees. And birds. You never seen so many birds.'

Sharon joined in from the back seat: 'We built our own place up there. Lived in a caravan on the block while we worked. How long was it, Pete? Four years?'

He laughed. 'Almost five.'

'We lived in a caravan in Adelaide,' Rachel piped up. 'With Gwen.'

'Who's Gwen?' Sharon asked.

'Our mum.'

'I thought you said she was in Melbourne.'

I changed the subject before Rachel got us in a deeper trap: 'Why'd you leave your house in the bush, if it was so nice?' I asked Pete. 'For the ferret business?'

Pete turned and looked at Sharon and then out the window. 'No, it wasn't the ferrets. A fire went through the valley we lived in. Biggest bushfire the state's seen in fifty years. We lost everything we had.'

'Everything?'

'Yep. But we got out with our lives, which was more than some. We left with nothing but the clothes on our backs. But we're still here.'

He waved his hand across the windscreen. 'So we come out here, where the land's even cheaper, where it's flat as a tack, and there's nothing much to burn.'

It was late afternoon when we pulled into their front yard. They had a wooden house, painted yellow, with flowers and fruit trees in the garden. Pete invited us to have something to eat with them. I didn't want to be ungrateful for the help they'd given us, but didn't want to stop either.

'That'd be nice, but we gotta keep moving.'

I waited in the yard with him while Sharon took Rachel inside to use the toilet.

'I've got to unpack this truck before it gets dark, hose it out and feed the mob out the back in their pens. Ferrets get all uppity if you don't feed them. You two could prop here tonight and I'll take you to the train station in the morning.'

'Na. We'll keep moving. We've got family expecting us tonight.'

'Fair enough. The highway's a couple of clicks that way. It's always busy. You'll get a ride in no time.'

It wasn't the same road we'd been on last night but I didn't feel good about heading back to the open road with the money on my back and Ray out there.

'Is that the only way back to Melbourne?'

He looked at me and smiled, like he knew I was holding something back. 'Well, you don't have to use the highway, if you don't want to.'

'We don't?'

He put a hand on my shoulder and pointed along the road. 'About halfway between here and the highway there's an old irrigation channel. You're lucky. It's concreted over, and mostly dry this time of year. Even with that rain last night, it won't be carrying too much water.'

'I can't see any channel.'

'That's because it's below ground. It cuts through the back of the farms, across country. It'll cut your trip in half. You can walk it –' he looked me in the eye – 'without being seen by anyone. In the old measurement it's about four miles between here and where it ends, just short of the oil refineries. If you two move quick enough you'll be there in around an hour, before dark.'

I looked across the flat and empty fields. 'Then what do we do? When we reach the end?'

'It runs smack bang into the train line. You can't miss it. There's a station for the refinery workers on shift. You can catch the train from there into the city. You got money on you? I could lend you a few dollars for the fare.'

'We don't need money. I got plenty of money.'

'Plenty? You could have caught a bus from that truck stop for Melbourne. Pulls in twice a day. Jesus, I thought you must have been flat broke to ask for a ride with us.'

He looked me directly in the eye, again. 'You in some sort of trouble?'

'No. I just want to take care of my sister and get her home.'

He offered his hand. 'Well, that's a good thing to do.'

We shook hands. 'How old are you, Jesse?'

'Thirteen. Be fourteen in a couple of weeks.'

'Well, you'd have to be the oldest thirteen-year-old on the planet. Your sister's in good hands. If you're ever back this way, look us up. You'd be welcome to stay.'

Rachel came out of the house carrying a large piece of cake in each hand and a cloth bag full of apples dangling from her wrist. She handed me a piece of cake.

'It's banana.'

When she said goodbye to Sharon, Rachel put her arms around her waist, squeezed tight and held on for as long as she could.

★

We ate two apples each as we walked along the road to the channel. We passed more roadkill, a bird, some rabbits, and maybe a wild dog, although I didn't look too close to see what it was.

'Hey, Jesse. What did you think of those people?'

'They were okay. He was a real help, that Pete.'

'She was nice too. And pretty. She smelled like soap.'

Rachel patted her braids. 'Do you like my hair?'

I didn't think much of it but told her she looked pretty anyway.

'Jesse, do you think there's a lot of people like Pete and Sharon? Nice people?'

I hadn't met a lot of nice people over the years. They weren't the kind of people that Gwen hung out with.

'Not too many like them, I don't think.'

In the channel a stream of water moved slowly in a straight line for as far as I could see. Weeds grew out of cracks in the concrete and the bottom was slimy and smelled bad. Walking along the bottom we couldn't see the land above us, which meant that nobody could see us either.

'We'll have to move fast, Rache. I don't want to be left out here in the dark. You can't get tired and slow us down. We'll rest when we get to Pop's.'

We walked for a long time without seeming to get any-where. The sun was low on our backs. We only stopped when we needed a drink of water or felt like another apple. I could see a bridge crossing the channel up ahead. It was a long way off and gave me something to aim for. I felt better when it got a little bigger. When we reached it we shared the last mouth-fuls of our last bottle of water. I should have asked Pete for a refill. I could smell shit and mud. I looked up at the underside of the wooden slats on the bridge. Bits of grass, dried mud and shit were caught in the cracks.

'Must be a cattle bridge. Or for sheep.'

Rachel rested against the concrete wall, held the bottle above her head and caught the last drops of water. She looked exhausted. So was I but I didn't reckon it would help letting on.

'We can't stop, Rache. If you give up now we'll never get back. Remember to be strong. Like Scout, in the movie.'

'I'm not stopping. I'm doing the same as you're doing. Having a drink of water. I can make it just as good as you. And I don't need to be like Scout. I'm just me. Rachel. And I can walk as far as you can.'

She didn't look like she could take another step. I hoped like hell I was wrong.

I slipped the pack off, dug out the last two apples and handed her one. I was sweaty and hot. I took off my t-shirt and tucked it into the front of my jeans. As I was putting the pack back on, Rachel tapped me on the shoulder.

'Those scars you have there, did you really get them from cigarette burns?'

'Of course I did. You know the story.'

'And you got them when you were in the foster home that time?'

'Who cares? It doesn't matter now.'

'I care. What if we go to Pop's house and he can't look after us? Last time he said he might not be able to keep us for good. If Gwen doesn't come back, then we'll be put in homes. Like you were that time.'

She touched the scar. 'I don't want that happening to me. Getting burnt. I'll run away first. It's scary, Jesse. And it's sad. When you were telling Jon the story that time, I wanted to cry.'

'But you'd heard it plenty of times before. I thought you liked hearing it.'

'I know. But it was more real when I heard you telling somebody else.'

We'd only walked on for another few minutes before I stopped again.

'I want to tell you something, Rachel. It didn't happen in the foster home. These burns. Well, I mean, it did. But the woman who ran the home, Claire, there was nothing wrong with her. She was nice. Just like those people back there we just met. She didn't do it.'

'You're just saying that to make me feel better, in case we get put away.'

'No, I'm not. The story's not true.'

'Why would you make up a scary story like that?'

I felt ashamed for lying to Rachel and for causing trouble for the lady who'd taken all those kids into her home. I sat down, hugged my knees and put my head down. Rachel sat next to me and wrapped her arms around my leg.

'Who did it then? Somebody must have hurt you.'

'I did it myself. I put the burns there.'

'You did? Why would you hurt yourself like that?'

I looked down at the water flowing under my feet. I could see tadpoles swimming and a grasshopper hitching a ride on a leaf. I pushed her arms away and got to my feet.

'Let's go. We have to beat the sun and get to the end before dark.'

'Why'd you do that to yourself, Jesse? I wanna know.'

'Now? Do you have to know now?'

'Right now.'

'Then we'll go?'

She nodded.

'Because of you. I didn't know where you were, and I got frightened.'

'For me? You hurt yourself for me?'

'No. For both of us.'

She touched the scar again. 'I'm sorry you had to do that.'

'Well, don't you be.'

'One day, I'll pay you back, Jesse. If you get in trouble, I'll pay you back.'

'You won't have to. Nothing bad is gonna happen to me, or you, again. We've got this money. It'll get us out of trouble.'

I noticed a flame in the distance, low in the sky above the channel. It glowed red and licked the sky around it. Rachel also spotted the flame.

'Is that a fire?'

'Pete said the channel ended where the oil refineries begin. It must be a fire from one of their chimneys.'

'How far away do you think it is?'

It still looked a long way off.

'Oh, I don't think it's too far.'

'You're lying to me, to make me feel better.'

I smiled as I thought that she'd finally worked me out.

We began passing graffiti tags scrawled on the channel walls. Pretty soon both sides were covered in them. Some of the drawings were as beautiful as paintings. Different colours, shapes and swirls. There were messages too, like 'Hoppers Hoods Are Fucked Up'.

Rubbish had been dumped and washed along the channel, mostly bits of scrap wood and sheets of tin. We passed a shopping trolley, lying on its side. It was packed tight with soft drink cans, bottles, plastic bags, and leaves and twigs.

Rachel pointed. 'That looks like a fish net, sort of.'

'Yeah, a net for picking up all the shit people don't want.'

A car wreck sat in the middle of the channel up ahead of us. Its wheels were missing, the windows were smashed in, and it was covered in more graffiti. Rachel had fallen behind. When I called her she ran after me and tapped me on the shoulder.

'See those boys?' She pointed.

Three teenage boys, maybe a little older that me, were walking along the edge of the channel, tracking us. They were wearing the same uniform: long hair, checked flannelette shirts and big shorts. They had skateboards tucked under their arms.

'How long have they been following us?'

'I don't know. For a little bit.'

'You could have told me.'

The boys ran along the top of the channel, single file, until they were ahead of us. The lead boy, who had long dark hair almost to his waist, leaped into the air, hitched the skateboard under his black gym shoes and dropped onto the wall. The other boys followed. They skated through the stream in the bottom of the channel and rode the wall back to the top.

They stayed ahead of us, skating from side to side, until we'd reached another bridge. The boys hung over the rail and waited for us to pass underneath. When we came out the other side they ran on again and zigzagged across the stream on their boards. They looked like water skiers as they passed through the stream.

They turned to face us. Two of the boys sat on their skateboards and the other one, the boy with the longest hair, walked forward with his skateboard under his arm. I had about fifty dollars in my pocket, nineteen hundred in my underpants and thousands in my backpack. I didn't want any trouble from them. But they didn't look too tough and didn't scare me at all.

'Where you walking from?' the boy asked, in a high-pitched voice.

'It's a girl, I think,' Rachel whispered.

I looked closer. It was a girl. They weren't big, but I could see that she had breasts under her shirt.

'That way.' I pointed back upstream.

'There's not much out there. And where you going?'

I pointed to the flaming chimney in the sky. 'We're heading for that. We have to catch the train to the city. Is it far?'

'Not as far as you've come.'

She reached into her pocket and pulled out a packet of cigarettes. 'You want a smoke?'

'Na. We gotta go.'

She spotted Rachel wiping her dry mouth. She called out to one of the other skaters: 'Sonny, get up here with the water.'

She hopped on her skateboard, pushed it gently forward and glided over to Rachel.

'You look thirsty. Sonny, my brother, he's the water carrier.'

Sonny pulled up on his skateboard and lifted his flannelette shirt. He was wearing a belt, made of a bicycle tube and the feet of old pantyhose. The belt held four bottles of water. The girl took one of the bottles and gave it to Rachel.

Rachel ripped off the bottle top and took a long drink. I reckoned she should have sniffed it first, in case they'd pissed in it, or something. The girl nodded to me.

'Good luck getting home.'

She jumped on her board and skated off in the direction we'd come from. Rachel passed me the water.

'She liked you.'

'You always say that stuff, Rache. She hardly said a word to me.'

'She was looking. I saw her. Girls have a good look before they talk. That's what they do.'

'How would you know? You're just a kid.'

'I just do.'

A little further on the channel broke to the left. We turned a corner and found ourselves in a wide concrete bowl. The water had completely drained from the bottom. The eyes of a pair of stormwater drains, big enough to walk in, stared back at us. It was almost dark and we'd reached the end. We climbed a concrete ramp to the world above, and found row after row of steel chimneys with flaming heads, shining fat metal tanks and towers decorated in fairy lights.

'Wow. Look at this, Jesse. Where are we?' Rachel was gushing. It was as if we'd finally made it to Disneyland.

'The refineries, I suppose.'

We headed along a road with high razor-wire fences and oil refineries on each side. I wasn't sure we were heading the right way until I heard the railway bells, saw the boom gates come down and a train pass by up ahead.

Rachel stopped to get a stone out of her shoe. When she sat down in the gutter to put it back on, I could see that she didn't want to move.

'It's not far now, Rache. If you're finding it hard, that's okay. You can say so. I'm finding it hard too. If you need to, I'll piggyback you the rest of the way.'

She tied her lace and stood up. 'I don't need a piggyback. I'm gonna get there on my own.'

The train station was deserted. We had plenty of money to buy tickets but the machine was broken. It looked like it had been hit with a sledgehammer. I ran my finger down the timetable. The trains ran every forty minutes.

'How long will it be?' Rachel asked.

'There's no clock here. All I can tell you is that it should be here in less than forty minutes.'

Rachel sat down, lay back and ate the last bit of her apple. It was saying something, but I'd never seen her looking so filthy. Her arms and legs were black with dirt. There was more dirt, mixed with my blood, on her singlet, and her face was smeared with food scraps.

I walked from one end of the platform to the other as we waited for the train to come. I stood on the end of the platform and looked back at the oil refineries. The sun was about to sink. It was blood red, as if it was on fire too. The flames from the chimneys in front of the sun looked like the candles on a giant birthday cake.

I could hear a train coming. The bells rang out again and the boom gates came down. I walked back to Rachel.

'This is it. We're nearly there.'

★

We fell asleep on the train and missed our stop at Flinders Street. The train whistle woke me and we jumped off at Southern Cross just before the train headed back to where we had come from. I found the ticket window and told the attendant that we had to get to Epping.

'Not tonight, you won't be. The last train on the Epping line has just left. You'll have to wait until the morning.' He pulled the blind down and stuck a 'CLOSED' sign in the window.

I slid down the wall and collapsed on the ground. I didn't know what to do next. All I wanted was sleep. I thought Rachel would burst into tears, hearing that we'd missed our train, but she had something else on her mind.

'Jesse, can you see that hamburger place over there, on the corner, we should go in there and eat. Come on. Get up, please. I bet you're hungry. I am.'

We ordered everything we thought we might want from the menu: hamburgers, chips, thickshakes, soft drinks and apple turnovers. We carried our trays to a booth in the corner, and sat and ate as people came and went. Most of them were drunks. They took their food outside and stood on the footpath smoking and drinking beer. Rachel burped real loud and wiped her mouth with a napkin.

'I didn't know I could eat three hamburgers until now. Do you think it might be a world record for a girl, Jesse? You're the tor champion and I'm the girls' hamburger champion.'

'Wouldn't bet on it. Have you seen some of them fat kids on TV, in America? I reckon some of them could eat ten hamburgers – with the lot. Maybe more. I saw a show once about a whole family of fat people, the mum and dad and three kids. And their dog, which was so fat it couldn't walk and had to shit where it lay. The boy in the family, he had two fat sisters who were twins. He was so fat himself he couldn't find any clothes that would fit him without splitting down the middle, so he went round in this dressing gown that belonged to his fat dad. He couldn't hardly tie it up in the front.'

Rachel drained the last of her soft drink. 'Was he allowed to go to school with just the dressing gown on?'

'Nup, he wasn't. Because he couldn't do it up properly his dick kept hanging out and frightening the girls, it was so fat.'

She caught me smiling. 'Is this one of the stories you make up?'

'Could be.'

Rachel asked if we could have one more go at the tarot cards.

'No, we can't. Look at the trouble they got us into climbing the silo. Nearly got us killed.'

'But we got out didn't we? And we didn't get caught. What about if we didn't climb up the tower, Jesse? Ray and Limbo would have seen us on the road and caught us. That card gave us luck. I want to do one more. For our future.'

I hadn't thought about it that way. She was right, sort of. The card had saved us.

'Okay. Last one. But then, we're giving the cards away for good.'

She took the pack out of her pocket and handed it to me.

'You shuffle and I'll pick.'

I shuffled the cards and fanned them. She picked one and held it out for both of us to see. It was 'Strength' and had a picture of a girl with flowers in her hair walking with a lion.

'Who is it, Jesse?'

'It's a girl. It must be you.'

She looked into the girl's face.

'Wow.'

I could hardly believe how bad I looked when I saw myself in the mirror in the toilets. My face was black and swollen and the cut over my eye had bits of gravel in it. I washed up in the sink and wet my hair. I didn't look much better when I'd finished. I shifted the roll of hundreds from my underpants to my pocket and walked outside. Rachel had gone to the toilet too, but hadn't bothered trying to clean herself up at all. Comfort was dripping wet, though.

'I stuck him under the tap and cleaned him,' she explained. 'I'm waiting till I get to Pop's to have a bath. Can you put him in the backpack? I'm tired of carrying him.'

'He stinks.'

'And so do you, Jesse.'

We walked outside and saw a sign pointing to a taxi rank across the street. It was empty. I asked a man in a railway uniform where we could catch one.

He looked at me, then at Rachel. I think he was wondering where our parents might be.

'A taxi? Well, this time of night your best bet is outside the casino.'

We headed down the hill, in the direction he'd pointed. We crossed the street at the bottom and stopped on a bridge that crossed the river. Our side of the river was dark and quiet. The other side was lined with tall buildings, all lit up, and lots of people and noise. It had to be the casino. Loud music was playing and people were clapping and cheering. A couple of taxis went by, and I stood on the road and waved to them.

They didn't stop. One had people in it, but the other one was empty.

'Why don't you just call Pop on the phone?' she asked. 'He would come and get us.'

'I don't know his number, I never wrote it down. Anyway, it's late and he would be in bed. We can get there ourselves.'

'Can we go over there for the taxi, where there are more people, Jesse? I don't like it here.'

It would have been a better idea to stay out of the way, but we weren't having any luck on this side of the river. We'd just about crossed the bridge when we heard a mighty roar and saw flames shooting into the sky from a steel tube on the bank of the river. People screamed and clapped. There was another shot of flame further along the bank. And then another. And another. Just like the oil refineries, but with an audience.

Rachel was excited. 'Let's go down and take a look.'

I was watching the traffic, looking out for a taxi. 'No, Rachel. We only have to find a taxi and we'll be back at Pop's.'

'Please, Jesse. Can we do what I want? Just this once. I've done everything you told me.'

By the time we reached the riverbank the flames had died, but there was plenty going on. A big crowd had gathered round a busker hurling swords in the air. He had a punk mohawk, dyed red, heavy chains around his neck, and was wearing a leather vest and pants. Some in the crowd were dressed up flash, like they were going to a ball. Others had the arse out of their pants, just like us.

Rachel tried getting a closer look at the busker. She'd

pushed her way to the front of the crowd before I could stop her. I stood on a bench at the back so I could get a better look myself and keep an eye on her. The busker was balancing on the back of a chair and playing a banjo at the same time. He then rode a one-wheeler bike, backwards and round in circles, while he read aloud from a book. And for his 'grand finale' he announced that her could juggle anything, 'including the kitchen sink'.

A kitchen sink flew into the air and crashed to the ground at his feet.

'Well, maybe not everything,' he said, laughing, and bowed.

The crowd slowly emptied. The busker packed up his gear then sat on the ground and started counting the money he'd collected in a bowler hat. Rachel ran over to me and asked if we could give him some money.

'It was fun, Jesse. Do you have some coins for him?'

I dug in my pocket. All I had was a fifty-cent piece and the roll of hundreds. I handed her the coin.

'That's all the change I've got.'

'But we've got lots of money. We should give him some.'

'If we go giving him a hundred-dollar note he'll get suspicious. Look at us, Rachel. He might call the cops.'

'I bet he won't. Let me give him one. Please.'

I felt the roll in my pocket. The busker had packed his gear, including the sink, in a wire trolley with wheels, hooked up to the back of a bike. He was about to pedal away when I walked over to him.

'We liked your show, and my sister wants to give you some money.'

He looked at us liked he felt sorry for the way we looked. 'You two on your own? You're out a little late. Keep your money. I've had a good night. Glad to hear that you got into it.'

'But we want to give you something,' Rachel butted in. 'We've got lots of money, don't we, Jesse?'

I could have kicked her.

'No we don't. She's just being silly.'

I showed him the fifty-cent piece. 'This is our money.'

I had the note in my other hand. 'And I saw somebody put this in your hat. It missed and blew along the ground. My sister picked it up, didn't you, Rachel?'

'Yep. I picked it up. And it belongs to you.'

He took the note from me and held it between a finger and thumb. 'A brick. Can you believe it? I've had a fifty before. Couple of times. Never a hundred. Why'd you give it back to me? You look like you got nothing yourselves.'

'It's not our money to keep,' I said, which was pretty much the truth.

He patted Rachel on the head. 'I'll be honest with you. I'd find it hard not to keep it, myself. You two on your own?'

'Nup. We're waiting for our dad. He's in the casino having a bet. We have to wait here for him,' I answered.

'Is he? See that all the time. Kids can sit here all night. You should go stand over there for him, where it's lighter near the door. There's a lot of shifty types around here. On the sniff for tackers just like you. Will you do that for me?'

I took Rachel's hand. 'We will.'

As soon as he'd pedalled off I jerked Rachel by the hand. 'We're getting out of here.'

We walked along the riverbank towards the bridge. A bicycle path ran under the bridge.

'We'll take a shortcut under here. It'll bring us out on the other side of the road.'

'But it's dark under there. I don't think we should go.'

'Don't go being a sook now, Rachel. There's no one around. We'll be okay.'

We were on pathway under the bridge when I heard voices talking, quietly. I could see two figures in the shadows to the side of us. One was a man in a suit leaning back against a wall. The other was a kid on his knees in front of the man.

'What are they doing, Jesse?'

'Don't look. Let's go quicker.'

We walked as fast as we could. We'd almost made it out when someone crashed into my back, threw me to the ground and pushed my face into the dirt. I could feel a hand going through my pockets and someone spitting on the back of my neck.

'What have you got there, prick?'

Rachel was screaming. I tried wrestling free, but couldn't move. A hand went into my front pocket and snatched the roll of notes, while the other tried ripping the pack from my back.

'I'll fucken have this as well.'

I heard a deep thud, like somebody had kicked the life out of a football. The mugger rolled off me and lay on the ground, moaning and holding his ribs. The mohawked busker was standing over him. He kicked him again, in the side, then bent down and took my roll of notes out of his hand. He helped me up. Rachel threw herself at me. She was crying.

The busker was big enough to wrap both of us in his arms. 'It's all right. You're safe.'

He dragged the man to his feet, slapped him around the face a couple of times and grabbed him by the shirt. 'Get your gear off.'

The man hunched forward. He could hardly breathe. 'What?'

'I said, get your gear off. Take your clothes off. Now.'

He looked up at the busker. 'You can get fucked, dickhead. I'm not doing that.'

The busker slapped his face again, a bit harder. 'Yes, you are. If you know what's good for you. If you don't I'll give you another kicking. And then I'll hand you to the cops. Now, take your clothes off.'

The man slowly undressed. When he was down to his underpants the busker picked up his shoes and threw them in the river. He went through his pants and pulled out a wallet. In it he found a twenty-dollar note: he put it in his own pocket then chucked the wallet in the river too.

'Hey!'

The busker told him to shut up, slapped his face again and threw his clothes in the water.

'I'd take your undies, but it'd be an ugly sight and I don't want you scaring these kids.'

He poked the man in the chest. 'I'm down here every day. This is my workplace, the riverbank. Don't come around here again. Now walk.'

'Walk?' he snivelled. 'Where to? I have no fucken money.'

'Hang around then, if you want. And I'll throw you in the drink after your stuff. Your choice, fuckwit.'

He pushed his hand against the man's chest to help him on his way. 'Now piss off.'

The busker walked with us until we were back on the street, where there were plenty of people. His bike and cart were leaning against a light post. He patted Rachel on the head.

'You've got a good set of lungs on you. I was pedalling for home when I heard you scream out.'

He handed me the roll of notes. 'You should thank your sister for this. She saved your life, and your money. You aren't waiting for no dad, are you?'

'We're on our own. But we have a grandfather. We were going to his place and missed the last train. We came down here for a taxi, and then we saw you doing your act.'

'That hundred you gave me didn't blow in from anywhere, did it?'

'No. But you can keep it.'

He laughed. 'Don't worry, I just earned it. I'm keeping it, all right. I'm not going to ask where you got it. Or the rest. You've plenty of dough for a cab. I'll get you one.'

He had no trouble hailing the taxi. We hopped in the back as he talked to the driver.

'You drop them where they need to go. And be sure you give them the right change.' The busker tapped the side of his head with a finger. 'I've got your rego and name, mate, up here. You get them home.'

He stuck his head in the back of the taxi. 'And you two desperados stay out of trouble.'

★

I asked the driver to pull over a few blocks from Pop's street. We walked along the footpath on the opposite side of the road to Pop's. When we passed Donny's house I was sure I saw a curtain move. We stopped on the nature strip, behind a tree. The blinds on Pop's front windows were down and the light in the lounge room was on.

'He's up late.'

Rachel was excited. 'Good. Let's go knock on the door. I wanna see him.'

'Not yet. We need to be sure. I'm gonna look around the back. You stay here.'

'But I don't want to. I want to see Pop. I can't wait longer.'

'Well, you have to. I just need to take a look around the back and be sure it's safe before we knock on the door. I'll be quick.'

'Let me come with you.'

'Wait here,' I said, and slipped off the backpack. 'Sit on this and don't move until I come back.'

She unzipped my jacket and handed it to me.

'Take this, Jesse, it'll keep you warm.'

I dropped it on top of the backpack. 'I don't need it now. We've made it.'

I snuck across the road and walked along the side of the house. The back gate was open. The kitchen light was on too. I wanted to look inside but it was too high up. I picked up the old wooden chair from under the clothes line. Pop used it to sit the washing basket on when he was hanging out the clothes.

I sat the chair under the window and crouched on it. I slowly lifted my head until I could see into the kitchen. It was a mess. The table was covered with empty pizza boxes, beer cans, a whiskey bottle and newspapers. As I stretched onto my tiptoes to get a look into the lounge room, I slipped from the chair and crashed against a box of glass jars and bottles. Maxie started barking from somewhere under the house. I got to my feet and ran back along the side of the house, through the open gate, straight into the arms of Ray Crow.

He lifted me off the ground and wrapped me in a bear hug.

'Hey,' he chuckled. 'The little rebel has come home to Grandpa's house. Well, say hello to the big bad fucken wolf.'

When he bit into my ear I screamed out in pain. He carried me to the front door with a tight grip around my chest. I was sure he would kill me.

'What kept you?' he asked, and laughed again. 'I was starting to worry you'd never get here.'

He kicked the front door open with his boot, dragged me into the lounge room, threw me on the floor and kicked me between the legs, straight in the balls. I pulled my legs into my chest. The pain was so bad I vomited up the hamburgers I'd eaten earlier.

I could hear someone sobbing.

'Look who I found snooping out back,' Ray said, chuckling.

'Leave him alone. He's just a boy.'

'Shut up, you old cunt.'

'I won't shut up. You leave him be.'

It was Pop. I rested my head on the floor and turned to the side. Gwen was sitting at one end of the couch, looking like shit. Her hair was a mess and her eyes were bruised and weepy. Pop was sitting next to her. The neck of the pyjama top he was wearing was covered in blood, and he had a cut over one eye, just like mine. He looked a lot older than the last time I'd seen him.

Ray circled me a couple of times and then knelt down next to me.

'You've got something belonging to me. Haven't you, little man? Let's get you to your feet and we'll have a chat about it.'

He lifted me up and dropped me into Pop's old armchair across from the couch. I could see the handle of his knife sticking out of the top of his boot. Gwen was shivering and rubbing her hands against her bare arms.

'Why'd you bring him here?' I shouted at her.

She was crying. 'I didn't, Jesse. It wasn't me.'

'You're a liar. You've always been a liar.'

Ray sunk the toe of his cowboy boot into my shin. The pain shot up my leg. When I screamed out he jumped on top of me and put a hand over my mouth.

'Be quiet now, son, or you'll wake the neighbours. And then I'll have to cut your throat. Your mother didn't bring us here. It was your own big mouth. Don't you remember bragging about your pop? I knew you'd find your way back here. Didn't bother looking for you once you got away from poor Lim. Rest his soul. Took a bit longer than I thought, but you did well to find your way.'

He grabbed a handful of my hair and pulled at it. 'I would have done the same thing. I bet you thought this old bugger could take care of you, if you could just get back here. Well, take a look at him. He's fucken useless. Gave him one whack and he pissed himself. Old Ray's the only one who can save your fucken skin now. Now, where's that little sister of yours?'

'She's gone. The cops picked her up at a railway station in the city, when I was in the toilet.'

He grabbed my face and squeezed my cheeks. 'You lying, boy? Where is she?'

'I'm not lying. I saw them take her. They put her in a car and took her away. I swear.'

He stroked the side of my face. 'Well, that's a pity. We could have had some fun, that girl and me. She was keen on me. But I've got your pop, and Gwen. Your *mother*. This is just like a family reunion.'

He slipped the knife out of his boot and held it front of my face, so I could get a good look at it.

'And we've got this friend of mine. Now, I should cut you from ear to ear just for what you did to Limbo. But that can wait.'

He rested the knife against my cheek. 'My money. Where is it?'

I looked across at Pop. He couldn't take his eyes off the knife.

'Pop. I'm sorry. I had an accident and broke the binoculars.'

'It doesn't matter, Jesse. It doesn't matter at all.'

'And I didn't mean to tell him about you. I was just talking about what a good time we had last summer. It's my fault.'

'No, Jesse. It's not your fault. None of this. This man, he's to blame, not you. You're a good boy.'

Ray walked across the room and punched Pop in the face. 'Shut up, old man, or I'll cut you too.'

Pop wouldn't shut up: 'Do what you like to me. Just leave the boy alone.'

'Don't worry, I will, granddad. As soon as he hands my money over. He'll tell me where it is. Or I'll fucken cut him open.'

Gwen fell from the couch, onto her hands and knees. 'Please don't, Ray,' she begged him. 'He's my son. Don't hurt him.'

Ray dug the heel of his boot into the back of her hand. She cried out in pain. 'I'll let him be, soon as we find out where the money is. So, Jesse, tell me where it is. Please.'

'I don't have it any more.'

'Bullshit.'

Gwen staggered to her feet and threw herself at him. He picked her up in one arm and threw her against the wall. She fell to the ground, crying. He pounced on me, dug his knees into my shoulders and put the knife to my throat.

'Last chance. Or you're dead.'

Pop begged him to stop.

'Please don't do this. I've got money. Savings. We can go into the bank tomorrow morning. You can take the lot. Twelve thousand dollars, I've got.'

'Twelve thousand?' Ray screamed. 'I had fifty fucken grand stolen by this little cunt.'

Ray jumped off me and ran at Pop with the knife. 'You're so popular, old man, I'll stick this in your guts and see if the kid's got anything to say.'

'Don't. Don't, please,' I cried. 'I've got the money, you can have it.'

'You have to get off of him now. Or I'll shoot this gun at you.'

Rachel was standing in the doorway, holding the revolver with both hands, pointing it at Ray. She was shaking. He looked over his shoulder and laughed at her.

'Hey, little girl, you came back too. Your brother here has been telling me lies about you. Said you'd gone for a drive with the Jacks. But here you are. And with my gun. I bet you've got my money too. Where is it, darling?'

'You get that knife away from my pop. You're hurting him.'

Ray held the knife above his head.

'I'm not hurting anyone, darling. Look. Now, put that gun down and tell me where my money is.'

'If you put your knife away I will.'

'Sure. If that's what you want.'

He stuck his knife back in his boot and showed her an open hand. 'See? I did what you said. I don't want anybody getting hurt. Now give me the gun.'

Her hands shook more and more. She was about to drop the gun.

'I don't believe you. And I don't like you.'

'That's no way to talk to me, honey. I like you, a lot.'

He threw himself at her. Rachel closed her eyes and pulled the trigger. The blast threw her body into the air.

Ray fell back against the couch and slid to the ground. There was a dark hole in the white t-shirt he was wearing, just where his heart should have been. As he sucked for air the white around the hole slowly turned red. Ray's eyes flickered and then closed and his head fell to the side. He looked like he was sleeping.

Rachel sat up, looked over at me, and then back at Ray. Her whole body shook as she burst into tears.

Carloads of detectives and uniformed cops with sirens blaring and guns drawn turned up within a few minutes. Two ambulances were not far behind them followed by a TV crew that set up in the street out front of the house with spotlights and cameras. I watched as the ambulance officers cut Ray's t-shirt open with a pair of scissors, put a mask over his mouth and looked over him. Police with bulletproof jackets and helmets moved from room to room, searching for the gunman.

I'd seen stuff just like this before, on TV, so it wasn't that unusual.

'He's dead,' one of the ambulance officers said, and took the mask away from Ray's face.

A tall skinny detective walked in and yelled at one of the uniformed cops for leaving us in the room with the body.

'Get these kids out of here, into the kitchen with the old boy. And get hold of Juvenile Services. Put the mother in one of the bedrooms on her own. Move. I need this room taped.'

I sat beside Rachel at the kitchen table while Pop made us some tea. She was white in the face and her eyes looked strange. Pop sat down next to her, wrapped his arms around her and rested her head against his chest.

'You okay?' he asked.

She nodded her head up and down.

'You don't look it.'

'I am, Pop. I am.'

She was holding something in her hand.

'What you got there?' I asked her.

She opened her hand and showed me a tarot card, the picture of the girl and the lion.

The skinny detective came into the kitchen carrying the backpack.

'This belong to anyone?'

He dropped the pack on the table, unzipped it, pulled out Comfort and held him up. 'What about this?

Rachel put her hand out. 'He's mine.'

The detective opened the bag a little wider and looked inside.

'You've got a rich bear, love.'

He counted each roll of money as he laid it on the table: 'Eighteen . . . nineteen . . . twenty bundles.' He searched through the bag to be sure it was empty.

I did some quick sums in my head. There were four rolls missing. Eight thousand dollars.

A crowd was standing on the footpath across the street from the house when we were led out. A barrier stopped them from getting closer. I could see Donny hanging over it. He was wearing my jacket over a pair of shorts. He smiled, waved at me and patted one of the pockets.

Rachel was rubbing a finger across the scar on the top of her thumb. I put my hand in hers.

Acknowledgments

I would like to thank my family and friends, both near and extended, for the support you have given me over the journey, with this book and those that came before. At University of Queensland Press, John Hunter is both a true friend and supporter of my work, while my editor, Rebecca Roberts, has cleared my mess with the eye of an artist. Thank you, Rebecca. I must also thank Charlotte Wood, who gave me important advice when I wrote and published the short story 'Blood' in a collection she edited, *Brothers and Sisters* (Allen & Unwin, 2009). To my kids – 'the famous five' – Erin, Siobhan, Drew, Grace and Nina, we did it again. I love you. And to beautiful Sara, I cannot tell you how it ends, 'It's [still] a mystery.'